But as he lowered his head to hers, the sultry night turned suddenly stifling hot. Her lips were summer warm and satin smooth, and in an instant his plan of offering her just one quick kiss was shot to hell. After ravishing her mouth for a full minute, he backed her against the railing and kissed her again…then again.

He meant to stop. He *would* stop. Soon, he told himself. But he was losing control, and she was letting him. And that was when it hit him.

He was no better than the man from her past—the one who'd hurt her so deeply.

"Dammit, *chérie*, what the hell are you trying to do to me?" Then, before she could answer, before her head had a chance to clear and grasp just how close she'd come, he melted into the shadows.

Dear Reader,

As Silhouette Books' 20th anniversary continues, Intimate Moments continues to bring you six superb titles every month. And certainly this month—when we begin with Suzanne Brockmann's *Get Lucky*—is no exception. This latest entry in her TALL, DARK & DANGEROUS miniseries features ladies' man Lucky O'Donlon, a man who finally meets the woman who is his match—and more.

Linda Turner's *A Ranching Man* is the latest of THOSE MARRYING McBRIDES!, featuring Joe McBride and the damsel in distress who wins his heart. Monica McLean was a favorite with her very first book, and now she's back with *Just a Wedding Away*, an enthralling marriage-of-convenience story. Lauren Nichols introduces an *Accidental Father* who offers the heroine happiness in THE LOVING ARMS OF THE LAW. *Saving Grace* is the newest from prolific RaeAnne Thayne, who's rapidly making a name for herself with readers. And finally, welcome new author Wendy Rosnau. After you read *The Long Hot Summer,* you'll be eager for her to make a return appearance.

And, of course, we hope to see you next month when, once again, Silhouette Intimate Moments brings you six of the best and most exciting romance novels around.

Enjoy!

Leslie J. Wainger
Executive Senior Editor

Please address questions and book requests to:
Silhouette Reader Service
U.S.: 3010 Walden Ave., P.O. Box 1325, Buffalo, NY 14269
Canadian: P.O. Box 609, Fort Erie, Ont. L2A 5X3

THE LONG HOT SUMMER
WENDY ROSNAU

Silhouette®
INTIMATE™MOMENTS®

Published by Silhouette Books

America's Publisher of Contemporary Romance

This book is dedicated to my husband, Jerry,
the hero in my life and partner in all things.
To Tyler and Jenni, for their love and bright smiles.
And to Lettie Lee, for her instincts,
support and always taking my call.

 SILHOUETTE BOOKS

ISBN 0-373-07996-6

THE LONG HOT SUMMER

Copyright © 2000 by Wendy Rosnau

All rights reserved. Except for use in any review, the reproduction
or utilization of this work in whole or in part in any form by any
electronic, mechanical or other means, now known or hereafter
invented, including xerography, photocopying and recording, or in
any information storage or retrieval system, is forbidden without
the written permission of the editorial office, Silhouette Books,
300 East 42nd Street, New York, NY 10017 U.S.A.

All characters in this book have no existence outside the imagination of
the author and have no relation whatsoever to anyone bearing the same
name or names. They are not even distantly inspired by any individual
known or unknown to the author, and all incidents are pure invention.

This edition published by arrangement with Harlequin Books S.A.

® and TM are trademarks of Harlequin Books S.A., used under license.
Trademarks indicated with ® are registered in the United States Patent
and Trademark Office, the Canadian Trade Marks Office and in other
countries.

Visit us at www.romance.net

Printed in U.S.A.

WENDY ROSNAU

lives on sixty secluded acres in the Northwoods of Minnesota with her husband and their two energetic teenagers. A former hairdresser, today she divides her time between the bookstore she and her husband opened in 1998, keeping one step ahead of her two crafty kids, and writing romance. In her spare time, she enjoys reading, painting and drawing, traveling, and, most of all, spending time with those two crafty kids and their dad.

A great believer in the power of love and the words *never give up*, Wendy's goal of becoming a published author is a testimony that dreams can and do come true. You can write to her at P.O. Box 441, Brainerd, Minnesota 56401. For a personal reply send a SASE.

IT'S OUR 20th ANNIVERSARY!
We'll be celebrating all year,
continuing with these fabulous titles,
on sale in March 2000.

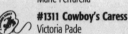
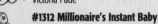

Chapter 1

The hell of it was, the parole deal stunk. But if Johnny agreed to the terms, he'd be breathing fresh air within the hour. It should have been an easy choice to make—he'd been rotting in Louisiana's maximum-security prison for six months. Yeah, it should have been easy—if only the terms of his parole weren't so ridiculous.

A buzzer sounded and the iron door electronically unlocked. "Come on, Bernard, put a wiggle in it," the guard ordered. "The warden wants to see you, pronto."

Contrary to the direct order, Johnny slowly got to his feet. Reaching into his shirt pocket, he pulled out his half-used pack of Camels, and passed the cigarettes to his cell mate, who lay sprawled on the top bunk. They exchanged a look; it said, Good luck, but don't bet too high on the odds. Then, in a lazy gait that had been a Bernard trademark for over half a century, Johnny sauntered through the open door and into the corridor of Cell Block C.

When Johnny entered the warden's office moments later, Pete Lasky looked up from the mound of paperwork scattered on his cheap metal desk. Lasky owned a pair of uncharitable blue eyes, and a false grin that exposed a row of coffee-stained teeth—an occupational hazard created by the monotony of ten-hour days sandwiched between a desk and a window overlooking a bleak, prisoner-filled court-yard. "So, Bernard, you wanna be cut loose today?"

The stupid question deserved a stupid answer, but Johnny didn't plan on getting cute; the sixty-year-old warden didn't own a sense of humor. "No chance for a fat fine and public service?"

"Sure would make life easier for you, wouldn't it?" Pete grinned. "Well, it ain't gonna happen. *Easy,* I mean. Never did like that word. *Easy* ain't gonna teach you when to keep your mouth shut or your fist out of some poor devil's face. And those are two lessons that would do you some good."

Johnny had heard it all before, and in most cases what was said about him was true. Only, in this particular instance—the one the warden was referring to—he hadn't been shooting off his mouth, or taking the first swing. Yeah, he'd retaliated, but only after Farrel had come at him.

"I've had two phone conversations with your hometown sheriff," the warden continued. "Looks like Sheriff Tucker's not any happier about these parole terms than you are. The way he tells it, you're about as popular in Common as a copper-belly at a Fourth of July picnic. But like I told him, I'm not in the 'happy' business." The warden opened his top drawer, then took out the paperwork for Johnny's release and laid it on his desk. "By the way, if you agree to this deal, that man—the one you damn near killed—is off-limits. Any criminal conduct will nullify your parole. Carrying a weapon will do the same. Failure to comply will earn you another six months inside. So what's it gonna be?''

Johnny jammed his hands in the back pockets of his faded jeans, and the image of Belle Bayou suddenly surfaced. With it came a treasured memory from his youth—his father teaching him how to fish cane-pole style at sunrise.

The truth was, if he agreed to the warden's parole deal, he would be waking up to that sunrise every morning for the next four months. He hadn't been back home in years—not until six months ago, anyway—but he'd never been able to forget the bond he'd formed with the bayou.

He knew the bayou as well as any of the old-timers. He knew where the best fishing spots were. Where the shy blue herons nested, and where every hidden channel in the bayou ended up. He also knew what a stir he'd cause by showing up in town again.

''Well?''

''I'll take the deal,'' Johnny said, glancing out the window behind Pete Lasky's desk. The sky was tauntingly clear, and maybe that's what had suddenly been the deciding factor. Or maybe it was remembering Belle. Either way, he heard himself say, ''Four months working for Mae Chapman at Oakhaven won't kill me, but staying in here another six just might.''

An hour later, Johnny walked out of Angola's front gate and into hell's kitchen. That's what his mama had always called the month of August in Louisiana. It was just after ten, and already the temperature threatened one-hundred. He headed north, his plan to catch the bus out of Tunica. A mile down the road, he pulled off his white T-shirt and ran the sleeve through an empty belt loop on his jeans.

He'd never intended to go back to Common when he'd

left fifteen years ago—both of his parents were dead and he had no other family—but after receiving that damn letter six months ago from Griffin Black, curiosity had overridden common sense. The letter had offered to pay him top dollar for his land. *His land?*

Now, everyone knew that Johnny didn't own any land in Common. True, his father had owned land years ago—a run-down sugarcane farm that had never earned him more than a sore back and a pile of headaches. But all things considered, delinquent taxes should have relieved him of the farm years ago. Only a week later, after strolling into Common city hall and telling the clerk what he was there for, Johnny had promptly learned that he did, in fact, own his daddy's old farm. But just how and why remained a mystery.

The truth was, there were only two people in town who cared enough to invest any time or money in him. Only Virgil didn't have any extra cash to speak of, so that left Mae Chapman. The question was, why would she do it?

Johnny left city hall with the intention of confronting the old lady with what he'd learned. But the day's heat was powerful, and he'd made a quick decision to stop by the local bar for one cold beer before showing up at Oakhaven. A bad decision, he realized, the moment he opened the door to Pepper's Bar and Grill and walked straight into his childhood enemy.

He hadn't been trying to kill Farrel Craig the way they had accused him of doing, as much as it had looked that way when Sheriff Tucker had shown up. Yes, he'd drawn his knife, but only after Farrel had come at him with a broken beer bottle.

It had looked bad, he couldn't deny that—but he hadn't been willing to roll over and let Farrel carve him up like a steak. Only, the authorities didn't see it that way. He'd been arrested and convicted for assault with intent to do bodily harm—the sentence: a year in Angola State Penitentiary.

So now here he was, six months later, faced with going back home to serve a lousy four-month parole sentence. And he would serve it. Only, by summer's end he intended to sell the farm and sever his ties to Common for good.

The sun was just setting as the bus rolled into Common and stopped on the corner of Cooper and Main. As Johnny stepped off the bus he glanced around the bare-bones town were he'd spent the first fifteen years of his life. The streets were nearly deserted. He supposed the sultry heat had driven most of the locals inside, or maybe they'd heard he was coming. He suddenly realized he could have been happy here if only the townsfolk would have given him a chance.

Gran would never willingly have agreed to hire such a disreputable man if she had seen the rap sheet that went along with him. Disgusted, Nicole tossed the paper on the Pendleton desk. She snapped off the old-fashioned floor fan sitting next to her, then picked up the phone and dialed the Pass-By Motel.

On the third ring Virgil Diehl answered in his thick cajun accent. "Motel. De coffee's black and dere's vacancies."

"Hello, Mr. Diehl, this is Nicole Chapman calling."

"Little Nicki! *Oui!* I heard yo' was back from de big city. Bet Mae's tickled pink, *ma petite.* Me, too. Yo' is de perdiest angel in all of St. James Parish. *Mais yeah.*"

"*Merci,* Mr. Diehl. You're kind to say so."

"Dat's me." Virgil chuckled. "Kind is good for business. But yo' kin't be wantin' a room, *ma petite,* so what yo' after?" He paused. "Maybe I already knows."

He no doubt did. By now the news of Jonathan Bernard's return and his newly acquired position at Oakhaven had most likely raced through the supermarket, the bakery, the corner drug, and both bars. "Sheriff Tucker told me Mr. Bernard is staying in one of your rooms," Nicole explained. "Is he registered?"

"Johnny? Yah, he's here. Fact be, he's jes' comin' through de door now."

"Could I speak to him, please?"

"Yah—sure t'ing, *ma petite*."

While Nicole waited, she turned the fan back on. A native of California, she was used to hot weather, but Louisiana's sultry heat was a new kind of hot. One that would surely kill her if she didn't acclimate soon—she had never perspired so much in all her twenty-five years.

She took another quick glance at the paperwork Sheriff Tucker had dropped by an hour ago. She hadn't read every word, but she really didn't need to. The gist was that Jonathan Bernard had been granted parole because of job security—thanks to Gran—and good behavior.

Good behavior. Nicole sniffed, taking another quick glance at the list of offenses the man had accumulated in the past thirty years. True, most of Jonathan Bernard's offenses dated back to when he was a teenager. And there was even a span of time—seven years, to be exact—when it appeared he had reformed. But when she'd mentioned that hopeful tidbit to Sheriff Tucker, he had assured her that Common's black sheep didn't know the meaning of the word *reform*.

That's why she intended to intervene. True, they did need someone to work a miracle on Oakhaven over the summer—the place was falling apart—but not Jonathan Bernard.

"This here's me. If it ain't free, I don't want it."

His phone manners spoke mountains for his character. The black-bayou drawl, however, sent an unexpected chill racing the length of Nicole's spine. She paused a moment, and in the process lost her train of thought. Scrambling to get it back, she settled for "Is 'me' Jonathan Bernard?"

"You got who you wanted. Only, folks call me Johnny. What you selling, *cherie?*"

A one-way bus ticket north, Nicole wanted to say. Instead, she said, "I'm not selling anything, Mr. Bernard. This is Oakhaven calling about your so-called job. The point is, the job is no longer available."

Silence.

"Mr. Bernard?"

"Let me talk to the old lady."

Nicole hadn't been ready for that. "I—ah, she's taking a nap in the garden." It was the truth.

"And she asked you to call me and say she's changed her mind, is that it?"

Nicole had hoped to settle this without involving her seventy-six-year-old grandmother. "I don't think—"

"The job is a condition of my parole," he drawled thickly. "The old lady signed papers agreeing to supply me with an eight-to-five job, five days a week for the summer. It's already been settled."

He was lying. Gran was too smart to sign anything without legal advice.

"I guess what I'm saying, *cherie,* is I'm nonrefundable."

Nonrefundable. Something in his voice suggested he was smiling. Narrowing her blue eyes, Nicole switched off the fan, then quickly flipped through the papers Sheriff Tucker had left. Sure enough, there it was, a copy of a legal agreement with her grandmother's signature on it. *Damn!*

"You still there?"

"I think there's been a misunderstanding." Nicole tried to keep her voice strong and confident.

"Is this where I get one of those sticky apologies over the phone?"

Nicole bristled, but she kept her mouth shut.

"I guess not. Well, I'll be moving into the boathouse sometime around four."

That bit of news was too alarming for Nicole to keep quiet a moment longer. "You're moving into the boathouse?" She nearly choked on the words. "I don't think so, Mr. Bernard! In fact, I—"

But it was too late for thinking or talking. Jonathan Bernard had already hung up the phone.

Chapter 2

Gran's garden was a blue-ribbon winner. Every kind of flower, in every color imaginable, from azaleas to camellias the size of grapefruits, flourished in the tropical heat. The old plantation-style house looked tired and desperate, the surrounding fields overgrown and empty of sugarcane, but the flower garden was breathtaking, the beauty so grand that Nicole couldn't help but sigh in wonder as she slipped through the wrought-iron gate.

She found her grandmother asleep beneath a hundred-year-old oak and knelt in the grass beside her wheelchair. Reaching up to brush a stray, snow-white strand of hair from Mae's wrinkled cheek, she whispered, "Do you plan on sleeping the entire afternoon away?"

The gentle touch and softly spoken words roused Mae, and she blinked open her blue eyes—eyes identical to her granddaughter's. "It must be getting late if you've ventured outside to wake me," she rasped, her solid voice a contradiction to her petite size. "Since your arrival two weeks ago I haven't seen you out much in the heat of the day. So what is it that has lured you away from that poor tired fan you've attached to your hip?''

Trouble, Nicole wanted to say, but she thought better of simply blurting out what she'd done. She glanced at Mae's ankle—a week ago the porch rail had given way and her grandmother had tumbled into the flower bed. She'd received a minor cut on her cheek, a few bruises and a sprained left ankle. ''How's the ankle?'' she asked. ''It doesn't seem as swollen today.''

''No, it doesn't. Thank the Lord, I didn't break it, or I would be in this chair longer than a month.'' She looked Nicole up and down. ''So, what brings you outside? We blow an electrical fuse?''

''Very funny.'' Nicole made a face.

Mae made an effort to simulate Nicole's cross-eyed contortion.

Nicole laughed. ''Okay, I've been a might excessive,'' she conceded.

''Clair and I have been trying to come up with a way for you to strap the fan on your back.''

''I didn't know you two were so ingenious.''

''There's a lot of things we haven't let you in on,'' Mae teased.

''Like hiring an ex-con for the summer?''

''So you've heard? Gossip, or from someone credible who hasn't twisted the entire story?''

''I assume Sheriff Tucker would be considered credible.''

''He certainly would not. He's always disliked Johnny.''

''If you took the time to read his rap sheet, you'd know why.''

''Are you upset with me?''

''Can you blame me? I'm the last to know about this.''

''It wasn't intentional. But honestly, I just forgot to

mention Johnny coming to work for us. I guess in all the excitement of your moving in, it slipped my mind.''

That might have been true of someone else, Nicole thought. But not of her grandmother. In her advancing years Mae Chapman might be losing a little of her agility, but nothing would slip her mind, which was as sharp as a razor blade and twice as quick.

''I would have remembered today, since this is—''

''The day he's moving in.'' Nicole stood and nailed her grandmother with a peeved look. ''So the truth is, you've hired an ex-con for the summer, and planned to tell me the day he arrived, is that it? Why so soon?''

''Now, Nicki, don't give yourself another headache. We old people get feebleminded from time to time.''

''You're about as feebleminded as I am,'' Nicole snapped, jamming her hands on her slender hips and narrowing her cool blue eyes. ''And don't you dare give me that sad, one-foot-in-the-grave slump. I'm serious. This man has an arrest record longer than a month-old grocery list. Sheriff Tucker says he's the dark side of trouble.''

''Bah! That's ridiculous. He's harmless.''

''Harmless? Sheriff Tucker says he nearly killed Farrel Craig at Pepper's Bar six months ago. I'd say he's about as harmless as a sunburned cottonmouth with a belly rash and a sore tooth.''

Mae chuckled. ''That was very good, Nicki. I must remember that one. Tell it to me again so—''

''Gran, I'm not trying to be funny.''

''I agree it was careless of Johnny to get caught fighting, but you see—''

''Caught? You condone his fighting. It's getting *caught* that you—''

''Don't put words in my mouth, dear. Farrel and Johnny were always going at it, but it wasn't all one-sided. None of us is perfect.''

No, no one was perfect. Nicole had certainly made her share of mistakes. Still, she needed to understand the reason behind what Gran had done. "So convince me we need him. Not just any carpenter, but Johnny Bernard."

"That's easy. Johnny's my friend and he needed out of that wretched place. In the bargain, we get a carpenter to restore Oakhaven."

"Friend?" Nicole felt her pulse quicken. "How good a friend?"

"Good enough to know it's time he stopped running and came home. There, I've said it. Said exactly what I've been feeling for years, and it's liberating to finally say it."

"Would he agree?"

"That he's been running?" Mae shrugged. "Probably not. I'll be honest with you, Nicki. You're going to hear a lot of gossip, most of it bad. But don't settle on an opinion until you've met him. I guarantee there is more to Johnny Bernard than what's in those reports. And far more than people in this town are willing to see, if they would just open their eyes."

Nicole could tell her grandmother believed wholeheartedly what she was saying. The question was, why would Gran feel so strongly about this man? What *wasn't* she saying?

"Actually, you and Johnny have more in common than you think, Nicki. He's not the only one the townsfolk have been gossiping about lately."

Her grandmother eyed Nicole's short cutoffs, then her hair. Self-consciously, Nicki tried to tame her shaggy blond hair into some semblance of order. "I'm from California, Gran. You know I'm—"

"A free spirit. Yes, I know."

Nicole smiled, not sure that was the word she would use. Or maybe it was, but in the past year she'd been reeducated on how dangerous being your own person could be. In fact, she'd lived through a nightmare and a half, and wasn't ashamed to admit her spirit had been broken. Snapped in half, actually.

Three months had passed since the miscarriage, but sometimes it felt like only yesterday. She still didn't sleep through an entire night, and she continued to experience depression—a condition the doctor believed would pass in time. Only, it wouldn't; Nicole was sure of it. Time could never wash away the guilt a woman felt over losing her child. Especially in this case, when Nicole hadn't been so sure she'd even wanted Chad's child. Not until after the baby was gone.

No, time would never erase her guilt, and she had told the doctor as much. She had told him she wasn't expecting miracles because, frankly, she didn't deserve any.

"The good news, Nicki, is that Johnny's an experienced carpenter. He'll be the perfect solution for our growing list of house repairs. Unless you've suddenly decided to buck up under the heat and learn how to pound nails and replace shingles. If not, I'd say we're in desperate need of a man around here. Someone who can swing a hammer and isn't afraid to sweat."

"And you're sure he's not afraid of hard work?"

"Johnny grew up hard, Nicki. There's no doubt in my mind he'll give us our dollars' worth. For the past two years he's been working in Lafayette for a construction outfit. The foreman told me he would hire Johnny back in a minute, no questions asked. He's that good. And he's a military man, too. An ex-marine. I suspect he's got hidden talents we don't even know about."

Nicole arched a brow. "And just how do you suppose we can utilize an ex-con who is an expert at warfare to his fullest potential?" She paused as if thinking. Finally, she said, "Funny, but I thought we were discussing restoring Oakhaven, not blowing it up."

"A regular funny-girl today, aren't you?" Mae shook her head. "I think you'll be surprised, my dear. Pleasantly surprised, that is."

Nicole didn't like surprises. Especially surprises that involved men. She said grimly, "He's arriving around four."

"You've talked to him? Wonderful!" Mae's excitement sent two birds nesting overhead into flight.

"I called the Pass-By Motel," Nicole admitted. "Sheriff Tucker said that's where I could find him." She purposely left out the part about trying to fire him over the phone. "He said he'll be staying at the boathouse."

"Yes, that was our agreement. Do you suppose, Nicki, you could send Bick down there to open the windows and air the place out? I'll scribble a message for Johnny. Bick can leave it on the table, since I can't get down there to meet him myself."

Mae's gaze traveled across the driveway to where a trail led to the boathouse. The trail was a quarter-mile through dense woods—a shortcut to Belle Bayou. "I haven't seen Johnny in fifteen years," she offered wistfully. "I intended to visit him in prison, but my lawyer advised against it."

Judging by the look in her grandmother's aging eyes, she was sorry she hadn't. Nicole found herself growing curious. She asked, "Is there some way I can help?"

Her grandmother reached out and patted Nicole's arm. "You already have—by coming home. First you and now Johnny. It's perfect." She paused. "When he left I had no idea it would be years before he came home. I wonder how he turned out in the looks department? If he ended up anything like his father or grandpa, watch out, dear. Gracious, but those Bernard men were handsome."

Nicole didn't need to see him to know how he'd turned out. The report on the desk in the study confirmed that Johnny Bernard had gotten his reputation the old-fashioned way: he'd earned every bit of it. And as far as his looks went, she didn't really care how handsome he'd turned out. They weren't shopping for a lawn ornament, just a simple carpenter. How he looked on a ladder was of no importance, as long as he could climb one.

She bent forward and kissed her grandmother's cheek. "When you get your note written, I'll see that Bick takes it with him. What do you say we have some lemonade? I'm dying."

"You're always dying," Mae teased. "Where should we have our lemonade? On the front porch?"

Nicole positioned herself behind Mae's wheelchair. "I've got an original idea. Why not relax in front of the fan in the study?"

An hour later, Nicole learned that Bick had taken himself off to town. Forced to run her grandmother's errand, she hurried along the wooded trail toward the boathouse. She checked her watch, glad to see that she still had an hour before Johnny Bernard would descend on them. She wasn't sure how she was going to face him after trying to get rid of him over the phone, but with any luck she wouldn't have to think about that until later. She would open the windows, leave Gran's note on the table and be gone before he even set foot on Oakhaven soil.

Within a matter of ten minutes, Nicole was through the woods, standing in a small clearing just west of Belle Bayou. All things considered, she was more intrigued by the moody swamp than frightened by it. It had a certain allure, a quality she had tried many times to capture on canvas.

It was an artist's paradise, she admitted. The colorful vegetation that grew out of the muck along the banks fascinated her as much as did the huge cypress trees with their gnarly roots and distorted branches. The branches dripping with Spanish moss along the water's edge reminded her of a travel brochure she'd once seen advertising scenic Louisiana.

Her gaze followed the grassy bank to the old wood and stone boathouse, this being the first time she'd come down to the bayou since she'd arrived from L.A. From an artist's point of view the place had immense possibilities. It was dark and eerie, straight out of a gothic novel, and when she decided to paint it, she would do so with that in mind.

She started down the overgrown path through the clearing, approaching the aging structure from the north side. She reached for the door's rusty latch, and as she pulled it open, it groaned loudly in protest. Inside, she ran her hand along the cool brick in search of the light switch. Relieved that it still worked, that she hadn't been greeted by any creepy-crawly surprises, Nicole followed the ray of light past the clutter and ascended the stairs to the second story.

To her surprise, what once had housed old tools and fishing gear now resembled a modest apartment. She recognized a few pieces of furniture from the house: a rocker, a bureau, a square table and two chairs. The dark red sofa, she remembered from the attic. An iron bed made up with a blue bedspread had been arranged in such a manner that one could lie down and still gaze out the window and enjoy the bayou's beauty at night. A partition wall cut the room in half. On one side, a small kitchen; on the other, an even smaller bathroom.

The window facing the woods, as well as the one overlooking the moody, black bayou, was already open. Puzzled, Nicole concluded Bick had second-guessed Gran's request and had opened the windows that morning. Not giving it any more thought, she placed Gran's note on the table and walked to the nearest window to gaze outside. She scanned the shoreline, noting the boat tied to the sagging dock, the cane pole resting across the seat.

Cane pole? Bick never fished with a cane pole.

She made the mental observation just as she heard something. A moment later, she identified the noise as footsteps—footsteps that had reached the stairs and were now steadily climbing.

She glanced at her watch. It was a little past three. *He* had said four. Nicole made a quick swipe at her blond bangs, swore silently at her bad luck, then forced herself to turn. Her first thought was that the black-bayou voice on the phone was a perfect fit for the dark and dangerous man who had suddenly filled the doorway.

Nicole's gaze drifted over Common's rebel, deciding that he was everything she had expected him to be, and more. A couple of inches over six feet, he stood shirtless, his long legs encased in ragged jeans. His broad shoulders looked hard as iron, his torso and stomach a series of layered muscles and corrugated definition. It was obvious he was in top physical condition. But then, what else did a jailed criminal have to do all day but get bigger and more dangerous by pumping iron in the prison gym? Hadn't she read a controversial article about that somewhere?

She had taken a few self-defense classes—living in L.A., it had been the smart thing to do. Even so, it would be almost funny trying to use what she'd learned against a marine who could add Angola State Penitentiary to his bio.

To be sure, he was a survivor. Of that, Nicole had no doubt—as she stared into a pair of rich amber, see-to-the-soul eyes that promised Johnny Bernard had seen it all, and possibly done it all, too.

She watched as he reached behind his back and closed the door. The movement shifted him slightly sideways, sending a stream of sunlight from the window into his straight, black hair. Loose, it would have touched his shoulders, but to combat the heat he had pulled it back from his face and secured it low at the nape of his neck.

If not for a straight high-bridged nose and a sensual mouth softening his otherwise hard features, he would have been almost too rugged to be referred to as handsome. Those two features, combined with a reckless thin scar trailing from his right eye to his temple, softened him and made him human, thus dangerously good-looking.

Clearing her throat, Nicole wrapped herself in false confidence—something she did often these days—and forced herself to speak. "I thought you said you were arriving at four o'clock."

"Did I?" He relaxed against the door and loosely folded his arms over his broad chest. The smile Nicole imagined him wearing earlier throughout their phone conversation appeared. He spared a quick glance at the plain silver watch on his wrist, then made eye contact with her once more. "Looks like you're early, too. Anxious to meet me, Nicki?"

She hadn't expected him to know her name, Johnny could tell by the surprise in her blue eyes. But he did know her name, and a whole lot more. He had pumped Virgil before he'd left the motel, and the old man had been eager to talk. In fact, he had claimed Nicki Chapman the "perdiest *femme*" he'd ever seen. And Johnny had to agree, she was the best thing he'd seen in a helluva long time.

Somewhere in her twenties, she was a little above average height, her body curvy and delicate. The delicate part warned him off right away—he avoided fragile women like they had the plague. They reminded him of glass figurines, and, frankly, they made him nervous. He did like looking at her, though. Liked her sexy long bangs and the way she let them play an intentional game of hide-and-seek with her eyes. Her honey-blond hair was shoulder-length and shiny. Her cutoffs, mid-thigh, flashed long, slender legs and sexy knees. Her short T-shirt was a distinct shade of blue, a perfect match for her eyes.

She'd been born in L.A. Her parents had died two years ago in a plane crash. This came from Virgil. She was an only child like Johnny, Virgil had said, but he couldn't remember what she did for a living. Apparently, she'd moved in with the old lady a few weeks ago with the intention of making Oakhaven her permanent home.

"I came to drop off a note from Gran." She gestured to the piece of paper on the table. "I had planned to open windows, too, but I see you already opened them." She thrust her hand out. "Ah, I'm Nicole Chapman. Mae's granddaughter. We met on the phone."

Johnny was surprised that she offered her hand. Most people were reluctant to get that friendly with him. Too bad he was going to have to decline the gesture. He wasn't sure what he had on his hands, but they were filthy. He unfolded his arms and showed her that both of his hands weren't even the same color. "I was catching supper, among other things," he explained. "Catfish."

Her gaze drifted to his dirty hands, then she promptly dropped the one she'd offered. "Since you're here and you'll be working for Oakhaven, I—"

"Will I, *cherie?* No new plan to fire me before I get started?"

"You made it clear over the phone that the choice wasn't mine, remember? I believe the word you used was *nonrefundable.* I checked with Gran and that seems to be the case." She broke eye contact with him and glanced around the room. "Gran took a lot of time to fix this place up. I guess that means something." She brought her gaze back to his. "You're a carpenter, isn't that right, Mr. Bernard?"

"Johnny. The name's Johnny. And, yeah, I'm a carpenter."

"Well, Oakhaven is in need of major repairs, *Johnny*, so it looks like there will be plenty to keep you busy."

Her concession to use his name amused him, and Johnny grinned. "So I've noticed."

She arched one delicate eyebrow, but didn't argue with him.

He gestured to the rocker, then shoved away from the door and strolled past her to the couch. Once she'd slipped into the chair, he dropped down on the couch and let his long legs sprawl apart. The day's heat had flushed her face, and he noted she looked miserably hot. He, on the other hand, had never felt better. He loved the Louisiana heat; it was in his blood, the hotter the better. He'd run away from Common years ago. Only he hadn't left the state. He'd been calling Lafayette home for almost two years.

"Will the job take the entire summer?" she asked.

"That depends on what's on the old lady's list."

A bead of sweat slipped past her left temple and down her cheek. She made a swipe at it, then lifted her right leg a fraction of an inch, then the other one. It didn't dawn on Johnny until he saw her go through the motion a second time that her bare legs were sticking to the wooden chair.

"Do you have a glass of water with ice?" she suddenly asked.

"Sure." Johnny stood and walked into the small kitchen. He scrubbed his hands, then retrieved a glass from the cupboard, filled it with water and dropped in a couple of ice cubes from the space-saving fridge. He returned and handed it to her. "One glass of water, served with ice."

She peered into the glass, then glanced at his clean hands. "Thank you. I haven't adjusted to the humidity yet," she quietly explained, "but I will eventually."

Johnny wasn't convinced—she looked about as miserable as she could get. He returned to the couch and watched her use the glass to cool her warm cheek. "Carpenters don't come cheap," he drawled, watching her slide the glass down her neck, then back up. She had a pretty neck, long and pale.

"No, they don't. But I imagine carpenters on parole are just happy to be working at all."

Johnny laughed out loud, liking her honesty. "So I'm supposed to work cheap, is that it? Or am I donating my time?"

She moved the glass to her opposite cheek and closed her eyes for a moment. "That's something you'll have to work out with Gran. She sprained her ankle a week ago and she's in a wheelchair. I imagine we can get our supplies at Craig Lumber, don't you think?"

"If they don't carry it, I'm sure they'll order it."

"Good, I'll call them tomorrow and make sure Gran's account is in order."

"Jasper Craig still own the lumberyard?"

"Yes, but I'm told Farrel— Ah, his son runs the business now that his father's retired."

By the look on her face, Johnny was sure she knew about the bar fight that had landed him in jail—at least, Sheriff Tucker's version. "My parole states no physical confrontations. What that means, *cherie,* is I'm not supposed to engage in any violent behavior. I don't plan on killing Farrel Craig the next time I see him."

"Should that make me feel better?"

Johnny shrugged. "For the record, I didn't start that fight at Pepper's. Even though I'm sure that's what you've heard. The truth is, if I had wanted Farrel dead, I would have killed him years ago. Leastwise, that's what I told the judge. Now, maybe after I've been in town awhile I'll feel different—Farrel being the number-one jackass that he is."

"So you're saying the bar incident wasn't your fault?"

"I'm saying, maybe I defended myself a little too good." Johnny paused. "Now about those repairs. The place looks like hell. Where do we start?"

For the next half hour, they discussed what Johnny would tackle first. The rotten roof and porch were the most urgent. But there was more: inside jobs for a rainy day, a dead tree in the front yard, painting, window repair.

After a while, Nicole stood, peeling her legs away from the chair one at a time. "If you could figure out some kind of a supply list, I would appreciate it. That's really not something I understand. If you can't—"

"I can." Johnny stood.

She looked nervous suddenly, and as she attempted to step around the chair she stumbled. Before she landed on the floor, Johnny took one long stride and reached out to grip her upper arm, quickly bringing her back to her feet. She was as lightweight as a hollow-legged bird, he noted, letting her go as quickly as he had rescued her.

Hastily she handed him the empty water glass then pulled herself together without delay, impressing him once more with how cool and collected she could be.

She crossed to the door, surprising him when she suddenly turned around in the doorway. "Gran called you her friend. I'm curious to know if it works both ways. Do you consider my grandmother your friend, Johnny Bernard?"

Johnny stayed where he was, his hands shoved into his back pockets. "I really don't think that's what you want to know, *cherie*. What you really want to know is if she'll be safe around me? The answer is, yes. I wouldn't hurt the old lady, or anyone she cares about. Good enough?"

"If you mean it," she said bluntly, and left.

Johnny listened to her light footsteps descending the stairs. And once the outside door creaked, he moved to the window to watch her cross the clearing.

Part of the reason the heat was eating her up so badly was that she moved too fast, he decided. In Louisiana, things were best done at half speed. She needed to learn that, if she was ever going to appreciate the tropical heat. He should mention it, but right now wouldn't do much good—she'd be too busy second-guessing his motives to take a suggestion from him.

The afternoon passed quickly. Before Johnny knew it, the sun had melted into the bayou and he'd spent four hours repairing the dilapidated dock that had been ready to float away in the next windstorm. Now as he walked along the trail in the dark, his thoughts turned to the old lady. He couldn't put off seeing her any longer, though that's just what he'd been doing. Why, he didn't know. Maybe because she was going to look at him long and hard with those knowing blue eyes of hers, and she was going to make him start feeling guilty for leaving fifteen years ago without saying goodbye.

The minute he emerged from the wooded trail and glanced across the driveway, he knew he'd put off seeing her too long. The two-story house was completely dark except for one lone light shining in the left wing. Relieved in a crazy way that made him feel like a vulnerable kid again, he crossed the driveway and ambled toward the big house. He could see the improvements Henry had made over the years. Mae's late husband had been a handy devil. The courtyard had been enlarged, and there was a swing in the backyard he didn't remember from when he was a kid. Two more sheds had been built west of the big field. The carport had been extended, and now accommodated not only Mae's '79 Buick, but a sleek-looking white Skylark.

Henry had died of a heart attack five years ago. Virgil had written the news to Johnny in the Marines. Johnny hadn't kept in contact with anyone else in town, but Virgil

was a persistent old bird and he had tracked Johnny down
years earlier. He had written faithfully over the years.
Johnny had never been much of a letter writer, but he'd
managed one or two a year, which had suited Virgil just
fine.

More than once, Johnny had thought about writing to
Mae. But he hadn't known what to say, so he'd just told
Virgil to let her know he was alive. The day he'd received
the letter of Henry's death, for one crazy second he'd
wanted to come back for the funeral. But then he'd remembered how hard it had been burying his father, and a
few years later his mother, and he had chickened out.

In the sheds, Johnny found old lumber and Henry's car-
pentry tools. In the older shed, he found Henry's tan '59
Dodge pickup. The memories the pickup resurrected were
unexpected. Johnny tucked them away after circling the
pickup twice, then wandered back to the house and found
a sturdy oak in the front yard to settle against.

While lighting a cigarette, he saw someone pace by the
French doors in the left wing of the house. Johnny knew
immediately who it was—the blue-eyed bird with the
shapely legs and long bangs was easy to spot. Smiling, he
slid down the tree to the ground and rested his back against
the sturdy oak. He ignored the steady hum of mosquitoes
overhead and the distant rumble of thunder. An hour
passed, and still he watched her pace the room anxious
about something, or someone. Was his arrival keeping her
up? It made sense; she must have heard some pretty wild
stories about him by now.

By the time she turned out the light and went to bed, it
was after midnight, and Johnny had smoked a half-pack
of cigarettes. He got to his feet and strolled out the yard
and down the driveway. Since leaving Angola he couldn't
get enough fresh air, and, although it was late, he decided
to walk to his parents' old farm.

The thunder continued as he reached Bayou Road and headed east. His pace, however, slowed steadily, his surroundings triggering memories from the past.

Johnny tried to shake them off, but in a matter of seconds he was a kid again, running so fast his lungs felt as if they would explode inside his chest, his bare feet pounding the dirt while Farrel chased after him waving a stick. He could hear Clete Gilmore hollering, calling him ugly names and encouraging Farrel to *"Get him!"*

As he ran, he could see Jack Oden out of the corner of his eye, could see him gaining on him. More than once Johnny had wished that the gangly kid they all called Stretch had been his friend instead of Farrel's.

Johnny stopped abruptly. He was breathing fast, as if he'd actually been running. He shook his head, forced the image back into the black hole where it belonged. He started down the road again, this time noticing that the potholes had gotten deeper, the ditches still waterlogged and ripe with decay.

A rusted-out mailbox signaled the farmhouse was just up ahead. He stepped over the rubble that had once claimed to be a sturdy gate, and walked steadily on. His heart rate picked up again, making his chest feel miserably tight. He didn't want to feel anything, he told himself. Least of all, vulnerable and scared. Lonely. Yet of all the feelings tugging at his insides, those inescapable emotions dominated.

He scaled the porch steps and stopped, his hand poised on the doorknob. He turned the knob—surprisingly it wasn't locked. He took a deep breath, preparing himself for whatever bleak remains still haunted the old house. Then, after fifteen long years, Johnny opened the door and stepped inside.

The floor creaked just the way it used to, the sharp smell of rotten wood swelling his nostrils in protest. He lit a match and glanced around the empty living room. The place had been ransacked, which couldn't have taken more than ten minutes—poverty keeping them from owning so much as a picture to hang on the wall.

He turned to his right and held the match toward the kitchen, and when he did, something scurried across the bare wood floor. He shifted his gaze to the shredded curtains at the window, then to the crude set of cupboards, the warped doors all standing open.

He walked past the kitchen and into the little room his parents had designated his. It was barely big enough to fit a mattress on the floor, and to his surprise the old ragged remains were still there, molding in the corner.

Despair overwhelmed him, and Johnny's stomach knotted. He hadn't expected to feel this way, hadn't wanted any part of the past to intrude on the present. But he was a fool to think that it wouldn't—there was just too much he had run away from.

The depth of poverty that had kept his family in a choke-hold continued to gnaw at Johnny once he returned to the boathouse. He stood at the window overlooking Belle Bayou, a cigarette cornered in his mouth, and closed his eyes. Not liking his melancholy mood, he willed himself to think of something else. The vision that popped into his head had silky blond hair and sexy blue eyes. Johnny took his time, treated himself to the perfect fantasy.

It was all too wicked and perfect to come true, of course. But a man could dream. And so he did.

Chapter 3

The dream was nasty, and *he* was in it.

Disgusted with herself, Nicole jerked awake and sat up
bed. A quick glance at the clock on the nightstand told
er it was barely six. She'd grown used to functioning on
ve hours or less these past few months, tormented by the
ghtmare she'd left behind in L.A. Last night, however,
er thoughts had shifted to the man with the river-bottom
awl and see-to-the-soul eyes.

She told herself it was because of Gran and the unusual
tuation surrounding Johnny Bernard's return. But was it?
he man had taken her completely by surprise yesterday.
e had looked dark and dangerous, yes—but not entirely
the way she had envisioned.

Disgusted that she was giving so much thought to the
bject, Nicole wrestled with the rose-colored satin sheets
d climbed out of bed. The sticky, warm air inside the
om settled against her, and she sighed with the knowl-
lge that she would have to find some way to cope with

the heat again today. Her gaze fell on the fan near the e
of the bed, and she almost reached out and turned it o
No, if she was ever going to adjust she would have to st
relying on that damn fan.

She swept her blue satin robe off the foot of the be
slipped it on and tied the sash around her trim waist.
quick glance outside had her wondering if the late-nig
rain had left a breeze behind. Relief an open door awa
she moved to the French doors that led on to the fro
porch and flung them wide in a sudden burst of hopef
energy.

At the very least, she had expected to hear a chorus
morning songbirds, but instead she felt a *clunk* and hea
a string of colorful cursing, half of it in French. In
instant she knew who owned that distinctive drawl. Drea
ing her next move, Nicole forced herself to peer arou
the door.

He was leaning against the house wearing beat-up jea
and scuffed brown western boots. His hair was tied ba
the same as yesterday, too. One of his hands was rubbi
his hip and the other was pinching his nose to stem t
flow of blood.

Blood. Oh, God!

Nicole ducked back inside, grabbed a handful of tissu
from the box on the nightstand and dashed back outsid
"Here," she said, shoving the pink tissues in his face.

He took the offering without saying a word and presse
the tissues to his nose. Within a few minutes the bloo
had stopped flowing, and he balled up the tissues an
jammed them into his back pocket. Giving her his fu
attention now, he said, "You carry accident insuranc
cherie? It looks like working for you could be dangerous.

Instead of anger, Nicole saw amusement dancing in h
dark eyes. He rubbed at his hipbone again, then flashe
her a crooked smile, which Nicole rejected with a stubbo

't of her chin. "If you're looking for fringe benefits, Mr.
ernard, you won't find them here."

His grin turned wicked. "Oh, I don't know. Insurance
n't everything." He gave her a thorough once-over.
And the name's Johnny. Remember?"

Nicole didn't care one bit for his sexist ogling. "Since
ou're in one piece, I'll leave you to whatever it was you
ere doing." She turned to go back inside, then hesitated.
Which was…?"

"Checking out the condition of the porch. You did say
was top priority, right?"

"Yes, I did. But this early?"

"I couldn't sleep. You, too?" He frowned. "Funny, I
ad you pegged for a snoozer 'til noon."

How he did it, Nicole didn't know. But as she turned
leave, he slipped in front of her and blocked the door
ith one of his long arms. It brought them in close contact,
rcing Nicole to acknowledge his hairy, bare chest cov-
ed in a sheen of sweat. He had powerful biceps, too, all
uscled and honed impossibly hard.

"I could use a glass of water. Got one?"

"Water?" Nicole was suspicious, and yet she couldn't
ry well deny him after asking for the same courtesy yes-
rday at the boathouse. "Wait here."

He dropped his arm. "I'll pass on the ice," he told her.

She hurried past him, through her bedroom and into the
rivate bathroom, where she filled a glass quickly. But as
e stepped back into her bedroom, she was brought up
ort—Johnny Bernard stood only a few feet from her bed.

He turned, saw her surprise, and said, "Red Smote just
lled in the front yard. Hanging around outside your open
or looked worse than just coming in. Should I leave?"

"I think that would look worse, don't you?" Nicole
anced at the clock. It was barely six. "If Red sees you
aving at this hour…" She didn't need to go on.

"Red's the biggest gossip in town," he agreed. "A least, he used to be. We wouldn't want the town specu lating on something that never happened." He relaxed h stance and shoved one hand into his left front pocke "Hell, if a guy's gonna be accused of something memo rable, he should at least have the pleasure of doing it first.

He was teasing her, his knowing eyes full of mischie But just for the record, to let him know she wasn't a push over, she said, "I know where to kick you to make it hu the most, so if you've got any ideas, I suggest you forge them."

He laughed. "You won't get any work out of me if can't walk, *cherie.*"

He had a point. Nicole took the necessary steps to clos the distance between them, and handed over the glass o water. Then, to make sure Red was truly in the yard, sh chanced a quick glance out the door. Sure enough, he wa leaning on the hood of his run-down, red Ford picku talking to Gran's handyman, Bickford Arden, the husban to their loyal housekeeper. Several mornings a week th two elderly men went fishing before breakfast. Hoping tha was the plan and that they would head to the bayou soor Nicole turned around to assure Johnny that he could leav shortly, only to find he'd moved closer to her bed and ha become very interested in the rumpled satin sheets wher she'd tossed and turned half the night.

Color swept into Nicole's cheeks, and Johnny turne just in time to witness it. "Restless night?"

"The heat," she responded.

He glanced around the room. Nicole was sure he ha no interest in floral wallpaper in Wedgwood-green an gypsy-rose, but his eyes seemed to miss nothing. Sh doubted that he would be able to quote what the massiv bed, bureau and matching vanity were worth on the antiqu collectors' market, but, still, his interest was keen as hi and brushed over each piece in obvious appreciation. Finally, he stopped in front of her vanity, his dark eyes finding her in the generous mirror. "Heard you're staying."

"Yes, I am," Nicole assured.

"And the heat?"

"I'll learn to love it."

He grinned. "You move too fast. Slow down some. That'll help." He emptied his water glass, set it on the vanity, then turned his attention to her lacquered jewelry box. With a flick of his wrist, he flipped the top open and looked inside.

Surprised by his boldness, Nicole stared speechless as he rummaged through her personal items, a piece at a time. Finally, his head came up to capture her reflection once more in the mirror. A minute dragged into two before he let his gaze drop back to her modest assortment of baubles, and he pulled out an inexpensive bracelet. "No shiny rocks, *cherie*." He looked at her in the mirror again as if waiting for her to say something. When she didn't, he returned the bracelet to the box and closed it. "So what's important to you, Nicki Chapman? It's obviously not a box full of gold and silver."

No it wasn't, Nicole admitted to herself. To some women, expensive jewelry was important, but not to her. Oh, she liked nice things, but she was more a simple pleasures kind of woman. She enjoyed painting a breathtaking sunrise. Walking in a warm summer rain. She thought a bona fide laugh, a beautiful smile, priceless. But those were her private thoughts and she didn't intend to share them with a stranger.

"Look, Mr. Ber—Johnny, what's important to me is my business. Yours is doing the job you were hired to do, not asking questions."

"Does that work both ways? You don't have any questions for me?"

"It's not the same thing," Nicole argued. "I'm not ᴏ parole. And I haven't earned a reputation in this town ᴀ a troublemaker."

Instead of being offended his dark eyes softened and ʜ wagged a finger at her. "Shame on you for listening to th gossip, *cherie*. You know what they say. Half of it usuall isn't true."

"And the other half?"

"Sometimes fighting back is the only way you can su vive."

It was clear that he was a man ripened by experienc and polished by a predatory edge. Still, was he saying a that was just a false front? That he'd reacted instead ᴏ acted? Nicole had done much the same thing, only not ɪ such a grand fashion. She'd donned her L.A.-cool facad to survive the pain she'd left behind, and even before she' lost her baby, when Chad had walked out on them, she' pasted a smile of indifference on her face.

She didn't want to dismiss his offenses so easily, but she was right, she couldn't help wondering who or wh had prompted his less-than-sterling reputation. Surely nᴏ just bad blood between him and Farrel Craig.

She asked, "Why did you ignore Gran's message to stᴏ by the house yesterday?"

"I didn't ignore it. I came by."

"You certainly did not."

"Yes, I did. I started to fix the dock at the boathous and lost track of time, but I showed up about nine." H shrugged. "The place was dark, except for this room. didn't knock at the front door because I figured the ol lady had gone to bed already."

Was he telling the truth? Nicole didn't know, but the why would he lie? "She waited all afternoon and into th evening. That was inconsiderate. Let's hope today you fin the time. After all, she is the one responsible for getting you out of prison early, Mr. Bernard.''

"Johnny. My friends call me Johnny.''

"Friends?'' Nicole arched a brow in a mocking fashion that she knew wouldn't go unnoticed. "So far, the only friend you have in this town—the only one I'm aware of, anyway—is my grandmother. And I'm still confused as to why she's so willing, when you don't appear to appreciate her kindness with even the simplest thank-you.''

Her chastising seemed to amuse him. He said, "Actually I have two friends in this town. Maybe in time I could add you to the list and make it three. What do you say, *cherie?* Think you could stop disliking me long enough to cut me some slack?''

"Cut you some slack?'' Nicole sniffed. "And then what?''

"Then we get on with the reason I'm here.''

"Whether I'm your friend or not, Mr. Bernard, you will do the job Gran expects of you. A full day's work, plus room and board, for the taste of freedom.''

"Yeah, that was the deal we made. But what about *our* deal?''

"I don't understand.''

He gave her another head-to-toe. "You're not exactly ugly, *cherie*. If you can get past the gossip and give me a fair shake, I'll see that I keep my hands in my pockets and my dirty thoughts to myself.'' He made a show of stuffing his hands in his back pockets.

Well, that was certainly blunt enough, Nicole thought. "Dirty thoughts are dirty thoughts, Johnny. Maybe the deal should be not having them at all.''

His laugh bounced off the walls. "*Cherie,* I've been in prison six months. My dirty thoughts are what kept me sane.''

There was no way she could respond to that withou
wading into dangerous water, so Nicole kept silent.

A moment later, he rounded the bed to gaze at the pain
ing hanging on the wall. She had painted the picture o
Oakhaven's private swimming hole three years ago whe
she and her parents had come for a two-week visit. It wa
the summer before her parents had been killed in a plan
crash.

"Nice picture. Someone local paint it?"

"No." In L.A. Nicole had been a rising star on th
gallery circuit. Or at least, she had been until a few month
ago. Lately, painting had become as difficult as sleeping

He turned around, reached into his back pocket an
pulled out a wrinkled slip of paper. "I've got a supply lis
started." He circled the bed, stopped less than a foot awa
from her and handed her the list. "They might have t
order some of this, so get on it right away."

Nicole accepted the paper, but when she glanced at i
and none of it made sense, she turned and laid it on th
nightstand. "I'll call today."

"The shingles come in different colors and styles
They'll have some samples at the yard you can look at."
He glanced outside. "The coast is clear."

Nicole walked to the French doors. Sure enough, Bicl
and Red had left for the bayou. She felt him come u
behind her, brush past. She said, "Will you see Gran to
day? She really was in a mood last night when she finall
gave up on you."

He turned around, waited as if expecting her to sa
more.

Finally Nicole gave in and said, "Please?"

A lazy smile parted his lips. "Yeah, as soon as she get
her hair combed and her teeth in, I'll come by." He starte
to leave again, then hesitated. "See how easy it is, *cherie*

A simple 'please,' and already you've got me eating out of your hand.''

He cut down the dead tree in the front yard before noon. Officially, he had two days before he started work, but the tree was an eyesore, and, anyway, it felt good to do some physical labor.

Sweat-soaked from the day's heat, Johnny took a good whiff of himself and wrinkled up his nose. A sour fungus growing on something rotten smelled better than he did right now. He glanced at the sky and decided it had to be around one o'clock. He hoisted the chain saw and axe and returned them to one of the sheds, then headed back to the house.

He found the old lady in the garden. He stopped just outside the gate, his chest tightening awkwardly as he assessed her asleep in her wheelchair beneath the old oak. She had always affected him strangely, touching that vulnerable part of him, that little-boy part that was attracted to someone who treated him like they cared. He still didn't know why she had bothered with him; he'd been a wild little bastard. But if he had any good in him at all, Mae Chapman could take credit for it.

She blinked awake as if sensing he was there, her blue eyes cloudy and content as they fastened on him. Her thinning wisps of white hair were pulled back in an attempt to make a small bun at her nape. She was thinner than he remembered, her frail body lost in the fabric of her simple yellow cotton dress.

''I expected to see you yesterday—this morning at the latest,'' she called out, her voice strong and lucid. ''You got a reason to avoid me?''

She spoke bluntly, but without rancor. Her raspy voice sent another burst of emotion through him as Johnny swung the gate open and strolled through. He noticed the bandage on her right ankle, smiled when on further inspection, he saw her small feet tucked into a pair of modern-looking tennis shoes meant for a woman half her age. "Heard you were laid up." He gestured to her injury. "Didn't see any need to bother you too early."

"My ankle's got nothing to do with my ability to get out of bed. And it hasn't affected my speech, either." She spun the wheelchair around to face him.

"No, it doesn't appear so." Johnny grinned. "Then again, you were never short on words, as I recall."

His teasing brought a smile to her gaunt face, exposing a row of perfect-fitting dentures. "Land sakes, look at you." She gave him a prideful once-over. "You still got your daddy's eyes. Kept his shiny hair, too. Delmar would have liked that."

At the mention of his father, Johnny's thoughts turned to the events that had lured him back to town six months ago, and what had happened since. "Are you the one?" he asked. "Have you been paying the taxes on the old farm?"

Her reaction to his question was a slow lifting of one thin white brow. "Now, why would I want to do that?"

"Beats the hell out of me," Johnny countered, still feeling far more emotion than he liked.

"I never invest in anything that isn't a sure thing."

"Oh? Then why did you waste your time on me all those years ago? Or have your lawyer hammer out a deal with the parole board? If you got a reason for dragging me back here, old lady, I want to hear it."

"Your manners are still gut rot, *boy*."

"Answer the question!" Johnny demanded, his patience stretched. "I got a letter from Griffin Black six months ago wanting to buy me out. Now I was sure he was crazy, that is until I came back here and found out I still owned the farm. Don't pretend you don't know what I'm talking about."

She looked crestfallen. "I had no idea this would cause so much trouble. I'm sorry."

She looked suddenly old and vulnerable. Ashamed of himself, Johnny said, "I was coming to see you that day. After I left city hall and I'd found out about that trustee business, I stopped for a quick beer and—I guess you know what happened after that."

"What always happens when you and Farrel get within ten feet of each other." She shook her head. "But I'm to blame this time. If I had let you know about the farm, none of this would have happened." She narrowed her eyes. "I would have told you if you had bothered to write, that is."

Johnny swore. "Keeping that land for me was a foolish mistake."

"I suppose me caring about you is foolish, too?"

Johnny ignored the question. "Virgil says you're going to be in a financial squeeze if you don't sell off your fields or start making a profit from them. You should be putting your money to better use than wasting it on that worthless farm on the hill."

"Virgil's got a big mouth. And speaking of old Big Mouth, how come you wrote to him and not me? It wouldn't have hurt you to write me a few lines every other year, would it?" She looked him squarely in his eyes. "You didn't have to leave, you know. Henry and me were prepared to take you in when your mother died. You could have lived here with us instead of run off like you did."

Yes, he knew she would have taken him in. And that's what had scared him the most. The people who had cared about him had never stayed very long in his life. It wasn't rational thinking, but he'd been scared to death to depend on Mae and Henry after his mother had died. It had been easier just to run away. To leave all his problems behind and start over where no one looked at him twice because his name happened to be Bernard.

"What did you tell Griffin?" she asked.

"He's offering a fair price. Besides, what do I need with a piece of land when I'll be gone in four months?"

"Do me a favor. Wait to make your decision until the end of the summer."

"It won't make any difference," Johnny insisted. "As soon as my parole is up, I'll be going back to Lafayette."

When she didn't argue with him, Johnny leaned against a nearby oak and turned his attention on the house. Ready to discuss the repairs on the porch, the sight of Nicole crossing the front yard in a black skimpy top distracted him. He let his gaze wander, his eyes fastening on her cutoff jeans, noticing once more how they hugged her backside like an overcharged magnet. "How come I never knew about *that?*" he asked without thinking the question through, a moment later wishing he had.

The old lady followed his line of interest. "Nicki? That would be Alice's fault. She was a stingy woman, my daughter-in-law. She didn't like sharing my son Nicholas, or my granddaughter. Henry and I were visited a few holidays a year, and we got Nicki one week each summer. It wasn't enough, but it was better than nothing."

Johnny heard the bitterness in the old lady's voice. "She says she's staying. That her idea or yours?" He glanced back just in time to catch the old lady arch both white eyebrows.

"It was my suggestion, but Nicki's decision."

Johnny followed Nicole's progress as she crossed the road. "So what's her story?"

"If and when she thinks you should know, I'm sure she'll tell you."

Johnny had hoped the old lady would feel generous and

offer a little free information. But it looked like she wasn't going to. Instead, for the next half hour they talked about how hot the summer was expected to be, the repairs on the house, and who had died since he'd been away.

Johnny didn't mention Nicole again, or the fact that he'd been in her bedroom that morning. It might be perverse, but he liked knowing something the old lady didn't. Liked keeping the memory of the slender blonde in her robe all to himself.

After a time, the conversation waned, and he shoved away from the gnarly oak. "I'll see you later." He took a step toward the gate.

"Not so fast. Will the boathouse do? You could never get enough of the bayou."

"Still can't," he admitted. "I fixed the dock yesterday. That's why I was late making it up to the house last night. You'd gone to bed. Guess I forgot you old people turn in early," he teased.

When he turned around to give her one last look, he caught her smiling. "You always had a smart mouth. But it's a good-looking one, to be sure," she conceded. "Join me for supper?"

Somehow, arriving on the back doorstep like a stray dog looking for a handout didn't sit too well. Johnny shook his head. "I don't think so."

She grunted, and she, too, shook her head, which sent the loose skin on her cheek into a slight tremor. "The more things change, the more things stay the same. Supper's at seven. Come through the front door, and put on a shirt."

A bar of soap jammed in his back pocket, Johnny left the boathouse and headed for Oakhaven's swimming hole. He didn't have to think twice how to find his way. He hung a left off the trail, ducked under a familiar leafy hickory, and the swimming hole came into plain view.

Small and secluded, the pond still looked like a well-kept secret in the middle of nowhere.

Johnny pulled off his boots, stripped his socks and unzipped his jeans. He was just seconds away from sending them to the ground when he heard a loud *splash*. He gave his jeans a tug back to his hips, yanked his zipper upward, then moved to the water's edge.

So this is where she'd gone.

Johnny watched as Nicole surfaced, then rolled onto her back and began kicking her way to the middle of the pond. Something blue caught his eyes along the shore. He slipped through the foliage and found her towel and cutoffs draped over a downed hickory limb. A pair of canvas sling-back shoes were perched on a stump.

She had no idea someone was there, and he could have sat and watched her all afternoon—something he would have enjoyed doing if he weren't so annoyed by the fact that she was so unobservant. He scanned the bank until he found two flat stones. Then, gauging the distance, he dropped down on one knee and let the first rock fly. It entered the water like a shot out of a gun, sailing past Nicole's pretty nose with deadly accuracy. By the time he'd sent the second rock zooming on its way, her feet had found the bottom of the pond, and she was searching the bank with alarm in her wide eyes.

When she spied him, her alarm turned to anger. "Are you crazy! You missed me by less than an inch." Her voice was shrill, irritation evident in the straining pitch.

"No, it was more like four," Johnny quipped.

She waded toward him, her breasts swaying gently in her swimsuit. She left the pond behind and kept coming up the grassy bank. "One inch or four—I don't see much difference, Mr. Bernard. It was too close and—"

"Johnny."

She stopped a few feet away and met his eyes disparagingly. "What?"

"You keep forgetting my name."

She glared down at him where he still knelt in the grass. "We've been all through that," she snapped.

"Yes, we have." He glanced around as if looking for something, or someone. "You haven't seen old One Eye around, have you?"

"One Eye?" She tipped her head to one side and began squeezing the water from the ends of her hair. "What's a 'one eye'?"

Johnny stood and hung his hands loosely on his hips. "One Eye's a gator. He used to take his afternoon nap in this here swimming hole years ago."

Her hands stilled. "An alligator? Here?"

Johnny told the lie easily. One Eye had always favored the privacy of the black bog deeper in the swamp. And he might still be there. But more than likely, the aging gator had been turned into a purse or a sturdy pair of boots by now.

He let his gaze travel the length of her delicate curves. Outlined in the skimpy, two-piece swimsuit, she was definitely hot. He wanted to stay in control of the situation, but his imagination was working overtime, and right now he would have liked nothing better than to run his hands over her satin-smooth skin, lick the water beads from her bare shoulders, lower her to the grassy bank for some serious one-on-one.

"You always run around half-dressed, or is this a sign my luck's changing? Twice in one day. I'd say that's—"

"Is there something you wanted besides stopping by to give me a hard time?"

Now there was a phrase. Johnny shifted his stance hoping to ease his discomfort, then reached for her towel and tossed it to her. She caught it, and after drying herself off, she picked up her cutoffs and slipped them on.

"Next time you think about swimming, it would be smart to tell somebody where you're going." Johnny glanced over Nicole's shoulder to where a snake hung camouflaged in the branches. It was a harmless variety, and yet it could just as easily have been poisonous. She was completely unaware of her surroundings, and, again, it angered him. "This isn't L.A., *cherie*. You got more to worry about here than rush-hour traffic and parking tickets. Here, you never know what might fall out of the sky."

She looked thoroughly annoyed with him. She said, "If that's all you came by to say, it's getting late. Gran will be—"

"Glad I came along to make sure you didn't drown, or worse."

"I'm a good swimmer."

With lightning-quick reflexes, Johnny shot his arm out past her head and yanked the snake out of the tree. As it dangled from his outstretched hand, thrashing to free itself, he drawled, "And just how good are you with curious snakes?"

To his surprise, she didn't go crazy on him and start screaming the way he'd expected she would. She did, however, take several steps back. "I didn't see it," she admitted.

"I know." He gave the mottled brown snake a mighty heave into the woods. "It's just a harmless milk snake, but until you see it, how would you know? By then, it could be too late." Lesson over, he changed the subject. "You call Craig about those supplies we need? Talk to him about ordering shingles?"

"I tried."

"What do you mean, tried?"

"Farrel Craig wasn't in his office when I called this

morning. It'll have to wait until Monday. I've decided to go into town, that way then I can order the shingles.''

His bar of soap must have slipped out of his pocket. She bent to pick it up and tossed it to him. ''When you decide to wash, don't forget to use it.''

She was past him before he had a chance for a comeback. Johnny watched her go, her hips swaying slowly. Each step she took appeared innocent enough, and maybe that was the turn-on. There was something erotic and very inviting about a woman who had no idea how completely she affected a man, inside and out. And there was no doubt Nicole Chapman affected him. He'd spent half the night thinking about her, and most of the morning.

Once she was gone, Johnny unzipped his jeans and shoved them to his knees. He was just stepping out of them when he saw her shoes sitting on the stump.

Nicole stopped to examine her injury. The inch-long cut on the bottom of her foot wasn't deep, but it hurt like the devil. Angry with herself for forgetting her shoes, she started back to the pond, limping like a lame bird. She wouldn't have forgotten the damn shoes if it hadn't been for that blasted snake. It had taken all the composure she owned to keep from screaming and acting foolish.

If she'd returned to the pond a second sooner, Nicole was sure, she would have caught Johnny Bernard buck naked. He looked as surprised as she did when she reappeared—his hair loose and hanging free to his shoulders, his jeans riding low on his hips, the zipper at half-mast.

She motioned toward the stump where her shoes sat. ''I—I forgot them.'' She took a step to retrieve them, and winced when a sharp pain shot into the bottom of her foot.

''What happened?''

''Just a scratch.'' Nicole tried to downplay her injury and the pain it was causing. Johnny Bernard hadn't come right out and said what he thought of a city girl moving to the country, but she sensed he didn't think she would last long.

His gaze sharpened. "You didn't step on something you shouldn't have, did you?"

Was he trying to be funny or was he serious? She had thought it was a stick that she'd stepped on, but now suddenly worried, Nicole hobbled to the nearest tree. Leaning against it, she raised her foot to examine the injury. The blood covering the bottom of her foot made it difficult. She wiped it away, trying to pinpoint the pain.

"Here, let me have a look."

Nicole glanced up and found him standing over her. "No, really, I'm fine."

"Let's make sure."

She slid down the tree and sat. "Just don't make it hurt worse."

He crouched in front of her and took hold of her foot. His hands were big and warm, rough from the kind of work he did. He wiped away the blood on his jeans, then carefully examined the cut. Finally he said, "You'll live, but you need surgery."

"What!"

Nicole tried to jerk her foot back, but he hung on. In fact, he tightened his grip. "Easy. There's a sliver in there, and you could drive it deeper if you're not careful."

"A sliver?" Relieved, Nicole sighed and relaxed against the tree.

"A good-size sliver," he corrected. "It needs to come out."

"And it will," Nicole assured. "Gran can—"

"I don't think you should wait." His dark eyes found hers. "If you put your weight on it, you could break it off or force it deeper. 'Course, I could carry you to the house…"

"Carry me? No. I—"

"Yeah, that's what I figured." He worked his hand into the front pocket of his ragged jeans and came up with a long sleek knife that unfolded into something that looked like it came straight out of a Rambo movie. That he owned such a knife was bad enough, but to think he was going to use it to probe the bottom of her foot was worse.

"Wait!"

He looked up. "You change your mind, *cherie?* You want a ride to the house?"

Damn him, but he almost looked as if he were enjoying this, Nicole thought.

When she didn't answer, he settled more comfortably in the grass, tucked his hair behind his ears, then took hold of her foot again. She wasn't expecting him to be gentle, but as she leaned her head against the tree and braced herself for what was to come next, she had to give him more than a little credit; he treated her foot like a piece of fragile glass.

She closed her eyes at the first prick of pain. "Talk to me," she insisted. "Say anything. Gran said you were a marine," she began, sucking in her breath as the pain began to build.

"For five years."

"Ouch!" Nicole bit her lip.

"Easy. This damn thing's twice as long as it is deep. Just breathe slow and even."

He sounded sincere. Nicole braced herself and tried to do as she was told. "Why did you quit the military?"

"I didn't quit. I was medically discharged." His hand stilled, and he glanced up. He offered her a smile before he lowered his head and went back to work. Quietly, he drawled, "I won't cut your toes off, *cherie.* I promise."

"I didn't mean to—"

"I spent some time in Kuwait." He looked up, laid the

knife in the grass. "This isn't working, *cherie,* but I know what will."

Before Nicole could ask him what he had in mind, he lifted her foot upward and pulled. The movement dragged her away from the tree, and, to keep her balance, she arched her back and rested on her elbows for support. He took in her sprawled position and said, "Now, don't move, no matter what. Okay?"

Nicole hesitated, then nodded warily.

He lowered his head, and a moment later his warm breath touched the bottom of her foot. Nicole had no idea what he meant to do until she felt his tongue slide over the cut. She clutched the grass at her sides in tight fists and craned her neck to see what was going on. He'd said don't move, but my God, he was licking the bottom of her foot!

She tried to sit up while at the same time pulling her foot away. He looked up. "I said, don't move. Trust me. I know what I'm doing."

He went back to work, and Nicole felt his tongue glide slowly over her foot once more. She decided to give him exactly one minute, and if he didn't—

"Ou-ouch!" Nicole jerked her foot away from him with such force that it sent her falling onto her back. She closed her eyes for a second, the pain momentarily stealing her breath. It had felt as if he'd sent the sliver clean through the top of her foot.

"You all right?"

Nicole slowly opened her eyes. Johnny was kneeling over her, the ends of his black hair almost tickling her face, those unnerving eyes smiling down at her. He opened his mouth and stuck out his tongue. And there it was—the wicked-looking sliver.

"It's huge," Nicole gasped.

He turned his head away from her and spit the splinter

nto the thick brush, then sat back on his heels. "When I was a kid, my mama used to take slivers out that way. We never owned a pair of tweezers." He reached for his knife and slipped it back into his pocket, then stood and held out his hand to help her up.

Nicole took his offered hand, and he easily pulled her up. She tested out her foot, the pain only slight now. "Thank you," she said softly.

"You're welcome."

Now that her crisis was past, Nicole once again became fully aware of Johnny Bernard. They were standing close, his chest gleaming and hard, his half-zipped fly exposing an appealing dark navel. Yes, she'd noticed his attributes yesterday and again this morning in her bedroom, but that didn't mean she wanted anything from him, because she most definitely did not.

"I need to get back," she announced quickly.

"Yeah, me, too. I've been invited to supper."

Nicole reached for her shoes and slipped them on. "I thought you said you didn't have many friends."

"That's right. Just so you know, *cherie,* the old lady invited me to join the two of you for supper. See you at seven."

Chapter 4

"A little warning would have been nice," Nicole insisted.

"Warning? Why would you need to be warned?" Mae asked. "You don't have to do any cooking. Clair will take care of that like she always does. All you have to do is show up. You don't even have to change your clothes or comb your hair if you don't want to. You look fine."

Gran had completely missed the point. She wasn't talking about her clothes, for heaven's sake, or the menu. She simply saw no reason for Johnny Bernard to share meals with them. He had a kitchen in his apartment above the boathouse. Wasn't that good enough?

"I still can't believe how much he's changed," Mae mused. "I tell you, Nicki, when Johnny stepped into the garden today, and I got my first look at him after fifteen years, I couldn't believe it was the same scrawny youngster. Oh, I knew it was him—he's got his daddy's eyes and his grandpa Carl's mouth." Mae plucked another wilted blossom off the azalea in the corner and dropped it into her lap, then focused her attention on Nicole once more. "Did you say it was at the swimming hole you ran into him?"

Nicole sat a little straighter in the white wicker chair on the front porch. "Yes. I went to cool off."

"Ninety-eight in the shade today," Mae confirmed. "Tomorrow is supposed to be even hotter."

"Oh, goodie."

Mae chuckled. "You'll get used to it, dear. Now then, down to business. Over supper, I think we should discuss our remodeling ideas with Johnny—the first being the attic. I know there are other things that seem more important, but it would make such a lovely studio for you, Nicki."

"I know you think so." Nicole did, too. It was a wonderful idea; that is, it would have been if she felt at all creative and focused these days. Only, she hadn't been able to do much of anything but feel sorry for herself the past three months. She wanted to return to work, she really did—but just thinking about painting caused her palms to sweat.

She stood and crossed to the porch railing, unwilling to let her grandmother see her anxiety. "I've been thinking about taking the summer off," she said, struggling to keep the emotion out of her voice. "I haven't had a vacation away from my career since I sold my first painting four years ago. I'm tired and—"

"The entire summer?" Mae gave a hollow whistle. "Do you think that's smart? You love your work, and the galleries…won't they be anxious to get something new on their walls?"

"I've taken that into consideration," Nicole assured, leaning against the support post. But she wasn't worried about the galleries; what she wanted most of all was the fever back. She wanted to wake up tomorrow morning

with a driving need to create something alive and beautifu
But what if she never felt the fever again? What if she ha
lost her talent? What if it had vanished along with every
thing else? She couldn't begin to describe the fear tha
daily clawed at her insides. And if she tried to explain i
to Gran, she would have to reveal everything. And righ
now she simply couldn't do that.

She closed her eyes and willed herself to think of some
thing else. She was successful in putting it out of her mind
but, in the trade-off, the topic circled back to another un
pleasant topic. Her grandmother asked, "Did you se
Johnny got rid of that old dead tree in the yard?"

Nicole concentrated on growing a nasty headache, th
kind that drained your complexion and dulled your eyes
The kind that would excuse her from the supper table.

"Nicki, did you hear? The tree's gone."

Nicole opened her eyes and glanced out into the fron
yard. "Yes, I noticed," she said without emotion.

"Make sure you comment on it at supper. Say he's don
a fine job, or something to that effect. A little praise i
what he needs to hear right now. It will boost his confi
dence."

"I think I'm coming down with a headache," sh
primed.

"Well, take something before it gets out of hand, dear
You wouldn't want it to spoil supper."

"No," she agreed, "that would be unfortunate."

A stingy breeze, slow and barely evident, drifted ont
the porch. Like a greedy beggar, Nicole raised her chin i
an attempt to cool her warm cheeks. She could smell th
potted azalea in the corner, the fried chicken Clair Arde
was preparing for supper. "Will it rain tonight?"

"No, but maybe tomorrow. So did we decide on gree
or gray shingles, Nicki? I think you said green, right?"

Nicole felt a tug on the uneven hem of her orange tank

top. She glanced down to see that Gran had wheeled up close.

"The shingles, Nicki. What color? I can't remember what we agreed on."

"We didn't, did we?"

"We certainly did." Mae arched a thin brow. "This drifting in and out that you do—is it a creative thing, or is there something on your mind I should know about?"

"What?"

"I keep telling myself it isn't that I'm a boring old woman, but that you're simply creating upstairs."

"Upstairs?"

"In the mind, Nicki. Honestly, one minute we're having a conversation, and the next you're lunching with the fairies."

"I was thinking about how to remodel the attic," Nicole lied.

Mae pointed at Nicole's splattered tank top. "Is this another one of those fashion statements? What do they call this one? Homeless, or the rag of the month?"

Nicole didn't feel like smiling, but Gran's comments were always amusing. The dress code in Common was definitely not as liberal as in L.A. "Have the ladies at the garden club been talking?"

"Of course," Mae admitted honestly, her eyes reflecting not a bit of censure. "No one moves to Common without getting a head-to-toe and a couple dozen opinions for free. Pearl Lavel tells me her son saw you last week at the post office and he's been talking about you ever since. Sounds to me like you made quite an impression on Woodrow. If you're wondering, he's single and twenty-seven. I don't believe he's a strong enough personality for you, though, and Clair agrees."

They'd had a similar discussion earlier in the week. Only, it had been in reference to Gordon Tisdale's son,

Norman. He was single, too. A thirty-six-year-old teacher at the grade school. Gran and Clair's assessment of Norman, however, was that he didn't have a sense of humor—a vital component for a lasting marriage.

Nicole rubbed her temple, the headache she'd been hoping for was going to be a reality very soon if they started talking about eligible bachelors, marriage and babies.

Mae glanced at her watch. "It's almost seven. Johnny should be coming soon."

The comment prompted Nicole to look across the road to the wooded trail. The sun was sinking, causing shadows to grow between the trees. Soon the mosquitoes would come, and like a gray cloud of doom they would chase anyone with half a brain inside. "Did you know his family well?"

"Yes. Delmar and Madie were good people, honest and likable. Madie was the prettiest girl in town, I always said. And the men agreed. They were all after her." Mae returned to the azalea bush and began plucking dead blossoms. "That old farm was a curse, though. Nothing ever grew in those fields, no matter how hard Delmar tried. Finally, he gave up and took himself off to town. Got a job at the lumberyard working for Jasper Craig. No one else in town would hire him, but Jasper surprised everyone and took Delmar on. It lasted a few months, then the accident happened."

"What accident?"

"Delmar was run over."

"Run over? Was he killed?"

"I'm afraid so. The driver of the car must not have seen him. It happened down the road about a mile. They never did learn who was behind the wheel. Henry found him early that morning. We called Sheriff Tucker, and he came out. Delmar was so badly mangled, they didn't show him at the funeral. Poor Madie cried her eyes out for months.

Johnny…well, after that, things just got harder for him. Then Madie got sick a few years later and died from cancer. Day after we buried her, Johnny ran off.''

Nicole turned to face her grandmother. ''You wanted him to stay, didn't you.''

Mae's eyes turned warm with affection. ''The first time I saw that boy something inside me melted. He was barefoot and so skinny he was all ribs and legs. He had a smart mouth and language like nothing I'd ever heard. 'Course his orneriness was just a front, you see, a way to cover up being scared. The kids in town were awfully mean to him. It's why I know that fight at Pepper's wasn't all Johnny's doing. I'm not saying he didn't participate, but I know in my heart he didn't start it.''

''And how can you be so sure?''

''Farrel Craig was on the other end of that fight. Anytime that boy got near Johnny, there was trouble. Farrel and those two puppets of his, Clete Gilmore and Jack Oden, used to chase Johnny home after school everyday. It started way back in grade school.'' A honeybee buzzed around Mae's head. She paid no attention as she went on. ''I've never told this to a soul, but Henry and I would have adopted Johnny if he hadn't run off. Yes, Nicki, I wanted him to stay, and I would be lying if I denied I want him to stay now. Running away from your problems isn't the answer. Deal with the demon, I always say. Or the demon will chase you all your life.''

Nicole gazed across the yard, not knowing what to say. The summer oak leaves began to rustle, and she angled her face to catch the elusive evening breeze. She closed her eyes and concentrated on the night sounds coming alive in the distant bayou.

Suddenly the feeling of being watched intruded on her, and she opened her eyes just as a shadowy figure broke through the oak grove and started across the road. She fixed her gaze on Johnny Bernard's slow, ambling gait, on the quiet strength he exuded with each step. No one else walked quite like he did, she decided. There was something mesmerizing about the unhurried way he moved. Something raw and earthy. Primal.

He wore a white T-shirt stretched over his iron chest. He'd even taken the time to tuck it into a pair of jeans that were in better condition than she'd seen him in so far, but even at this distance, she could see they weren't hole-free. He was crossing the yard now, his shiny black hair moving slightly in answer to the sultry summer breeze. She hadn't wanted to think about their afternoon meeting at the pond, but suddenly she could think of nothing else. The memory of how easily he'd handled the snake, the way he'd gotten her attention by skipping rocks practically under her nose. The way his silky tongue had slid over the bottom of her foot.

Aware that her heart had begun to race, Nicole quickly spun away from the railing.

"Nicki! Nicki, where are you going?"

"He's coming." Nicole headed for the open French doors that led into the study, her voice straining to sound normal. "I'll tell Clair supper will be on time."

Mae arrowed her wheelchair in front of the open French doors leading into the study. "You don't mind wheeling an old lady in, do you? Nicki went to tell Clair we're on our way."

Johnny had seen Nicole shoot inside like someone had lit a fire under her. Instead of commenting on it, though, he sauntered up the steps and positioned himself behind the old lady's chair. "You trust me to keep it under the speed limit?"

"Trusting you was never a problem, dear boy." She reached back to pat his arm.

Johnny felt her warm fingers, and it brought back a mountain of memories. He'd never liked being touched as a boy. But that had never stopped Mae Chapman. She was one of those affectionate types, always patting him and tousling his hair. Once or twice she'd even hugged him. He had tried to figure her out, had at first been suspicious of her motives. Finally, he'd given up, and no matter how crazy it sounded, decided that she just liked him. Still, it humbled him. No one in Common liked the Bernards.

He pushed the wheelchair through the study and into the oak-paneled hall. Even though he'd lived only a few miles from Oakhaven, he'd never been inside the twelve-room house. Not until today, anyway, when he'd slipped into Nicki's bedroom uninvited. Oh, he'd been asked as a boy, or maybe *coaxed* was a better word. The old lady used to tempt him with cookies and apples. He never liked taking charity, though, and had preferred a trade if it was something he wanted badly enough. Most of the time he'd bartered for food. But one time it had been for a pair of shoes Mae's son, Nicholas, had outgrown.

Nicholas had been tall and blond like Henry and big-hearted like Mae. Virgil said he'd become a lawyer. It must have damn near killed the old lady to lose him in a plane crash only three years after losing Henry, Johnny thought. And Nicole—it must have devastated her to lose both her parents at one time.

They passed a small parlor and entered a dining room with high ceilings and papered walls in a light shade of green. The house was just as he'd imagined it would be, full of antiques and pictures. Spit-polished until even the floors shined. The oak table in the middle of the room could seat ten people, easily. Johnny noticed an end chair was missing so he steered Mae to the open space. Then he sat in the vacant chair to her left, leaving him a clear view of the open door.

"I was glad you tackled that dead oak," Mae said. "I was just telling Nicki on the porch about this idea I have for the atti—"

"Green. We've decided on green shingles."

Johnny glanced toward the door, as Nicole stepped into the room. She was wearing a yellow sleeveless shift, short enough to see her bare knees and just straight enough to accent her narrow waist and shapely backside. She'd twisted her hair into a messy knot on top of her head, and her exposed neck drew his attention to a small mole just below her left ear.

Usually he preferred his women dark and sturdy enough to go the distance. Nicole was fair, and curvy in a delicate way that would make a man want to take his time. The image of slow and easy lovemaking sent a shudder ripping through him, and Johnny tore his gaze away from her. Even though he knew he shouldn't be thinking what he was thinking, he'd been thinking it all day. And after what happened at the swimming hole, he'd been thinking about more places to put his tongue than the bottom of her foot.

"Water, anyone?"

"Yes, please," Mae said.

Johnny nodded in agreement with the old lady. Clair Arden hurried in and deposited a platter of fried chicken and dumplings in the middle of the table. The compact housekeeper, who was in her late fifties, barely stood five feet tall. She had round cheeks and warm brown eyes. She smiled at Johnny, and it was one of those smiles that hinted she knew something he didn't. He pondered that, while she made two more trips, leaving a basket of corn bread, coffee and a dish she called *maque choux*—corn served with tomatoes, green peppers and onions.

Mae's heavy sigh drew Johnny's attention, and he turned just in time to see her sway forward.

"Mae?" It was Clair's voice. "What is it?"

"I feel light-headed all of a sudden," she complained.

"Gran!" Water forgotten, Nicole hurried back to the table. "What's wrong?"

"I'm sure it's nothing. Oh, my." She placed her hands on the table to keep from tipping out of her chair.

"Gran! Is it the heat? It is, isn't it?"

"Now, Nicki, don't blame the weather," Mae scolded gently.

"Maybe you should go lie down," Johnny suggested.

Mae waved a hand in rejection of the idea. "I'll be fine in a minute."

But one minute slipped into two, then three. Nicole said, "I'm phoning Dr. Jefferies."

"Nonsense," Mae protested. "I don't intend to bother that busy man with something so foolish as a little dizzy spell."

Nicole exchanged a look with Johnny. He could see she was worried. Not sure what to do, he finally stood, pulled the wheelchair away from the table and hunkered down in front of it. He was just about to insist that she let Nicki call the doc when he noticed the old lady's eyes—they were as sharp and clear as a blue sky, certainly not the eyes of a woman suffering from a dizzy spell. Her skin was its normal color, too. Was she faking being sick? It sure as hell looked that way.

Johnny thought for a minute, then made a show of examining her face. "Yeah, you really don't look good," he said. "I thought I noticed it earlier in the garden. Only, it's worse now. You remind me of a catfish dangling on a hook just before it goes belly-up."

Nicole gasped from somewhere behind him. He didn't have to look to know her eyes would be wide with stark surprise. Mae gave him a suspect look, and he countered it with one of his own. They were reading each other perfectly, and neither needed to elaborate on the message.

Suddenly he felt Nicole's hand on his shoulder, shoving him out of the way to plant herself in front of Mae's chair. "Don't listen to him, Gran. He doesn't know what he's talking about. I'll take you to your room and get a cool cloth for your head. You'll be fine," she assured. She turned and shot Johnny a frosty glare. "In the future, don't try to help. Obviously, you don't know the first thing about it."

"That's not how you felt this afternoon. As I recall, you even said 'thank you.'"

"Thank you? What did she say 'thank you' for?" Mae asked.

"It was nothing," Nicole insisted, glaring at Johnny.

"Now children, don't fight," Mae intervened. She gave Nicole a weak smile, followed by a long sigh. "Oh, you win. I'll rest in my room if you promise to sit down and eat with Johnny. Clair, go get Bick. I'll have him take me to my room so the children can have a nice, quiet supper."

"I'll take you," Nicole insisted. "I'm not hungry."

"Nonsense," Clair piped up. "You can't afford to miss a meal if I'm going to win my bet with Mae and put five pounds on you by the end of the month. You're much too skinny, honey."

Johnny watched the two old women exchange a look. It was obvious the housekeeper was in cahoots with Mae and that they had anticipated Nicole's argument and rehearsed their lines. He watched Clair hustle out the door, and return a moment later with Bick.

Bickford Arden was as tall as Clair was short. He strolled into the room wearing baggy tan pants, a blue cotton shirt and a beat-up blue baseball cap. He smiled at Nicole, nodded in Johnny's direction, then grasped Mae's wheelchair and spun her toward the door. Clair said, "I'll make you a cool lemonade and bring it to your room, Mae."

The entourage left, with Nicole following. Johnny returned to his seat to wait and see if she would join him. A few minutes later, she came back through the door wearing a thin-lipped scowl that clearly warned she wasn't too happy with the way things had turned out.

At the sideboard, she retrieved their water glasses and brought them to the table. Without a word she plopped his down, splashing water onto his plate. While Johnny reached for his napkin and mopped up the spill, she seated herself.

"A hooked catfish going belly-up?" she said. "Why don't you just get the shovel out and start digging a grave in the backyard?"

"I had my reason for saying that. Would you like to hear what it was?"

Instead of letting him vindicate himself, she said, "She's an elderly woman. A sweet, sensitive—"

"Sneaky."

"Sneaky?" She glared at him. "Gran is the most good-hearted person I know."

Good-hearted had nothing to do with it, Johnny thought. A woman who could con a man back into town when he had promised himself never to return was sure capable of staging a little dizzy spell. It made him wonder what was coming next. Discarding his manners, he reached for the chicken and dumplings. After serving himself, he passed Nicole the platter.

She dished up a small helping, set the platter down and reached for her napkin. Johnny watched her snap it open and lay it in her lap. It prompted him to look for the wet ball he'd laid beside his plate. He decide to forgo it, and left it where it was.

While she cut her chicken into small pieces, Johnny devoured his first piece using his fingers. He was on the second when he glanced up and caught her watching him.

He wasn't eating like a well-mannered gentleman, but he wasn't exactly foaming at the mouth, either. "Something wrong?"

"No."

Johnny grabbed up the wet ball and made a quick swipe around his mouth. When she became preoccupied once more with her own food, he forked a healthy helping of dumplings into his mouth, then reached for another piece of corn bread. The bread was addicting, but he curbed his desire to make a pig of himself.

He noticed she was eating more slowly than he was, and he tried to pace himself. Maybe if he said something... "Does Henry's old Dodge run?"

She looked up. "Why do you want to know?"

"I sold my wheels from inside prison. Thought I could use the pickup while I'm here. I could drive you into town Monday morning and pick up those supplies we need."

She stopped her fork on its way to her mouth, set it back down. "You want the two of us to go to town together? To Craig Lumber? Why?"

"Why not? You afraid to be seen with me, *cherie?*" Johnny reached for another piece of chicken.

"Of course not."

"Afraid I'll start trouble or something?"

"Or something."

Johnny leaned back in his chair and rested his arms on either side of his plate. "I don't plan on making trouble."

"It sounds like you don't really have to, it just follows you." She speared a small piece of chicken and brought the fork to her mouth.

"What if I promised to stay in the pickup?" Johnny offered.

She left half her food and slid the plate back an inch.

A moment later, Clair came through the door with two slices of pecan pie. She frowned at Nicole's plate, but removed it anyway, replacing it with a large piece of pie. "My husband wanted to know if you're a card player," she asked, giving Johnny her full attention.

The question caught Johnny by surprise. Still, the idea of a few hands of cards on a hot summer night had a certain appeal. "I can hold my own," he said.

"Red don't play so good," Clair confessed. "Bick usually heads into the kitchen around nine-thirty for a cup of coffee. If it suits you, you're welcome. The coffeepot's always on." She turned to Nicole. "Mae's feeling better, honey. It must have been a touch of the heat, just like you said. Be a good girl and eat your pie, now. I've only got two weeks left to win my bet."

They finished dessert in silence. Nicole left her crust; Johnny was tempted to lick the plate. When she laid her napkin beside her plate and stood, Johnny had just sucked the last of his coffee down. She said, "If I don't see you tomorrow, I'll meet you Monday morning on the front porch at ten o'clock. You can drive me to town, but when it comes to the lumberyard, I'll handle the order. Deal?"

Johnny hadn't expected her to give in so easily. "You've got a deal." He stood when she did. She was halfway to the door when he said, "The old lady faked it."

She stopped, one hand on the door frame, and turned slightly. "What did you say?"

"The dizzy spell was all an act." He closed the distance between them. "It's the truth. She faked it, and Clair Arden was in on it."

"That's ridiculous. Why would they do that?"

Johnny hooked a thumb into the waistband of his jeans and relaxed his broad shoulder against the doorjamb. It brought them within a foot of each other, and he caught a whiff of her light, spicy perfume. "I got my own theory, but maybe you should ask her."

"And just what is yours?"

"I'd rather not say until you've had a chance to discuss it with her."

She stared at him for a minute, then took a step closer to the door. To leave she would have to brush past him, or get him to move. Johnny wasn't surprised when she said, "You're blocking the door."

"Is it just me, or do you hate all men, *cherie?*"

"Get out of my way," she insisted.

"As soon as you answer the question. Do you always pace the floor half the night, or is it just since I moved in? Is it because my name is Bernard?"

Her eyes went wide. "You admit to spying on me?"

"Not intentionally. I was out walking and noticed your light."

"So you stopped and watched!" Her voice had turned accusing.

"That's not the way it was."

"I'll just bet it wasn't."

Her eyes had turned a stormy shade of blue-gray. She was more than simply angry. "You still haven't answered my question. What's keeping you up nights?"

"None of your damn business."

"Were you trying to think of another way to get rid of me?"

She turned away and walked back to the table. With her back to him, she said, "I made that call yesterday to protect Gran. I had no idea you two knew each other. I made a mistake." She turned around and faced him. "Haven't you ever made a mistake…*Johnny?*"

"Dozens. Did you tell her you tried to fire me?"

Her hands went to her hips, and she glared at him. "No. And if you think it will give you a few extra points with her, go ahead and tell her."

"I'm not interested in making points—" Johnny

grinned "—unless they're with you. How about it, *cherie?* How about a truce?" He shoved away from the door and moved toward her. "Doesn't taking that sliver out of your foot count for something?"

Without responding, she sidestepped him and headed for the door. Johnny turned to follow, but she stopped. "If Gran was faking it, why didn't you confront her with it?"

"Because I agree with you and think she's a decent person. I'm willing to bet if you ask her, she'll admit the whole thing was concocted."

"You could have told me this during supper."

"I tried. You cut me off. After that—" he shrugged "—I saw my chance to have supper with a pretty woman and decided to sit back and enjoy it. It's been a long time."

"I don't believe you. Gran wouldn't make me worry needlessly." That said, she turned and walked out.

Nicole took a deep breath and summoned her L.A.-cool facade back in place. It had taken an hour to regain her composure after leaving the dining room, but now that she could breathe normally again, she was going to confront Gran with Johnny's absurd accusation.

She rapped lightly on her grandmother's bedroom door. "Gran, are you still up?"

"Come in, Nicki."

Nicole opened the door and stepped inside. Gran's room, like her own, was a mix of old lace and polished oak furnishings. A single lamp glowed on a nearby night-stand, and it spilled just enough light into the room to guide Nicole to the bed. Mae was braced against the head-board with a fluffy pillow at her back. She was in a white nightgown, her hair brushed out, the strands thin and fly-away in the dim light.

Nicole didn't want to believe Gran had feigned the dizzy

spell, but she looked for signs that would convince her otherwise and found none: Gran looked perfectly fine.

"I waited up for you," she said, patting the bed to encourage Nicole to sit.

"I want to ask you something," Nicole said, taking a seat and getting right to the heart of the matter. "Did you—"

"Yes."

"Yes?" Nicole frowned. "How can you answer a question you haven't heard yet?"

"Because I know what you're going to ask. Johnny saw through my hoax tonight and he told you, didn't he? I expected he would."

Confused, Nicole asked, "Why did you do it? Why did you pretend you were sick?"

"I've sensed for two days that you haven't been happy with my decision to bring Johnny here. I thought once you got to know him, you'd feel differently. He really is a good boy, Nicki. But it takes time to warm up to him. I was giving you that time."

"It's not going to happen, Gran. I believe he's a chameleon."

"Aren't we all. It depends on the time and place and who's standing next to us, but I believe we all are changing constantly. That boy has seen a lot, Nicki. I'm surprised he's still in one piece."

"He's not a boy," Nicole reminded. "He's a man. A man you haven't seen for fifteen years."

"It doesn't matter. I'm not wrong about him, Nicki. You'll see I'm right, once you've decided to give him a chance."

Nicole threw up her hands. "You sound just like him. 'Give me a chance,'" she drawled in a bad imitation of Johnny's dark voice. "Well, I don't trust him. Or any other man, for that matter."

"And why is that, dear?" Mae reached out and brushed Nicole's bangs out of her eyes. "What has happened to make you so bitter?"

Nicole didn't want to discuss her reasons, but now that she'd said too much, how could she avoid it? She stood and moved to the window overlooking the backyard and a row of giant oak trees. "You were right, there was a man in L.A. His name was Chad Taylor. I fell in love, and he… He walked out on me." She turned around. "I know I'm bitter, but it hurt."

Mae said nothing, as if she sensed there was something else. Nicole groaned, then relented. "You need to know something else. When I called the Pass-By Motel yesterday, it wasn't to find out when Johnny was arriving—it was to fire him." Before her grandmother could say anything, Nicole rushed on. "I didn't know he was a friend of yours. I thought he was some ex-con on parole, is all. A stranger the people in town referred to as 'bad-boy' Bernard. You can understand how that would color my opinion, can't you? Anyway, I apologized for that, and though I'm still not convinced he should be here, I'm prepared to go along with whatever you want. Only, I won't be swayed into liking him. And no more surprise suppers or fake dizzy spells. Agreed?"

A slow grin creased Mae's soft cheeks. "You tried to fire him? And how did he take that?"

"Actually, he told me he was nonrefundable."

Mae clutched her frail chest and laughed heartily. "That's what I would have expected."

"It's getting late." Nicole moved back to the bed and kissed her grandmother on the forehead. "I'll see you in the morning. And remember, no more tricks."

Johnny steered clear of the house on Sunday. He woke early and escaped into the bayou with his cane pole and the quart of White Horse he'd won the night before playing poker with Bick. Letting the boat take him wherever it wanted to go, he dozed until noon, then went hunting for the best fishing spot for the afternoon.

He hadn't eaten anything all day, so, when he started on the whiskey around supper time, it was no surprise that it hit him harder than it normally would have. But he didn't care. If the whiskey took his mind off Nicole, it would be worth it. Then maybe tonight he could get some sleep.

When the sun had set, and the day was almost gone, instead of heading back to the boathouse—not tired enough, or drunk enough—he thrust the pole into the black water and sent the boat deeper into the bayou. A slice of moon was all that guided him as he turned the boat into another narrow channel and slipped through a maze of live oak and tall cypress trees shrouded in thick moss. The bugs were bad, but Johnny paid them no mind as he pulled a cigarette from his T-shirt pocket.

A clap of thunder sounded, promising a rainstorm before morning. Undaunted, Johnny shoved the pole into the water and headed north. He saw the light a moment later. At first he thought he'd gotten turned around, only he knew he hadn't; the house on the hill was definitely the old farmhouse, and the light was coming from inside.

"What the hell?" Johnny flipped the butt of his cigarette into the water, dropped the pole into the muck and turned the boat into the marshy shoreline. He climbed out of the boat, still keeping his eyes on the house through a veil of leafy oak limbs. There was no electricity at the house. Was someone inside with a flashlight? If so, why?

He didn't know how long he stood there, watching and waiting. A full minute, maybe two. He crept up the bank, but as he reached the rise, the light went out. He dropped to his knees and flattened out in the grass. It was so damn dark out, he couldn't see three feet in front of his face. Still as the night, he waited, listening.

Minutes ticked by slowly. Out of frustration, Johnny swore, wondering if he should rush the house and see who was inside. Another minute passed before he heard a car roar to life. He jerked to his feet, and in an instant he was running flat out. He saw headlights come alive at the end of the driveway, and he steered himself in that direction. The car was backing up onto Bayou Road, turning around. He was too far away to stop it, but too determined to give up. Cutting across the uneven yard and into an overgrown field, pumping his arms and legs, he sprinted through the field as fast as he could in hopes of cutting off the car before it reached the sharp bend on the county road.

At the edge of the field, he jumped the ditch. He could hear the car as it downshifted to make the bend. Relieved that he had made it in time, Johnny stepped onto the dirt road, just as the car came around the corner. The headlights zeroed in on him. Any second, Johnny expected to hear the driver downshift and swerve to the side of the road. Only the car didn't slow down. To his surprise, the driver gunned the engine, floored it, and sent the car into fourth gear.

"Damn!" Johnny scrambled to get out of the way, but he wasn't fast enough. The car clipped him high on his right leg and pitched him into the air, tossing him into the water-logged ditch.

Then everything went black.

Chapter 5

The thunderstorm Sunday evening had been reduced to a misting rain by Monday morning. Nicole dashed off the porch and raced to the pickup the moment she saw it pull into the front yard. The passenger door swung open just as she reached it, and she jumped in quickly, slamming the door behind her. "Thanks, I— Oh, my God!"

Nicole didn't need to ask what had happened. It was all too obvious what had happened to Gran's *good boy*—he'd been in a fight. "'Just give me a chance,'" she mimicked. "'I don't plan on causing any trouble,'" she singsonged. "I can't believe Gran can be so naive where you're concerned."

He let her rant and rave for a minute, then put Henry's old pickup in gear and headed down the road. While Nicole fumed, she chanced another look at the bruises that marred Johnny's face. There was a cut on his chin, and a purple welt on his right cheekbone. The long gash on his arm looked nasty. The doctor who had sutured the cut had done a good job: the stitches were small and even. Once it healed, the scar left behind would be no more than a thin white line.

As bad as his wounds looked, Nicole noticed his hair had been freshly washed and tied back. He wore a clean black T-shirt with the sleeves ripped out and another pair of beat-up jeans. He looked impossibly tough and unbelievably composed. Handsome, too, though she wasn't willing to explore that any further than for observation's sake.

She wanted to ask him who the fight had been with, but she kept her curiosity to herself. Remembering what Gran had said about Farrel Craig, she wondered if Johnny had paid the man a visit. If so, she hoped Farrel Craig looked worse than Johnny. She shouldn't care one single bit about who had come out on top, but for some unexplained reason she did. Which was just plain crazy.

"You ask the old lady about the dizzy spell she faked?"

Nicole knew sooner or later he would get to that. She said with as little emotion as possible, "You were right. She invented it."

"She say why she did it?"

Nicole glanced at him. "She thought if we shared some time, I would change my mind about what a 'good boy' you are."

The mockery in her voice made him glance her way. "But that's not going to happen, is it?"

Nicole pointedly eyed his bruises. "I don't think so."

The lazy grin he offered her said he had expected as much.

"If Gran wants to offer you her blind loyalty, that's her business. But don't expect that from me. Gran and I are not made the same way."

He gave her curves the same pointed assessment she had

just given him, then directed his gaze back to the road. "No," he agreed, "you certainly aren't made the same."

The sexual implication behind his words had Nicole feeling self-conscious again. She looked out the window, glad she had picked jeans and a lightweight denim shirt to wear to town instead of cutoffs.

"I need to stop by Tuck's office for a few minutes. You mind if I do that first?" he asked.

"Tuck? Who's Tuck?"

"Sheriff Tucker," he explained.

Nicole shot him a surprised look. "You're going to see the sheriff? Don't tell me you were stupid enough to get caught. I mean, it's bad enough that you were fighting, but if there's a witness who can point a finger, you can kiss your parole goodbye."

"Yeah, that would pretty much screw me."

He appeared perfectly calm. Nicole wanted to scream at him. "Does the sheriff know what happened? Did he order you to come by this morning?"

"No."

"Then why, for God's sake, are you going to see him? If he doesn't know about the fight, he will the minute he sees you. How are you going to explain the bruises? Have you thought about that?"

He rolled his shoulders in a lazy shrug. "I'll have to tell him the truth, I guess."

"The truth!" Nicole's blue eyes went wide. "That's the stupidest thing I've ever heard. The sheriff feels the same as the rest of the town does about you."

Just as they reached the city limits, a flash of lightning cut through the dismal, gray sky, followed by the distant rumble of thunder. Without warning, Johnny pulled the pickup off the road and parked across from Gilmore's Gas and Go.

"What are you doing?" Nicole asked.

He turned slowly and slid his arm along the back of the seat to give her his undivided attention. "Just what do you think I should tell Tuck, *cherie?*"

Nicole scooted closer to the door to avoid his thigh coming in contact with hers. He was staring at her boldly, taking in every detail of her face. She didn't like it when he did that. She wet her lips, thinking. "I don't exactly have a story in mind. Maybe you should just avoid him for a few days. Or maybe tell him you had an accident. You know, walked into a door or something."

"An accident?"

Nicole narrowed her eyes, completely frustrated. "Well, say whatever you want. Say you were in the bayou biting the heads off poisonous snakes and wrestling alligators for no other reason than to count their teeth. Do you think I care what you tell him?" Unable to hold his hard gaze a moment longer, she looked away. Softer, more in control, she added, "I just don't think the truth in this case is going to do either one of us any good. Gran's already making another repair list for you. What about her? If you're sent back to prison, she'll be devastated."

When the silence grew, Nicole looked back and found him staring at her so intently that it made her shiver. "I thought that's what you wanted," he drawled. "For me to pack my bags and disappear."

He was backing her into a corner and trying to get her to say something she had no intention of admitting. "Stop fishing for me to say it," she demanded. "The only reason I care one way or the other is because of Gran and because Oakhaven needs a carpenter."

"There are other carpenters."

"Well, tell that to Gran. She wants you, and I promised her I wouldn't interfere." Nicole didn't want to belabor the point. Besides, they were getting away from the real issue. "It hardly seems worth it," she said.

"What's that?"

"Was one night of raising hell worth another six months in prison? Does your freedom mean so little, then? Does Gran mean so little?"

His eyes narrowed. "Are you so sure that I'm guilty?"

"Are you going to blame *this* fight on someone else, too?"

"No."

"Look, it doesn't really matter what I think. Sheriff Tucker is the man you're going to have to convince, or avoid." Nicole shrugged and tried to sound nonchalant. "The rumor in town is that you're a long shot, anyway."

"You really don't want to know the truth, do you?" He shook his head and sighed. "Siding with the popular vote is understandable, but it's dangerous and gutless, *cherie*."

"I'm not gutless," Nicole exploded. "I just don't take chances on bad investments. Like it or not, that's what you are."

Without warning, he shifted into the middle of the bench seat and slid his arm along the back. He was giving her that look again, only this time it made her feel as though he were burning the clothes off her body, a thread at a time. Nicole tried to look past his battered handsome face, to ignore the heat being generated between their bodies. So much heat that the windows had completely fogged up, and the air inside the cab had turned warm and moist. Finally, he said, "What would you say if I told you I did have an accident? That there was this car and—"

"I'd remind you that it's not me you have to convince," she cut in. "Save the story for the sheriff."

He stared at her for a long moment, then returned to the wheel. He put the pickup in gear, but before he pulled back on the road, he said, "Okay. Have it your way, *cherie*. I'm guilty as hell."

* * *

Johnny stepped inside the police station and tried not to think about the iron cell down the hall. He'd taken Nicole to the drugstore, then dropped her off at the bakery. She told him she was going to be at least a half hour due to the fact that Clair's daughter-in-law, Dory, worked there, and she liked to talk. That had suited him fine—the police station was just around the corner, and he didn't need more than thirty minutes of Tuck's time.

Johnny heard the noisy air-conditioning unit knocking in the window, and realized it had weathered the last fifteen years, as had the creaking wood floors and the dingy gray walls. It seemed nothing had changed in Common.

Well, almost nothing. For years Millie Tisdale had been Tuck's secretary. Now the woman behind the scarred oak desk was Daisi Lavel. She had been a few years younger than him in school, but he still remembered her as the redhead who liked to flirt with him when no one was looking.

She didn't acknowledge him, even though Johnny was sure she had heard the door open. Preoccupied with applying nail polish to nails that were too long to be much good for typing with any speed or accuracy, she had her lips pursed and her eyes glued on her task.

Johnny moved closer to the desk. "Steady as she goes, Daisi."

A glop of polish landed on her cuticle, and her head flew up, ready to chastise the person responsible. Her intention died the instant she recognized who was standing in front of her desk. "Johnny Bernard. My God, you look... You look like your daddy."

"That's what I hear." Johnny grinned. "How are you, Daisi?"

"I'm fine, but I see black and blue are still your two favorite colors. After all this time I would have thought you'd have smartened up."

"Slow learner, I guess."

"No, I don't think that's it. School came easy, as I re-call. And physically—" Her eyes drifted over his body with female appreciation. "You look like you could really do a number on somebody if you wanted to, so what's the problem?"

Johnny chuckled. "I don't have any problem, Miss Lavel."

"It's Daisi Buillard now." She leaned back and rubbed her swollen belly. "I married Melvin. You remember him, don't you? The cute one in the family. We're havin' our second in three months. Got a little girl, named Sally. She'll be two this fall. You got any kids?"

"No."

"You sure? A handsome devil like you?"

"No, I don't have any kids." He gestured to the grow-ing puddle on her nail. "Sorry about that."

Daisi reached for a tissue and wiped the glob off her nail. "No biggie."

"I came to see Tuck." Johnny glanced down the hall. "Is he in?"

"Oh, he's in, all right. But he ain't smilin'. Hasn't been since he found out you were comin' back here for the summer. He still hates your guts, you know. But then, I'd hate you, too, if you busted all the windows in my house and stole my dog."

"I suppose I did get a little carried away the night before I left town."

"A little?" Daisi rolled her big brown eyes. "I'd say sprayin' red paint on half the businesses on Main Street and settin' fire to that dead oak in the center of town was more than just a little carried away."

Humbled by the magnitude of what he'd done, Johnny had the decency to flush. "You wanna tell him I'm here?"

One of Daisi's fingers pointed to a metal box tented with

old mail. "The intercom broke a couple months ago." Her eyes danced with mischief. "Why don't you just go on back and surprise him. It'll serve him right for chewin' off one of my ears already this mornin' for not makin' his coffee strong enough."

The phone rang. "Dang." Daisi waved Johnny down the hall. "Good luck. And if I hear any gunshots, I'll remember to duck."

Johnny ambled down the hall. When he came to Sheriff Tucker's office he stopped, his hand poised on the doorknob. He'd gone over what had happened on Bayou Road a dozen times since last night. He figured it had been Farrel behind the wheel. He hadn't seen him, and he couldn't make out the car, but his gut told him it had to be his old enemy, Farrel.

Johnny wasn't expecting Tuck, however, to do anything about it. But a record of the incident on file couldn't hurt. That way if there was more trouble—which there no doubt would be—he'd have a paper trail to fall back on. It might be the only thing that would save him and keep him out of jail if things took a turn for the worst.

If he'd learned anything during his stint in the military, and then in prison, it was that keeping quiet wasn't always the smartest thing to do. Sometimes the more people who knew your business, the safer you were.

He decided to dispense with knocking and took Daisi's suggestion of surprise. Slinging the door wide, he stepped inside unannounced.

The minute Tuck looked up from his desk and saw the condition Johnny was in, he laughed outright. "Well, now. Looks like we got ourselves a problem. Guess your stay is going to be cut short—shorter than even I figured."

Johnny closed the door behind himself, and took a seat in the chair in front of Tuck's desk. Just like the rest of the police station, this room looked in need of more than just paint. A long line of file cabinets ran the length of one dingy white wall. Overhead, an ancient ceiling fan whirled at top speed, vibrating as if it might come apart any minute. A couple of dozen messages and newspaper clippings, some yellowed with age, fluttered on a bulletin board behind the desk.

"So, should I make the call to your parole officer, or do you want to?"

"I already called him," Johnny drawled. "That's why I'm here."

Clifton Tucker leaned back in his chair and crossed his arms over his bulky chest. The fifty-four-year-old man had put on at least twenty pounds since Johnny had seen him six months ago. He resembled a well-fed bulldog, with dull gray eyes and aging curly hair to match.

"So, Bernard, what's your excuse this time? Not that I'll believe it, but we'll go through the motions to keep it all legal-like."

Johnny came to the point quickly. "Someone tried to run me down on Bayou Road last night."

"You got witnesses?"

"No."

The sheriff made a rude noise. "Figures."

Johnny reined in his temper. It would do him no good to antagonize Tuck; the man could make his stay in town miserable if he had a mind to. "I told my parole agent what happened, and he made a record of it. Now I'm telling you and expect you to do the same. That's the only reason I'm here."

Again, the sheriff made a disgusted noise. But he pulled open his top drawer and took out a paper to file the report. "You say this happened when?"

"Around ten last night," Johnny offered.

"Guess it could have happened. Somebody wanting to get even, I mean."

"Like Farrel."

"He's not the only person in town who'd like to see you six feet under, boy. He's just a little more verbal about it than the others." The sheriff narrowed his eyes. "Recognize the car?"

"No." *But it had a sweet engine,* Johnny wanted to say. One that had been worked over and juiced up. The kind of car a grease monkey like Clete Gilmore could put together with his eyes closed. And why not? If Johnny's memory served him correctly, Clete had been tearing cars apart and putting them back together in his daddy's gas station since he was twelve.

Clifton scratched his head, then looked over the few lines he'd written down. "That it?"

Johnny didn't intend to mention the light he'd seen in the window of the farmhouse. He'd gone back to the house to investigate once he'd regained consciousness, but there had been no signs that anyone had been there. He said, "That'll about do it."

Clifton swiped at the sweat hanging from his bushy dark brows, then gave the fan overhead a dirty look. His wilted, tan shirt and the deep circles of sweat ringing each armpit held proof that the fan was failing him miserably. "I'll check around, talk to Farrel and see where he was last night. If I find out that he's got no alibi, and you wind up dead in the meantime, I guess you were telling the truth. How's that?"

No, nothing had changed, Johnny thought, shoving to his feet. But he really hadn't expected a party picnic to welcome him home. And it was doubtful Tuck would get anywhere with Farrel. But that didn't matter. He'd come to make his report and that was all.

He was two steps away from the door when it opened, and a skinny, old man hurried inside. "I need to see you, Cliff."

Johnny thought he recognized the voice. He looked again, studied the man's gaunt face and sharp green eyes. The man was Jasper Craig, he decided. The voice was a little shaky, yet it had a faintly educated ring to it—a drunken educated ring. When he thought about Jasper, he thought about fancy clothes and polished shoes. About an educated man who had made his money too easily, and had spent it in the same breezy manner.

Johnny stared, unable to believe the ragged man standing in front of him could be Farrel's father. What the hell had happened to him? He remembered Nicole saying Farrel had taken over the family lumber business. But he'd just assumed it was because Jasper had retired early. Now it seemed more likely that it was because the man had turned into a pathetic drunk. Johnny eyed his soiled clothes. They reeked of stale whiskey, and there was dirt clinging to him as if he'd just crawled out of a hole in the ground.

Suddenly the old man locked eyes with Johnny. He didn't say anything for a minute, then finally he gave up a lopsided smile. "Hello, boy. You grew up."

"It happens," Johnny answered.

"Plan on staying out at your place, do you?"

"No. The boathouse at Oakhaven."

Jasper nodded, his smile spreading. "The boathouse. Well, that's real nice of Mae. That old farmhouse is in bad shape. Not really fit for staying in." He glanced at the sheriff. "Didn't mean to interrupt, Cliff." He started to back out the door.

"J.P., I thought you needed to talk to me."

"Ah, no. No, that's all right. I can wait."

"Johnny was just leaving."

"No, I'll come back. I just remembered something I got to do."

* * *

She came through the bakery door the minute he pulled the pickup to the curb. Nicole was carrying a small white bag between her teeth, a loaf of French bread tucked under her arm, and a paper cup of coffee in each hand. Despite his best intentions, Johnny couldn't keep his eyes from straying to the rain-spattered shirt clinging to her breasts, or her hip-hugging jeans. She was a sight, and there was no sense denying he was attracted to every inch of her.

He reached over and opened the door. She handed him the cups, then removed the white bag from between her teeth and set it in the middle of the seat. The long loaf of bread went on the dash just before she climbed in. "Dory insisted I take the coffee and doughnuts. She's just like Clair, trying to fatten me up."

Johnny glanced at Nicole's slender curves. She was thin, all right, like a sleek, fine-boned greyhound. He swore silently, then handed her back one of the cups.

"Waiting long?"

"About ten minutes. Did you go see the sheriff?"

"Yeah."

"And?"

"And I'm still here."

She arched a pretty brow, set her cup on the dash, then opened up the white bag and angled it in his direction. He hadn't bothered to eat breakfast. After last night's excitement, just getting up and moving had been all he'd wanted to tackle. He was sore in a dozen places. His right leg and hip were black and blue clean to his butt.

He reached inside the bag and pulled out a cake doughnut. Johnny savored every bite. She offered him another, then another. When the bag was empty and the coffee gone, he draped his wrist over the steering wheel and asked, "Where to now?"

"I have two stops left," she told him. "The post office and Craig Lumber."

Johnny pulled into the lumberyard parking lot moments later, and killed the engine. It was still raining out, the sky still dark, the rumble of thunder in the distance.

"I'll run this letter to the post office," she said. "Then I'll go order the shingles and anything else they don't have on the list." She handed him back the list he'd given her two days earlier. "Why don't you check it over and see if there's anything else you want to add. I'll be right back."

Johnny took the list. He allowed himself a few minutes to appreciate the view of her hurrying into the post office—her long legs and sexy backside giving his heart rate another jolt—then got out of the pickup. He slid the list into his back pocket, and in his normal lazy gait, sauntered through the front door of Craig Lumber.

A quick glance at the desk told him Willis Lavel was half asleep behind the counter. But not for long—the doorbell gave a hellish *clang,* and Willis let out a holler and jumped a good two feet off the high stool he was perched on. He grabbed the counter to steady himself, his gaze searching out the customer who had disturbed his sleep. When he realized who it was, all the color drained from Willis's pudgy face. "Oh, hell."

"Nice seeing you too, Will."

Johnny dug into his T-shirt pocket for his smokes. After lighting up, he took a leisurely drag.

"I got a knife," Willis finally warned. "Try somethin' and you'll be sorry."

If Willis owned a knife, it had to be the size of a fingernail file. Johnny glanced around, noticing for the first time that the office door behind the counter stood ajar. The light was on. Loud enough so whoever was inside could hear him, he said, "Came to pick up supplies for Oakhaven. Think you can put an order together without screwing it up, Will?"

Willis had started to sweat. He swiped at his bald pate,

then reached for his half-used black cigar in the tarnished ashtray on the counter. With shaky fingers, he lit a match and struggled to relight it. "You're gonna have to talk to Farrel about that," he said, puffing long and hard to get the cigar fired up. "But that ain't likely, on account I don't think—"

"That's good, Will. Don't think," Johnny cut in. "Just call your boss out here. I'll do the asking."

The older man gave up trying to light his cigar and disgustedly tossed it aside. "Farrel ain't gonna agree to nothin' that involves you, Johnny," Willis whined. "I ain't never seen one man who can hate another as much as he hates you."

"I've come on business, Will. Oakhaven business."

Just as Johnny expected, his voice carried into the office, drawing Farrel Craig out as if he'd thrown in a baited line and bagged himself a sucker. Farrel was almost as tall as Johnny, but fair where Johnny was dark. His tanned face followed the slender lines of his trim body. His eyes, distinctly green, were deep-set. Insolent.

He wore jeans, snakeskin boots with silver toe caps, and a red shirt too flashy for any kind of real work. Except for an inch-long scar on his jaw and a jog in his nose—both Johnny's doing—Farrel didn't own a blemish, a mole or a freckle.

"You got a lot of nerve coming in here, Bernard," Farrel snarled. When Johnny said nothing, he taunted, "What's the matter, *beggar boy,* they cut your tongue out in prison?"

Like a puppet who had just had his string jerked, Willis started laughing. Once his chuckle petered out and the silence stretched, he nervously picked up his dead cigar and stuck it in his mouth.

"I still got my tongue," Johnny finally said, "and I see you still got a crooked nose."

Instead of getting angry, Farrel grinned. "You look in the mirror this morning? You got more than that. Welcome home, Johnny."

The doorbell clanged once more, and both Johnny and Farrel turned simultaneously to see Nicole hurry through the door. She looked rain-spattered and out of breath, as if she'd made a mad dash from the pickup—which no doubt she had, the minute she learned Johnny wasn't inside waiting for her like some obedient puppy. Before she got her pretty mouth open, Johnny said, "You finished at the post office already, *cherie?*"

He gave her a lazy smile, and in return she gave him a look that could have turned stone into smoldering ashes. "Didn't we agreed you would stay in the pickup, Mr. Bernard?"

She took the necessary steps to close the distance between them. Johnny waited a few seconds before he answered, but when he did he leaned close, whispering, "The lesson here is, if you want to treat a man like a dog, you should remember to bring along a collar and leash so you can chain him up like one. That way you'll always know where you can find him."

"Such a useful tip," she hissed softly into his cheek. "Next time I'll be prepared."

"Could be fun...you trying to put one on me," he drawled.

She didn't appreciate him baiting her, or his smug smile. "We'll discuss it later," she insisted, her eyes shifting to Farrel, then back to Johnny. "Where's my supply list?"

"In a safe place," he assured. "I'll take care of this. All you have to do is choose a color for those shingles we talked about."

"I'll take care of all of it," she insisted. "Now give me the list."

"Is there trouble, Miss Chapman? Something I can help ut with?"

Farrel's voice was friendly. Too friendly, Johnny hought, not liking the way his enemy raked Nicole's body vith hungry appreciation.

"You can call me Nicole," she told him, "and no, I on't need any help. I do apologize, however, if my worker as been bothering you." She gave Johnny a nasty side-ong glance. "He was told to stay in the pickup."

"It's hard to find good help these days, that's a fact," 'arrel agreed, giving his own man a disappointed look. He an a hand through his cropped blond hair and leaned his rm on the counter. "So, what is it I can help you with, Jicole?"

"I need some building supplies and to order new shin-les for my grandmother's house."

Suddenly Johnny was aware that Nicole was leaning nto him, her hand on his backside. His body tensed just efore her fingers climbed into his right back pocket and tole the supply list. She gave him a pleased look, then loated to the counter with that hip action she'd perfected or the sole purpose—Johnny was sure—of scorching a nan's blood and frying his insides.

"Morning, Mr. Lavel," she purred sweetly, charming ld Willis into a heated frenzy. "Remember me? We met ast week at the bank."

"Sure do. You look mighty fine this mornin', Miss Jicki. It's sure nice, you movin' in with your grandma. /ly son, Woodrow, thinks so, too."

Johnny was sure Woodrow Lavel wasn't the only man n town thinking he'd just hit the jackpot. Nicole was def-nitely the apple that would get picked first in this town; he was shiny and new and ripe in all the right places.

She offered a friendly smile to the older man, then un-olded the list and laid it on the counter. Her attention

refocused on Farrel, she asked, "I assume Gran's accoun
is up to date?"

"Sure is." Farrel glanced down, half interested, at th
material list. "Doing some major repairs, I see. That'
quite a list." He slid the list toward Willis. "See to this
Will. And get the boys to tarp the load so the lumber stay
dry. I can pick up the tarp next time I'm out that way."

"But you never lend out—"

"Tarp the load, Will!" Farrel's eyes left Nicole's fo
just a split second and shot Willis a *Get moving!* look tha
nearly levitated the older man up and pitched him out th
door headfirst.

Farrel said, "I've got shingle samples in my office. Hov
about you and me picking that color out over a cup o
coffee?"

"That would be fine," Nicole answered.

Farrel escorted Nicole around the counter and into hi
office. Then, just before he closed the door behind them
he turned back, grinned at Johnny, held up his middle fir
ger and mouthed the words.

Chapter 6

The moon's guiding light vanished the moment Nicole entered the woods. She glanced around warily, then started down the blackened path, ducking from time to time to avoid whatever might be hanging in the tangled foliage overhead. She didn't want to think about the many eyes that were, no doubt, watching her. If she did, she would be struck once again by how crazy it was for her to be going to the boathouse after dark.

Just as she reminded herself of the fact, she stumbled, barely catching her balance in time to save herself a hard tumble. Swearing softly, she stopped to brush her hair out of her eyes.

"Should have brought a flashlight along. That way you could see what kind of snake you're kickin' in the head."

Nicole gasped, then whirled around so fast she nearly fell on her face again. Squinting in the darkness, she saw a match spark. A moment later the glow from a cigarette illuminated Johnny Bernard's handsome face.

He was leaning against a tree, looking relaxed and ever bit the bad boy he was. Still, she owed him an apology and she hadn't wanted to put it off until tomorrow.

"What are you doing out here?" she asked stupidly "You nearly scared me half to death."

"That must be the question of the night, 'cause I'n wondering the same about you. What brings you ou *cherie?* It's late. Too late for a stroll."

"But not for you?"

"I know these woods. I used to live around here, re member?" He took a drag off his cigarette and sent th smoke into the black night.

"I would have called, but the boathouse doesn't have phone," Nicole explained, "and I wanted to…" She too a deep breath and let it out slowly. She hadn't been lookin forward to this part, but it had to be done. "To apologize."

"Ah, an apology."

She couldn't see his face very well, but she heard th amusement in his voice. "Why didn't you tell me the trut about last night? Why did you let me assume the worst?"

"Did I do that? Funny, I thought I tried to explain. A I recall, you didn't want to listen. Sound familiar?"

"I suppose I deserve that."

"Yes, you do. You've been thinking the worst of m since I got here." He dropped his spent cigarette an ground it out with the heel of his boot. "The bottom lin is, you don't know me, and you don't want to."

"That's not true." Nicole swatted at the dozen mos quitoes swarming around her head, glad she had worn sweatshirt even though it was much too warm. "It's jus that—"

"The gossip that arrived later today wasn't what you' expected. Does that mean you're ready to listen? To trus me?"

Listen, yes; trust him, no. Frankly, she didn't think sh

would ever be able to trust a man again. "You knew your visit to the sheriff's office would circulate. That the entire town would be privy to the information before long?"

"That's the way it works around here."

"You think you know everything, is that it?" Nicole was furious. "Did you also expect an apology? Am I playing right into your hands?"

When he didn't answer, Nicole spun around to leave, only to be pulled up short by his hand on her arm. "Easy. Don't go running off all mad."

Nicole pulled her arm free and glared at him. "You set me up."

"No, you did that all by yourself."

She swatted at another swarm of mosquitoes. He reached out and pulled up the hood on her sweatshirt. "Come on. The bugs are making a meal out of you."

Boldly, he took hold of her hand and started deeper into the woods. Momentarily surprised, Nicole followed, as he easily maneuvered the twisted trail as if he shared some secret with the nocturnal animals that thrived on darkness. When they reached the clearing, Nicole saw the bayou in the faint moonlight, and knew where they were.

Inside the boathouse, he ignored the light and guided her through the maze of clutter. Once they reached the stairwell, he let go of her and said, "Wait here."

In the dark, Nicole listened as his booted feet took the stair treads two at a time. Suddenly a muted stream of light brought him into focus at the top of the stairs, and she saw him clearly for the first time since he had frightened her in the woods. He wore trashed jeans, the worst pair she'd seen so far, and a brown T-shirt stretched over his chest. His black hair was damp and loose, as if he'd showered or, maybe, gone for a swim at the pond.

Nicole sucked in a ragged breath, wondering why she

had allowed him to bring her here, why she wasn't in flight
back to the house.

"*Cherie,* you coming?"

Nicole pushed the sweatshirt hood off her head, hesitated.

"I don't bite. That is, not unless that's what you like."

His teasing was followed by a suggestive smile. If she
had any sense, she thought, she would turn and run.

At the top of the stairs, Nicole slipped past him into the
apartment. The day had turned blisteringly hot after the
rain, and without any fan the small room felt stifling even
with the windows open.

She unzipped her sweatshirt and slipped it off, leaving
her in a white T-shirt and jeans. She glanced around, noticing that he had made several changes in the past couple
of days. A worn rug lay on the wood floor in front of the
rocker, an old-fashioned, metal reading lamp stood behind
it. She hadn't thought of him as the type to read, but a
paperback novel on the floor beside the rocker claimed
otherwise. He had scrounged an old flat-topped trunk from
somewhere and turned it into a makeshift coffee table,
which sat between the sofa and the rocker. It was all very
homey and neat, and she couldn't help but be impressed
by the fact that he had invested some time in a few creature
comforts.

"You want something to drink?"

Nicole turned in time to appreciate his lazy gait as he
sauntered into the small kitchen.

"Soda? Water?" he called out.

"No. Nothing."

While he went to the sink, ran himself a glass of water
and drained it, Nicole moved to the sofa and perched on
one corner. Another glance around brought her face to face
with one of her paintings. It hung over his bed—a picture
of Belle Bayou. She'd painted it a few years ago. She

emembered sketching for hours near the secluded inlet where the night herons made their nests. Bick had taken her there, and while she had become enthralled with her subject, he had caught a string of catfish. She'd gotten the worst sunburn of her life that day, but it had been worth t; she'd captured the bayou's mystery and its beauty perfectly. She'd sold a number of prints, and afterwards she'd given the original to Gran for her birthday. She was curious as to why it was here.

"Sure you don't want something?" He came out of the kitchen.

Nicole shook her head. "No. I'm fine."

He strolled across her line of vision and seated himself n the rocker. "I'm going to start tearing the roof off the house tomorrow, if it doesn't rain. The yard will be a mess for about a week or two."

Nicole laid her sweatshirt on the sofa beside her. "We'll put up with whatever we have to," she assured him. She paused. "Tell me about last night."

"Like I told Tuck, a car tried to run me down on the county road."

"Are you sure? Maybe the person just didn't see you."

"No, they saw me. I was at the old farm. I still own it, thanks to the old lady and—"

"Wait! Back up. What do you mean, thanks to the old lady?"

"Your grandmother is the reason I came back," he told her. "She's been paying the taxes on the farm ever since I left. Don't ask me why. The place is worthless." He ran his hands through his hair, frustration evident.

"How did you find out you still own it. Did she write you?"

"No, Griffin Black did. He wanted to buy it. I got the letter six months ago. At first I thought there had to be a mistake, so I came here from Lafayette to check it out. I left the courthouse and was headed here when I decide to stop for a cold beer at Pepper's. After that, as they say all hell broke loose."

Nicole was beginning to understand—that's *if* she coul believe him. "Do you think it was Farrel who tried to ru you down last night?"

"Maybe. Early this morning I called my parole office and he suggested that I report the incident to Tuck. H thought having a record of it would protect my position That is, if something like that ever happens again."

"Do you think it will?"

He shrugged. "I'm not going to pretend my being bacl doesn't matter to some folks. I have a lot of enemies i this town."

"Why?"

"That's the sixty-four-thousand-dollar question. Som of it I understand, even deserve, but there's a lot that ha never made any sense."

"So now what? What if this person—Farrel or who ever—tries again?"

"I'll be ready next time."

Nicole sighed. "What does that mean?"

"Relax. It doesn't mean I'm going to go looking fo trouble. I'm not."

"Maybe that's what this guy is hoping for. Maybe he' just waiting for you to lose your temper like before. Fron what I've heard, you have quite a temper when you're—' Nicole clamped her mouth shut. She was doing it again listening to the gossip and expecting the worst of him "I'm sorry."

"You get that from Farrel this morning?"

Nicole flushed. "He did warn me about you. Somethin; about breaking windows and killing a dog."

"I did break a few windows when I was younger. Th

dead dog is bull. Should I take my turn and warn you about Farrel?''

Nicole leaned back into the couch cushions and relaxed a little. "You don't need to. One thing you should know about me, Johnny, I'm no chump. I'm not inexperienced when it comes to men with easy smiles, or who know just the right thing to say nine times out of ten. But that's getting away from the point. If you screw up your parole, you'll be sent back to prison. Don't do it. If you don't have a good enough reason to for yourself, think of Gran. She's the happiest I've seen her in years. I don't pretend to understand why exactly, but I do know your being here is very important to her. And loving her like I do, I'm willing to do whatever it takes to keep her happy. You can't let anyone ruin it for her, you just can't!''

"Take it easy. It won't come to that."

He started rocking the chair slow and lazylike, his hands resting on the arms, his blunt-tipped fingers dangling limp over the edge. Nicole stood and planted her hands on her hips. "You bet it won't, because you're going to avoid Farrel Craig and anyone else who might try to draw you into a fight. Do you hear? Better yet, there is no reason for you to go anywhere near town."

"I'm a free man, *cherie*. I'll go where I damn well please, when the hell I feel like it."

"That would be fine if you only had yourself to think about, but you don't. You owe Gran. You'd still be rotting in prison if she hadn't offered you a job and a place to stay."

"There's another way of looking at that," he countered angrily. "If she hadn't kept my name on that worthless land deed all these years, none of this would have happened at all. I had no intention of ever coming back here until I got that letter from Griffin Black."

His bluntness made Nicole clamp her mouth shut. She

turned away, unable to hold his potent gaze a moment longer. Finally, she walked to the window overlooking Belle. The moon had slipped through the clouds, and the picture it made was breathtaking. "Are you holding a grudge? Because if you are—"

"I'm not holding a grudge. The old lady didn't make me break Farrel's nose or pull my knife that day at Pepper's."

The sound of the rocker scraping along the floor warned Nicole that Johnny had gotten to his feet. She waited for him to say something, but instead he came to stand behind her at the window. She could smell his earthy scent, feel his breath next to her ear.

"I'm glad you read Farrel this morning," he drawled. "He's not to be trusted."

"But you are?" Nicole's gaze remained focused on the moon hovering over the bayou, casting gnarly shadows across the still water. She felt him shift his body, his thigh brushing her hip. "Are you trustworthy? Or are you working this situation to your advantage?"

He leaned in, closing the last inch. He was so close, Nicole could feel his warm body against the length of her own. "What would that gain me?"

Nicole turned, and wished she hadn't; it put her practically in his arms. "Not a thing. I told you, I'm no chump." He was too close. She suddenly felt in need of air. "I've got to go." Seeing her sweatshirt on the sofa, she moved around him quickly and picked it up. When she turned back around, he was standing in the doorway.

"Put it on," he said. "Your skin is too delicate for the woods this time of night. Then I'll walk you back."

"I know my way to the house."

"I'm sure you do, but as you pointed out earlier, I don't only have myself to think about these days."

"I was talking about Gran, not me."

"Just the same, I'll walk you back."

Two days later Nicole stepped inside Pepper's wearing a baby-blue, straight jersey shift. The bar was wall-to-wall people. Tonight there was a live band, and everyone for forty miles around had turned out to hear it.

She scanned the crowd looking for Dory. Normally, Nicole avoided bars, but Dory had convinced her that tonight was special. She found an empty table and took a seat—amazing, since every booth was bulging with serious party-goers.

"Hi."

Nicole turned to see a redheaded woman standing in front of her. A pregnant woman. Her gaze fastened on the woman's swollen stomach. She didn't want to stare, but she couldn't help it. She forced herself to smile and cleared her throat. "Hi. I'm Nicole Chapman, and you are…?"

"Daisi Buillard. Mind if I join you?"

"No. Not at all."

Daisi pulled out the only other chair at the table and took a seat. She was dressed in slacks and a cute T-shirt with Baby on Board written on it. "I noticed you right away. I've been meanin' to give you a call and introduce myself, since we're close to the same age—but you know how it is. What with workin' and tryin' to keep the house clean and hubby happy, the days just fly."

Nicole smiled, her eyes straying again to Daisi's pregnant stomach. She tried not to think about her own baby and what might have been, but that was impossible.

Daisi continued to talk, unaware that Nicole was becoming melancholy. "Are you waitin' for someone. A guy?"

"No." Nicole leaned back in her chair and crossed her legs. "I was supposed to meet Dory at seven. She's late. You must know Dory from the bakery? She's—"

"I know Dory. We went to school together. It's not like her to be late. Maybe somethin' came up."

That's all she needed, Nicole thought. If Dory didn't show up, she'd feel foolish sitting alone. She flagged the waitress and ordered a white wine. "Do you want something to drink?"

"A diet cola," Daisi told the waitress.

Another fifteen minutes passed without Dory showing up. While Nicole flagged the waitress for another drink, Daisi motioned for her husband to come over. He was tall and lean. He wasn't the most handsome man in town, but he had kind gray eyes, and it was clear he loved his wife.

"Daisi and I are glad to see someone our age move into town," he said. "There's not many young people making Common their home these days. The norm here is to leave the minute you get out of school."

"Mel and me like it quiet," Daisi interjected. "We bought the corner house on Mill Street." She sipped her drink. "I heard from my mother that you're an artist. That must be excitin'."

Nicole nodded, wishing Gran had kept quiet about her career. "It is," she agreed.

"How's Johnny working out?" Mel asked. "He staying out of trouble?"

Daisi elbowed her husband. "I told you, Mel, those bruises were from an accident. Why do you always have to make somethin' out of nothin'?"

"Maybe because anything having to do with Johnny Bernard usually ends up to be something," Mel challenged.

Daisi and Mel headed for the dance floor a short time later. Nicole watched as Mel pulled Daisi close, and together they cradled their unborn baby between them. It was painful to watch, but she couldn't look away, the past returning with such force that her entire body ached.

She ordered another glass of wine in the hope that it would numb her pain. To her surprise, it wasn't a waitress who brought it, but Farrel Craig. "Hiya, pretty lady." He set the drink down in front of her. "Mind if I join you?"

Nicole had given up on Dory, but as she looked up and saw Farrel staring down at her, she wished her friend would suddenly appear out of a crack in the wall. Trying to be friendly, she faked a pleasant smile. "I don't think I'll be staying too much longer, but you're welcome to the table."

"You don't need to rush off. The fun's just getting started." He pulled out the empty chair and sat. "I've been watching you all evening, and I finally figured it out."

Nicole raised an eyebrow. "Figured out what?"

"The reason you're here. You're dressed for dancing." He held up his hand when Nicole was about to refute his declaration. "Just so you know, it's not you, Nicole. The guys are interested—they're just scared. Not too many women in this town have been educated past high school. You being from California and all, they don't know how to approach you. So they're sitting confused, waiting for someone else to make the first move, to see how he does."

"So you're the designated ice-breaker?" Nicole asked, aware that Farrel was on the verge of asking her to dance. He was smooth, but not the smoothest she'd encountered—no one could be as smooth as Chad Taylor had been, she thought.

"I guess. I've been enjoying the sight from over there." He motioned to a prime booth that had a view of everyone who came in and out. "And just so you know, I came to dance, too."

Nicole glanced toward the band just as they cut loose with another fast-paced, raucous song. Around the stage blinked two rows of pink neon lights. The accordion was loud, the guitar fast-paced, and the fiddler knew just when to challenge the beat with a reckless tempo that turned the crowd wild.

Maybe it was seeing Daisi Buillard pregnant and so happy that made Nicole feel blue, or maybe it was just Farrel Craig's coaxing smile and one too many glasses of wine, but, moments later, Nicole found herself in the middle of the dance floor wrapped in the arms of a man she didn't even like. As he locked his hands around her waist and twirled her into the crowd, he said, "We're going to clear the dance floor, sweet thing. Hang on."

He wasn't kidding about chasing the other couples back to their tables. Nicole thought about the spectacle they were making, then quickly traded one concern for another—maintaining her balance and staying on her feet.

Two songs later, they were the only ones on the dance floor, and the center of attention. Steadily the music grew more frenzied. Ribald hoots came from a nearby table as Nicole's dress inched higher and higher. Worse, the wine decided to kick in all at once, and her heart began to race.

Nicole, face flushed, wanted to stop. She wanted—no, needed—air. But the crowd kept clapping, stomping their feet and shouting encouragement from all sides of the room. On the next song, a slow, steamy Delta Blues, a dozen brave couples took their chances battling Farrel for room on the dance floor. The neon lights were doused, and it was then Nicole realized Farrel was, in fact, the consummate con man Johnny had warned her about. Within seconds, he'd wrapped his arms around her with great care and brought her in to him. Tenderly he began whispering compliments as he stroked the damp hair at her temple.

It was well past midnight by the time Farrel ushered Nicole into the parking lot in front of Pepper's. They had danced for hours and indulged in several drinks, and once outside, Farrel pulled Nicole close and stole a kiss.

His mouth felt hot and invading. Hard. "What do you

say we keep the night going," he whispered. "I know a place where we can be alone."

Nicole struggled out of his arms. "I don't think so." She checked her watch. "I didn't realize how late it is. Gran will be worried sick."

Farrel angled his head. "That's a brush-off if I've ever heard one, Nicole."

"Sorry." Nicole suddenly felt light-headed. "The truth is, I'm not looking for an involvement at the moment. Not even a brief one-nighter. I didn't really come to dance tonight—I came to listen to the music with a friend. But she didn't show and—" Nicole's stomach rolled, warning her she didn't have long before she'd be too weak to make it to the car without help. "I've got to go," she said in a rush. "Thanks for the fun."

"You're welcome. Anytime you feel like another night of dancing, let me know."

"I'll remember that." A car door slammed from somewhere in the middle of the dark parking lot. Nicole squinted and tried to focus, but she wasn't sure if she was seeing the flicker of a match...or nothing at all. She pushed her bangs out of her eyes and started to walk slowly to her car. Not too slowly, but slowly enough that Farrel wouldn't suspect she was teetering on the verge of collapse.

She reached her car, dug her keys out of her purse and unlocked the door. Inside, she started the engine and turned on the air conditioner. She glanced toward the bar's front door, relieved when she saw Farrel sauntering inside. She leaned her head back against the seat and closed her eyes. Her head was spinning, and she knew the last glass of wine had been the culprit.

A sudden rap at the window gave Nicole a start. Her eyes flew open, and she let out a cry of surprise that surely was heard through the closed window. To her distress, seeing Johnny Bernard staring through the window at her made her feel worse. She didn't need those soul-searching eyes analyzing her just now. She didn't need him making some wisecrack about her condition, either. Right now, all she wanted was to be sick in private, and without an audience.

He motioned for her to buzz the window down, and after gazing at the panel of buttons for a confused couple of seconds, Nicole turned off the air conditioner, then pressed the upper-left button and watched the window disappear inside the door.

"You all right?"

The warm night air drifted into the car to attack Nicole's flushed face once more, and she instantly felt as weak as a kitten. "I'm fine," she lied. "What are you doing here?" Her words sounded strange, she thought, and the idea had her clearing her dry throat.

He took an impatient drag off his cigarette, then flicked the butt in the opposite direction of the car. Angling his head, he sent a cloud of smoke over the hood of the car. When he locked eyes with her once more, his expression was hard to read. "It's late," he drawled. "The old lady's worried. Especially since Dory called hours ago and said she couldn't meet you. So, what have you been doing for five hours, *cherie?* Or shouldn't I ask?"

"Dory called?" Nicole frowned. "Did she say why she couldn't meet me?"

"There was a small fire at the bakery."

"A fire?"

"Nothing serious. How much?"

Nicole gripped the steering wheel. "How much what?"

"Booze. How much did you have to drink?"

"Excuse me?" Nicole tried to sit up a little straighter. Her stomach did a sudden flip, but she would be damned if she'd let him see just how rotten she felt. She simply wanted to go home, pop a couple of headache pills and fall into bed.

"Drinking and driving is a bad combination."

Did he think he was telling her something she didn't already know? Incensed, she reached for the panel of buttons to buzz the window back up, but he read her intention and had the car door open in an instant.

"Slide over."

Nicole peered at him through narrowed eyes. Suddenly seeing two of him, she groaned softly and blinked in an effort to chase one of him away.

He gave her a nudge. "Come on. Move that cute butt of yours over a few inches, *cherie.* You're in no shape to drive."

"I'm fine," she insisted.

"Like hell."

Before she could argue, the upper part of his body was suddenly inside the car, and he was working his hands beneath her backside.

"Stop that!" Nicole protested.

With little effort, he half lifted, half slid her to the middle of the seat, then climbed in. "You ought to be tanned good for worrying the old lady needlessly," he scolded, slamming the door shut. "And of all things to drink, wine is the worst."

The last comment gave her pause. "And how would you know what I was drinking unless you were spying on me." When he didn't deny it, Nicole clutched at his black T-shirt sleeve so he would have to look at her. "Were you?"

He glanced down at her fine-boned little fist, then locked eyes with her. "You have a nice time dancing with Farrel Craig? Rubbing yourself all over him?"

"I wasn't doing that," she protested.

"Then maybe that grin he was wearing all evening was

just in anticipation of what might happen later if he got you drunk enough. You suppose?''

Nicole wasn't going to dignify that vulgar crack with so much as a peep. Changing the subject, she asked, ''Did you drive the pickup into town?''

He pointed to the middle of the parking lot. It was in the same general area where she thought she'd seen the match spark earlier.

''I'll come back in the morning and get it.'' He put the car in reverse, backed up and left the parking lot.

Once they were headed out of town, Nicole leaned her head against the seat and closed her eyes. She was willing to concede that it was for the best that Johnny drive her home. She was even ready to admit that drowning her misery in a bottle of wine had been idiotic and the most reckless thing she'd done in a while. But seeing Daisi Buillard's swollen stomach had brought the entire nightmare flooding back, all the pain and empty feelings. The helplessness. Her stomach knotted, and she laid her hands there and tried to chase the nausea away. But it wasn't going anywhere.

Johnny glanced at Nicole and saw her holding her stomach. Her head was resting at an odd angle against the seat, and he maneuvered his arm around her and pulled her close so she could use his shoulder for a pillow.

Damn her. What the hell was she doing wearing a dress that showed off every curve she owned, and dancing crazy with Farrel Craig as if they were old friends? He felt his insides tighten, and again the sight of Farrel stealing a kiss outside the bar flashed before his eyes.

He'd never been a jealous man, but at that moment he had been ready to put Farrel's face into a car window— and to hell with his parole. He didn't want to want Nicole Chapman the way he did, and yet there it was. She was a fragile woman, not at all his type, but still he wanted her. He wanted her in his bed, willing and saying his name. No, not just willing, but hot and aroused as hell.

When he had laid eyes on her at the boathouse that first day, all he had wanted was the physical contact, to satisfy himself with a warm, soft female body. Now he realized it was more complicated than just sex. Seeing her tonight with Farrel had been damn painful. He didn't understand it, and he wished to hell he could make it stop. But how?

He heard her moan softly and he pulled her closer to him. "Easy, *cherie.* We'll be home in just a few minutes."

They left the highway and turned off on Bayou Road. When Oakhaven came into sight, Johnny cruised up the driveway as quietly as possible, pulled the Skylark alongside Mae's Buick in the carport and turned off the ignition.

He shifted slightly and looked down at Nicole. She was so beautiful. He couldn't really blame Farrel for making a move on her. A man would have to be crazy not to try. He noticed her hands were still holding her stomach and wondered just how much she had drunk before he'd arrived at Pepper's looking for her. She didn't appear to be the type to get carried away with liquor. Then again, he didn't know her well enough to make that kind of call.

"Hey, *cherie,* wake up," he whispered. "We're home." She moaned and opened her pretty blue eyes, and that's when he saw the tear. Concerned, he wiped it away, then asked, "What is it? Upset stomach? Headache?"

She straightened to sit up, looked away from him as if she were embarrassed. "I'm fine."

He opened the door and climbed out. When he turned around, she was already sliding out his side. He reached out to help her, catching her around the waist. When her feet hit the ground, she swayed slightly. "Come on, *cherie,* get your feet underneath you."

She managed to stand, one arm looped around his waist,

one soft breast pressed into his rib cage. They crossed the yard and scaled the porch steps to the private entrance of her bedroom. Once there, Johnny propped her against the wall to open one of the French doors. Before he got it open, she was leaning against him again, all warm and vulnerable.

He got the door open, then glanced at her. She had angled her head to one side and was looking at him curiously. "Are you really a nice guy, like Gran says?" She pressed her hand to his chest where his heart beat strong and fast. "I hope not. I don't want to like you, Johnny Bernard. Not even a little bit. I want you to be just like Chad, selfish and dishonest."

Her face contorted with raw emotion. She looked like she was one step away from crying again. Johnny didn't know what to say, but it was obvious this guy, Chad, was someone from her past and that he had hurt her. Johnny also figured that if she were thinking clearly, she wouldn't be talking like this, telling him things she deemed her private business. He was curious to know more, just not this way. Not when she was feeling so low. He said, "Come on, *cherie,* it's time for you to go to bed." He untangled her from his body and set her away from him. "You'll feel better in the morning. Now go on."

He gave her a little nudge toward the door, then started off the porch. He didn't get far before she said, "He didn't ask me if it was all right."

Johnny turned. "What?"

"Farrel. He didn't ask if he could kiss me."

Johnny didn't want to be reminded of that kiss, sure it would haunt him throughout the night as it was. He shook his head. "Go to bed, *cherie.*"

"I will. Only, I can't stop thinking about it. I—"

"Dammit, I don't want to hear it!" Johnny turned away from her, determined to leave.

"You're mad. I'm sorry. It's just that there's this sour taste in my mouth—"

Johnny spun back around. "And just what the hell am I supposed to do about that, *cherie?* I'm fresh out of mints."

At that moment he would have done anything to get her inside so he could get the hell out of there. He was on the verge of doing something stupid, and the longer he hung around—

"I don't want a mint," she said simply, softly. She took an unsteady step toward him, then another and another until they were toe to toe. Slowly, she leaned into him, her sweet scent filling his nostrils, branding him and guaranteeing he was going to spend another sleepless night in hell. "Offer something else, Johnny. Use your imagination."

The thought of kissing away Farrel's taste and leaving her marked with his own had Johnny turning stone hard. God, he wanted to kiss her. Wanted to do that, and so much more.

Her hands stroked up his chest, and she swayed into him. The sultry night suddenly turned stifling hot. Johnny knew he shouldn't do it, even as he lowered his head to meet her halfway. One quick kiss, he promised. Just one…

Her lips were summer warm and satin smooth, and in an instant his plan of offering her *one quick kiss* was shot completely to hell. He slipped his hands around her and brought her slender body in full contact with his. After ravishing her mouth for a full minute, he backed her against the new railing he'd built and kissed her again…then again.

He meant to stop.

Soon he would.

She made a little mewling noise, wiggled against his arousal.

Desire burned hotter than Johnny had ever experienced in his life. He coaxed her mouth open and thrust his tongue deep inside. She wrapped her arms around his neck and clung to him. Her ready response sent another jolt of desire ripping through his aching loins; at the same time blood surged hot through his veins. His heart knocked against his chest like a jackhammer.

His hands moved to her hips, his fingers working her dress up her slender legs to caress her velvet thighs. Boldly, his fingers found the elastic edge of her panties. He was losing control, and she was letting him.

He was breathing fast—too fast, he thought. He stopped for a moment to catch his breath, and that's when it hit him: she was drunk, and he was climbing all over her, making him no better than Farrel Craig or that man from her past. Grounded, Johnny pulled his hand out from under her dress and took a giant step back.

"Dammit, *cherie,* what the hell are you trying to do to me?" Swearing again, he thrust his hand through his loose hair. Then, before she could answer, before her fuzzy head had a chance to clear and grasp just how damn close she had come to ending up on her back, Johnny melted into the shadows.

Chapter 7

Nicole left for New Orleans before breakfast. She didn't want to take a chance on running into anyone: not Gran, not Clair nor Bick. Least of all, Johnny.

Johnny.

Nicole ran a finger over her lips as another sharp mental image assailed her. Had she really begged him to kiss her?

She wanted to believe it was just another naughty dream. But she knew that was just wishful thinking. The entire kiss, every heat-filled moment, could still be felt. She was burning inside and out, floating on some strange, erotic wave of pure bliss. A never-before experience, which made it all the more distressing.

How could she have sunk so low?

She really had had no business staying at Pepper's after Dory hadn't showed. And the wine had been mistake number two. The doozy had been allowing Farrel Craig to control the evening, then steal that miserable kiss.

Looking back, she realized the entire evening had disaster written all over it. And Johnny showing up to witness the whole thing, then playing white knight and chauffeur all in one, had been the *coup de grâce*. It was more than just humbling to know she had allowed him to see her in such a pathetic state. She felt not only ashamed, but humiliated.

And considering what had happened between them on the porch, she feared her disgrace wasn't over yet. Surely he would make an issue out of that wicked kiss he'd planted on her lips. And more to the point, of how readily she'd accepted.

Furious with herself, Nicole snapped off the radio, pressed her sandaled foot to the floorboards and sent the speedometer well past what the county road could handle. Anxious to forget last night, she turned her thoughts to New Orleans and the new gallery Gran had told her about. Maybe if she started working again things would get back to normal sooner.

Since she had been a little girl she had wanted to paint pretty pictures and to be taken seriously for her artistic talent. She'd wanted the reality of snaring her dream and building on it. She'd worked hard for it, battled the odds and prevailed. And the heady pleasure she had gotten from her first sale had been euphoric. She would never forget that phone call or the overwhelming feelings that had nearly choked her and rendered her speechless. Yes, if only she could paint again, she knew she would be able to get back to her old self.

She saw *him* just as she careened around a curve in the road. She was two miles from town, planning to hook up with highway 18 and take the river road straight into New Orleans. Too late, she realized she should have gone crosscountry.

He wasn't hitchhiking, simply walking with purpose toward town. *I'll get the pickup in the morning* is what he'd told her last night. Why hadn't she remembered that until now?

Evidently hearing the car approach, he slowed his pace and glanced over his shoulder. Nicole cursed her luck, sped past him, then slammed on the brakes. Her flashy car did a little dance as it came to a screeching halt. She tried to remain calm as she glanced into the rearview mirror and watched him stroll to the passenger side, using that famous loose-limbed gait he appeared to have owned since birth.

Nicole took a deep breath and braced herself as he opened the door and climbed in. When he slammed the door shut, she winced and wished the four headache pills she'd taken before leaving the house would hurry up and corral the pounding behind her eyes. She managed to put the car into gear, and sailed off down the road. Out of the corner of her eye, she saw him roll his broad shoulders against the leather seat and stretch his long legs out in front of him.

His beat-up jeans and T-shirt hugged him shamefully, only serving to make her more nervous as she remembered how wonderful it had felt being pressed against all that hard muscle. His boots were dusty, his jaw unshaven. He looked great, his hair loose and shiny in the morning light.

He slanted her a look, and she jerked her eyes back to the road. She could feel his gaze drift slowly over her. The gallery she was going to was on Julie Street in the warehouse district. Nicole had dressed for the occasion in a straight skirt in orange sherbet and a silk tank in white. She hadn't felt up to fussing with her hair, but she'd managed to twist it into a stylish knot. And though her hands had been a bit shaky, she'd bravely attempted the five-step make-over regime she'd picked up from an old friend that promised a miracle in just ten minutes.

"Thought you'd be sleeping in today."

Nicole braced herself for the attack. "No. I'm going into

New Orleans today. And where are you off to this morning?'' she asked before she realized the question was a loaded one.

''To fetch the Dodge.''

He gave her another long look. Nicole gripped the steering wheel and tried to breathe more quietly. Keeping her eyes on the road, she said, ''I want to apologize for what happened last night. I wasn't myself. I was…''

''Drunk,'' he said bluntly, when words failed her.

''No. That's not exactly true. I was…I never meant to let things get out of hand. I was just trying—''

''To get Farrel Craig's taste out of your mouth. Yeah, I remember.''

His tone was sharp, harsh, the words ending the subject with finality. Nicole gave him a sidelong glance. Was his anger directed at her? She frowned, annoyed with the idea. Actually, he should share some of the blame. He was the one who had insisted on driving her home.

No. She couldn't blame him for what had happened last night. She had been the one to let her emotions lead her astray. She was the one who'd had too many glasses of wine. And in the end, she was the one who had asked him to kiss her.

No, she hadn't asked. She'd begged.

''Sleep all right?''

They were on the outskirts of town, passing Gilmore's Gas and Go. ''I did, yes,'' she lied. Actually she'd gotten sick not five minutes after he had stormed off the porch. She'd sat by the toilet for two hours before dragging herself to bed.

The town was still half asleep when she swung into the deserted parking lot at Pepper's Bar and Grill and pulled up next to the pickup. She left the car idling in the hope that he would get the hint she was in a hurry, but he didn't budge. Instead, he reached across the seat and slipped her dark sunglasses off her face. In slow motion, his arm slid along the back of her seat, bringing his body close, his face mere inches from hers. He drawled, "Let's have a look-see."

Nicole blinked her bloodshot eyes and prayed her makeup covered the dark circles outlining them.

"Wine's no good when you've got serious drinking to do, *cherie*. You feel all right?"

"Just a little headache," Nicole admitted. "I'll be fine."

He looked at her, his eyes searching hers. Finally he said, "That's what counts."

He gave her back her dark glasses, and Nicole gladly slipped them on. "Johnny, about last night—"

"If anyone was to blame, it was me," he said quickly. "I had the clear head, remember? I should be the one apologizing, only—" he offered her a lazy smile "—I've never been any good at saying I'm sorry if I'm not. Holding you felt real nice. It's been a long time, and I'd be lying if I said I wished it hadn't happened."

"But—"

"Thinking about it too much and trying to analyze it to hell isn't going to change anything. If you want to forget it happened, *cherie,* that's your right. Me, I don't intend to forget any part of it. In fact, I don't think I could even if I wanted to. You drive safe now, you hear?"

The gas gauge shouldn't have been sitting on empty. Johnny's first thought was that someone had siphoned the tank dry overnight, but as he drove into Gilmore's he knew better—they were waiting for him, just like old times.

Knowing he'd been set up, Johnny stepped from the pickup without the slightest hesitation. As in the old days, the three of them were wearing smug grins—Farrel standing in the middle with Clete on his left and Jack Oden on his right.

Johnny wasn't really surprised. He'd always known Farrel would bring a fight to him sooner or later, only he'd hoped for better odds. But he shouldn't have. Farrel had never been much of a fighter; he was always too worried about getting dirty and feeling pain.

No, it didn't look as if Farrel had changed his tactics. He still didn't know how to fight any other way than behind a couple of front-runners. The truth was, no one had taught him how to take pride in his own ability. He needed to win, and that was all that counted. But sooner or later a man had to lose.

Only, Farrel wouldn't lose today. The question wasn't *if* Johnny was going down, it was how soon. There was no denying he'd be kissing the dirt before this was over. No doubt in his mind at all.

Well, hell, nothing like a little discussion between enemies early in the morning to get a man's blood pumping and put his life into perspective, Johnny decided. Only, this time he wasn't a vulnerable kid anymore. He'd learned a few moves of his own.

He sent the cigarette he'd had pinched between his lips to the asphalt and crushed it out with his boot, then stepped away from the pickup. Henry's Dodge was in good condition, and he didn't like the idea of scraping the paint or putting a dent in it once the party got rocking.

With a five-star smile, Farrel pushed away from the wall of the gas station. He was wearing black jeans and a black T-shirt. "Kinda feels like old times, don't it, Johnny? I've got you cornered, and there's nowhere to run." He gestured to his sidekicks, and they pulled wide, fanning out as if it were high noon at the O.K. Corral. "You remember the fun we used to have—you, me, Clete and Jack? It's like a reunion, don'tcha think?"

Johnny didn't answer, but he had to agree—it was exactly like old times. Except that Clete's body had gone to

fat—about three hundred pounds' worth. And Jack looked
like life had played a cruel joke on him—his red hair had
gone completely gray and had thinned to a mere ten hairs
on top of his head. His teenage pockmarked face had wors-
ened, too, giving him several hellish scars on both cheeks
and across his forehead. He looked meaner than ever and
angry at the world, with plans on getting even that very
minute.

"I think he's gonna run," Jack warned, cracking his
knuckles. He turned his head and spat a stream of tobacco
a good ten feet.

"He ain't gonna run," Clete assured. "Not *Swampy.*
He's treed and he knows it. And you know what we do
when we tree a coon, don'tcha, *Swampy?*"

"You girls plan on standing around sweet-talking me
all day, or are we gonna get to it?"

Johnny's wisecrack had Clete jerking his crooked hat
down farther over his ears and Jack snarling like a wild
dog. But Farrel only chuckled. "All right, then, let's do it,
Johnny."

The joke put the boys back in a better mood, and when
they saw Farrel start to advance they followed his lead.
Hands loose at his sides, Johnny watched as Clete started
to circle left while Jack moved right.

Farrel hung back. But that was no surprise; he always
moved in after the dust had settled.

It was after dark when Nicole wheeled into the driveway. Her arms loaded down with packages, she sprinted
across the yard in the rain to reach the house. The day had
gone better than she had ever imagined it could, considering the way it had started out. She had met Frank Medoro, the new gallery owner in New Orleans. He was
maybe thirty-five, good-looking, and spoke with a refined
French accent. Best of all, he had recognized her name

and had even seen some of her work. Excited, she had accepted his lunch proposal, and before she had left the Palace Café on Canal Street, he had invited her to his summer exhibition in a few weeks.

"I'm so glad you're home," Clair said as she greeted Nicole at the door.

Nicole let Clair take her packages. "The French Market bag is for you." She pointed to the wrapped package. "That one's for Bick. It's some of those special cigars he likes from Dumar's. Is something wrong? You found my note this morning, didn't you? You knew I went to New Orleans, right?"

"Yes, we knew. I'm sorry about last night, honey. Dory felt bad about not being able to meet you. One of the ovens caught on fire at the bakery. You know how it is when you're in business for yourself. She appreciated the call you left on her answering machine this morning."

"I'll give her a call again tomorrow." When Clair's worried expression remained, Nicole realized there was something more. "Clair, what is it? Is it Gran?"

"No, Mae's fine. But something is wrong, honey. It's Johnny."

"Johnny? What's wrong with Johnny?"

"Mae's in the study. I'll let her tell you."

A wave of panic flooded Nicole's senses as she hurried past Clair. When she reached the study, she flung open the door. "Gran? What's happened to Johnny?"

Mae turned away from the French doors where she had been sitting in her wheelchair half the day. Her cheeks were tear-stained. "Nicki, dear, I'm so glad you're home. Johnny's gone. No one has seen him since last night, and I'm terribly worried."

Nicole immediately felt a rush of relief. "Don't be," she soothed. "I saw him this morning."

"You did? Was he all right?"

"He was fine." Nicole was determined to ease her grandmother's mind. Gran looked awful. She didn't want to detail her morning conversation with Johnny, but if she had to, she was willing.

"Did you talk to him? Did he say anything about what his plans were for today?"

"No. I just assumed he would be working." Nicole crossed the room, crouched in front of Mae and took her hand. "Don't worry, Gran. Johnny is more than capable of taking care of himself."

"I know. But I keep remembering what took place a few days ago on the road. If anything happens to that boy, I'll never forgive myself. It's my fault he's here, my fault for everything."

"Gran, you're not responsible. Yes, I know about the land deed and your paying the taxes. Johnny mentioned that, but you didn't make him draw his knife at Pepper's. Really, you're getting all worked up over nothing."

"Then where is he, Nicki?"

That was a good question, one Nicole couldn't answer. "Maybe he took the day off and went fishing," she offered.

"No, he wouldn't do that," Mae argued.

Nicole stood and walked to the French doors. Through the screen she could hear the active nightlife in the distant bayou. She scanned the woods beyond the road. It had stopped raining, and the air was ripe with the smell of magnolia blossoms. "Where are you, Johnny," she whispered. "Stop worrying Gran and show yourself."

She turned, wanting to ease Gran's mind, but she didn't know how. The only thing that would make her grandmother breathe easier would be Johnny walking through the door.

It was odd how he had wormed his way into their lives, she thought. He hadn't been there a week and already most everything that happened centered around him. Gran's mood hinged on whether he came to breakfast and showed up for supper. Clair's menus had been altered to satisfy Johnny's palate. Even Bick searched him out and tagged behind him like an awestruck admirer.

What was it about this man that had attracted the people in this household so easily? What was it about him that had attracted her?

Yes, she admitted she was attracted to him, only not in the way everyone else was. Her attraction was based on something more, something far more dangerous. She couldn't deny she'd had a wonderful time in New Orleans today, but Johnny hadn't been far from her thoughts. His dark, intense gaze—the one he had offered her before he'd climbed out of the car—had been with her all day. And then there was that burning kiss that hadn't stopped smoldering since he'd planted it on her lips last night.

Ironically, even his slow-moving style and lazy drawl made him more exciting than any other man she knew. She hadn't thought she would look at a man with a sense of desire ever again, but she'd been wrong. Until a few days ago, she had promised herself she would never allow another man into her life, but somehow she had.

"How was New Orleans?" Mae managed to ask.

"Hot and crowded. I met the owner of that new gallery. I'll tell you about it tomorrow." Nicole faced her grandmother. "Did you call Sheriff Tucker and report Johnny missing?"

"No. I was afraid to. I didn't want him thinking Johnny skipped town."

"Could he have?"

"No. Johnny's a good boy."

Nicole could hear the pride and love in her grandmother's raspy voice. It was clouded with emotion and worry, and her heart went out to her. "He'll turn up, Gran. He will."

"Bick's out searching for him. I've been hoping and praying. That boy walked out of my life once before, and now that I've got him back I don't want to lose him a second time. I failed him once, but not this time, Nicki. I won't let it happen this time."

"Failed him? What are you talking about?"

"I should have tried harder. Made him feel welcome here. I should have insisted."

"He knows you care about him. I'm sure he knew back then, too."

Mae let out a long, tired sigh. "I'm not so sure, Nicki. And it's something I've lived with for fifteen years."

Without warning, Clair swung the study door open and rushed into the room. "Bick found him," she nearly shouted. She looked at Nicole, then Mae. "He found him at the farmhouse. He's been beaten badly."

"Oh, dear Lord," Mae gasped.

"Beaten!" Nicole cried. "Why? How?"

"Bick didn't give me any details. He just said I should tell Mae that Johnny's at the boathouse. He said not to worry, but you know Bick. He never stutters unless he's riled good. And he was making a mess of his words."

"Nicki! Where are you going? Nicki!"

From the porch, Nicole shouted, "To the boathouse! I'll let you know how serious he is as soon as I can." Then she was off the porch and running toward the woods as fast as her sandals would allow.

By the time she made it to Belle, Nicole was panting and clutching her side. She didn't remember when her hair had slipped from its knot, but when she reached the boathouse it was hanging in her eyes and the gold clip was gone.

Inside, she met Bick coming down the stairs. "How is he?" she asked anxiously.

"They kn-knocked him around p-pretty good, Miss Nicki."

"Who are they?"

Bick shrugged as he moved past her. "He w-won't say. But to do damage like th-that, th-there had to be more than one walking on him at the s-same time. Whoever done it s-sure got more than one piece of him." Bick jerked his baseball cap lower on his head. "Don't l-look so worried. I-I'll fix him up best I c-can."

"You? Shouldn't we take him to the hospital?"

"He said no fuss."

"I don't care what he said," Nicole snapped. "This is no time to be stubborn."

"Well, you b-best talk to him. He said no doc."

"I'll handle it. You go back to the house and fill Gran in. Assure her that he'll be all right." Nicole paused. "He will be, won't he?"

"Oh, h-he'll make it," Bick guaranteed. "It's just gonna slow him d-down for a spell."

"He did tell you what happened, didn't he?"

"I know what happened," Bick declared. "H-he got beat."

Nicole sighed in exasperation. "Just explain it as best you can to ease Gran's mind. Tell her I plan on taking Johnny to a doctor as soon as possible."

"Good luck with that, Miss Nicki. You want me to head back here in a little while, after I talk to Mae?"

Nicole was losing patience. "No. If he doesn't agree to a doctor, he'll have to settle for me."

"You got any training in busted ribs?"

The color drained from Nicole's face. "Busted ribs?"

"My guess is two, maybe three."

As Bick headed back to the house to do as she asked, Nicole climbed the stairs and let herself into the room. She hadn't expected it to be so dark. Brought up short, she waited a minute while her eyes adjusted to the darkness.

"Bick, that you?"

The pain in his voice sent a spasm of fear through Nicole's entire body. She took a deep breath to calm her nerves and made her way farther into the room. "No, Johnny. It's me, Nicki."

Silence.

"Johnny?"

"Dammit, *cherie,* get the hell out of here."

"I'm not leaving." He was on the bed; she could see his shadowy figure. She stopped by the rocker and turned on the small lamp. "Oh, God!"

He was lying on his back, shirtless in a pair of faded jeans. His face was badly bruised; one eye, his good one, was blackened and completely swollen shut. His lower lip was split, and blood had dried in the corner of his mouth. He had a cut on his forehead, and his bare chest and stomach were a mass of dark ugly bruises. A three-inch cut started to the left of his navel and disappeared into the waistband of his jeans.

There were two empty whiskey bottles on the bed beside him.

Yes, he'd definitely been beaten. But amazingly enough, he still looked tough and resilient lying there sprawled the length of the bed.

Nicole marveled at his durability; at the same time she felt angry and sick over what had been done to him. She glanced at the empty bottles, sure the liquor had been used to ease his obvious discomfort.

She moved to the bed and eased down beside him.

"You need a doctor, Johnny. Bick thinks you have broken ribs.

"It looks worse than it is. I don't need anything but a day off." He offered her a half smile. "You think the boss lady will give it to me?"

Nicole studied his face. He was a little drunk, but not inebriated. "Let me call Dr. Jefferies. Please?"

"How was New Orleans?"

"I didn't come here to talk about what I did today. I've come to drive you to the hospital." She held out her hand to offer him help in getting up. He made no move to take it.

"Did you come by yourself?"

"Yes." Her nursing skills were limited, but if he wasn't going to go to the hospital, Nicole would be forced to use them. "Come on, let's go. You can't—"

"Shh. My head's pounding. Don't be a nagging wife."

Nicole clamped her mouth shut and glared at his battered face. "I wouldn't have to be if you would listen to reason."

"You look good," he drawled. "What I can see of you. So when are you going to start patching me up so I can feel your hands on me and think about something else besides how much I hurt?"

Instead of getting angry, Nicole went into the bathroom and quickly put together some supplies to clean his wounds. She found a small enamel pan beneath the sink and filled it with hot water, then collected several towels, antiseptic and a bottle of pain relievers from the medicine cabinet.

"You could have internal injuries," she scolded, returning to the bed. "I still think—"

"I'd know it, if I did. And I don't."

She'd have to take his word on that, Nicole decided,

because she couldn't very well carry him through the woods and put him in the car by herself. She got busy cleaning the cut on his forehead and washing the dried blood from his face. She tried not to think about his comment earlier, even though she knew he was conscious of her touching him.

She eyed the cut on his belly, hesitated as to whether she should unzip his jeans. When she glanced at him, she found he'd opened his eye and was watching her. "You can leave it if you want," he said.

"So you can get an infection?" She forced her hands to move. After she'd unsnapped his jeans, she slowly slid his zipper down halfway. Luckily, the cut wasn't deep and only moved past his waistband an inch. She dipped the cloth in water once more and began to remove the dirt carefully from the wound. "How did you get this?" she asked.

"Don't remember."

"Sure you do. Why won't you tell me?"

"Because it's not important."

She rinsed the cloth and went back to work. He sucked in his breath when the cloth brushed over the cut. "Sorry. I've never been any good at this kind of thing."

"You're doing fine."

"Well, it's the least I can do. After all, you took that sliver out of my foot, remember? And last night you rescued me from driving home intoxicated."

"But I was already rewarded for that."

Nicole was fully aware of the heat that had surfaced between them. He reached up and brushed her bangs out of her eyes so he could see her better. "Does remembering our kiss make you uncomfortable, *cherie?*"

"Yes. You make me uncomfortable," she admitted. "Especially when you look at me like you're looking at

me now." She knocked her bangs back into place, then
went back to work. After she'd put a bandage on his belly
she reached for one of two elastic wrap bandages she had
brought from the bathroom. "I'll help you sit up, then I'll
wrap your ribs. I think that's all they would do at the
hospital. That and X-ray them. Are you sure you don't
want to go to the hospital?"

"No." He groaned as he struggled to sit up. Nicole
quickly reached out and gripped his shoulders as he
dropped his bare feet to the floor. Disgusted with his in-
ability to handle the task on his own, he cursed crudely.

When he finally looked as if he was going to stay upright without falling over, Nicole kneeled between his legs.
"You'll need to tell me if this gets too tight."

She could feel his heavy breathing on the side of her
neck as she leaned forward and started wrapping his ribs
as carefully as possible. Being this close to him only
served to remind her of last night, and a little shudder went
through her.

"You smell good," he drawled lazily, lowering his head
so that his face brushed her hair. His cheek slowly moved
against hers.

Nicole's hands stilled. "Johnny, please don't."

Ignoring her plea, he slipped his arms around her and
locked her between his hard thighs. "What did you do in
New Orleans today? Bick said you were gone all day. Meet
someone?"

"Actually, I did. A very nice man," she admitted.

His mouth brushed her ear, and Nicole sucked in her
breath and closed her eyes. "Want me to wipe the taste
of him away?"

"It wasn't like that."

She was treading in dangerous water again. Frightened,
she jerked hard on the bandage.

"Ouch! What the hell was that for?"

"To remind you that I'm trying to be nice, and you're trying to take advantage of the situation." She finished the job quickly, then stood and went into the kitchen. When she returned, she offered him a glass of water along with our pain relievers. "Here. Your body is going to hate you in the morning, but at least this will get you through tonight. Tomorrow we'll move you to the house. It'll be easier to care for you there."

"The house? No way. I'll be fine right here."

"We'll talk about it tomorrow. For now, you need to get back in bed. Only—"

"Only what?"

She lowered her gaze, a solid lump forming in her throat.

He followed her interest. "If you're worried about getting me out of my pants, don't be. You can close your eyes and feel your way through it."

It amazed her how he could make jokes when he looked so awful. Still, Nicole didn't want any part of what they were discussing. "If you have enough strength to be a wise guy, then I imagine you can't be as bad off as I first thought. The pants are your problem."

That said, she busied herself rinsing the pan out at the sink. Luckily, by the time she returned, he had somehow gotten his jeans off and was back in bed. She picked up his discarded jeans from the floor and draped them over the foot of the bed. His eyes were closed, and she didn't say anything to him for fear he'd fallen asleep.

Bick came by and asked her if she wanted him to stay, or if there was anything she needed. She told him no, and that he should go and get some rest himself. In the morning they would move Johnny into the house. She suggested

her room, since she didn't think climbing up and dow
stairs would do Johnny's ribs any good.

"Have Clair pack a few of my things and put them i
my old room upstairs," she told him. "And tell Gran n
to worry. Tell her Johnny hasn't lost his sense of humo
It's safe to say he's going to live."

Chapter 8

Johnny slowly climbed out of bed and pulled on his jeans. It had been three days since his run-in with Farrel and the boys. He could see out his blackened eye now, and it no longer hurt to take a breath, though he sucked air with more care than usual. He'd been staying in Nicole's bedroom at the house. He felt funny about it; making her move out hadn't been necessary.

All the fuss had actually embarrassed him. He had told the old lady and Nicole more than once that the boathouse was where he wanted to be. Yes, he looked like hell—that he hadn't debated. But he would mend whether he stayed at the boathouse or the big house. All he needed was time.

The process would be slow when it came to his ribs. He was sure a couple were busted, but he had denied it to the women, saying they were only bruised.

When the knock at the door came, Johnny wasn't surprised. A morning routine had been established, and about this time Nicole brought him breakfast in bed. Only, this morning she wasn't going to find him there.

Angry all over again that she continued to wait on hir like a slave for hire after he'd told her time and again no to, he put on his best ugly face and nailed her with a loo that said *I eat little blondes for breakfast* the minute sh swung the door open and stepped inside. She ignored hi exaggerated scowl from where she stood by the window and carried the breakfast tray to the nightstand and set down.

"Clair made pecan waffles," she announced. "She tell me they're one of your favorites."

"I'm getting out of here, today," Johnny told her.

She turned and looked at him where he stood soakin up the morning sunshine. "I think that's an excellent ide. Maybe it'll improve your mood. I'll have Bick come b and take you for a walk."

He turned back to the window. "I'm not some dam dog. I don't need to be 'taken' anywhere. My legs wor just fine. I don't need a nurse any longer, either, so con sider yourself fired."

"Has the maid service been that awful? What, the sheet not crisp enough, sir? Or is it the food? Clair will b crushed to hear you don't like her waffles."

She was mocking him, and he had a mind to…what He turned away from the window, his eyes fully on he molded curves straining the confines of her slippery whit shift. What she'd said was anything but the truth. Actually the service had been the best he'd ever had. He couldn' remember anybody ever bringing him hot food and wor rying about crisp sheets. But it was something he coul get used to real fast if he let himself. Only he wasn't goin; to. As soon as his parole was over, he was on his way ou of Common for good.

"What I'm saying is all of you have better things to do I'm just the hired help, remember?"

She shrugged, then headed for the door, stopping before she opened it. "Can I get you anything from town?"

"Like what, a color book?"

She laughed. "I was thinking more on the lines of a magazine or a book, but if you have your heart set on coloring…"

So that's why she was dressed up: she was going into town. He gave her another slow head-to-toe, stopping when he spied her pink toenails. Her white sandals showed off her slender feet and narrow ankles. Her knees were a favorite with him. But best of all, he liked her naughty long bangs, and the way they half hid her beautiful blue eyes. "What are you going to do in town?"

"Gran's garden club meets today. I told her I would drive her."

"Come here."

"What?"

"You heard me."

"No." She shook her head. "I'll bring you food, a color book from town if that's what you want. But you've been scowling at me since I came through the door. In fact, you've been downright mean for days. I'll keep my distance, thank you."

Johnny dragged a hand through his hair, then started toward her. "So why have you been putting up with me if I've been such a bastard?"

"Because it makes Gran happy."

He'd hoped for a different answer. "You won't have to too much longer."

"Shall I start celebrating now or after I buy the party balloons?"

Johnny stopped a foot away from her. "Since I've taken your bed, how do you like sleeping upstairs?"

"I was only using this room until Gran's ankle got better. Actually, I like the room upstairs." She checked her watch. "I've got to go. Clair should have Gran ready by now, and your breakfast is getting cold."

She turned to leave, but Johnny reached out and caught her hand. "When I talked to Mae yesterday, she said she didn't think you had been sleeping very well." He brushed his thumb beneath her right eye. "Dark shadows, *cherie*. Still pacing late at night?"

"Mae? Since when did you start calling Gran anything but 'old lady'?"

"Since yesterday," Johnny admitted. "She asked me to do her a favor. Made me promise before she told me what it was. I was conned before I knew it."

She smiled, and Johnny was reminded of how much he liked her mouth, of how soft and sweet it was. Of how many times in the past three days he'd wanted to drag her down on the bed and kiss her.

"So, tell me why you don't sleep."

"I'm sleeping fine. It just takes me a little time to unwind." She slipped her hand out of his.

"And why is that?"

"There are millions of insomniacs out there."

"Good answer, but I don't think you're one of them."

"Let's change the subject. Is this going to get to be a habit? Are you going to get beat up weekly or monthly?"

"That depends."

"On Farrel?"

Johnny had never given any names. But the situation being what it was, he supposed Farrel was everyone's logical choice. "Has he confessed to something I should know about?"

"I don't think so. Should he?"

Johnny shrugged guardedly, knowing she was trying to get him to falter.

"You've had plenty of opportunity to tell me what happened. I've asked often enough," she prompted. "I'm beginning to wonder if what Bick said isn't closer to the truth.''

"Oh?" Johnny shifted his stance, his hands finding his back pockets. "And that would be…?"

"Bick says there was more than one. He said the only way anyone would get the jump on you was if you were outnumbered or caught by surprise."

"Sounds like Bick talks too much and shouldn't be scaring little girls with such tall tales."

"Oh, he wasn't telling me," she announced. "He was talking to Gran. I was eavesdropping. Was he right?"

Again Johnny didn't answer. The truth was, he didn't want Nicole, or anyone else at Oakhaven, involved in his problems. Choosing sides would be dangerous for her, especially if she chose his.

He had asked her to give him a chance days ago, but now he wasn't so sure that had been a good idea. He didn't want to put Nicole in an awkward position—not when she was intending to make Common her home.

"Not giving up their names doesn't make this go away," she continued. "If anything, it's just letting those men off the hook so they can do it again. And next time—"

A sudden rap at the door cut Nicole off. "Nicki?" It was Clair. "Pearl Lavel called for a ride to the church. Mae says you better hurry along. Pearl will huff like a steam engine the entire way if she's late."

"You better go," Johnny said.

She glanced at his breakfast tray. "I hope the food isn't too cold."

"It'll be fine," he assured.

"If you're feeling cooped up and restless, maybe you could spend some time in the study figuring out renovation costs. Gran's been after me to get some totals for her, but I'm not very good with figures. I hear you are, though."

When Johnny made no comment, she continued, "I don'
expect you to do it for nothing. The hours would be adde
to your paycheck."

"I wasn't thinking about that," he told her. "I'll si
down this afternoon and see what I come up with."

"Nicki?" Clair was again in the hall. "I'm putting Ma
in the car."

"Bring me back some cigarettes, would you?" Johnny
asked. "I ran out last night and—"

"I think a color book would be healthier. Maybe thi:
would be a good time to quit blowing smoke."

Johnny rested his shoulder against the wall and studiec
her bloodshot eyes. "I'll quit the day you go to bed before
midnight and sleep straight through the night. Deal?"

"You're offering that deal because you think I can't do
it."

"No." Johnny gave up a lazy smile. "Call it incentive
Wouldn't you like the satisfaction of seeing me suffer from
withdrawal?"

"It does have a certain appeal. Especially since you've
been such a nightmare of a patient." She opened the doo
and stepped into the hall.

"Cherie?"

"Yes?"

"Keep your opinions about this mess to yourself while
you're in town, would you. These folks are funny. They
might not always like everything their own do, but if ar
outsider starts riling them up they usually band together
like wolves. You and Mae don't need to be caught in the
middle of the war against me."

"It's called Red Flame." Daisi struck a pose, her long
fingernails wiggling against her cheek.

"They look stunning," Nicole complimented, noting the

color was a perfect match to Daisi's red-striped maternity dress.

"I love red." Daisi giggled, then glanced appreciatively at Nicole's slender figure. "I wish I was that thin, but even before I got pregnant I didn't look like that. God, you must eat practically nothin'."

"I'm just naturally thin, I guess," Nicole admitted.

Daisi wrinkled up her button nose. "I hate that line, but I won't hold it against you. I'll be the first to admit bein' pregnant doesn't do a woman's figure any favors, but it sure makes my nails grow."

Nicole's gaze shifted to Daisi's swollen stomach. She tried not to dwell on the fact that there was a baby nestled inside, growing and gaining weight. A healthy baby. It was so hard getting past the emptiness, the deep ache that never seemed to go away for very long. The guilt.

"It was real nice of you to give Mama a ride to the church."

Nicole kept her smile fixed. Pearl Lavel was not one of her favorite people. Daisi's mother had huffed and sniffed and evil-eyed the back of her head the entire way from her house on Willow Street through the short five blocks to the Saint and Savior Baptist Church. That the woman had a daughter as nice as Daisi was a God-given miracle.

"How did you know I drove her?" Nicole asked.

"One thing you'll get used to around here is that everybody knows everybody else's business. Just like what happened to Johnny. We all knew about that by breakfast the next mornin'."

"And just what version did you hear?" Nicole knew she shouldn't have said anything. Johnny had warned her to keep her opinions to herself, but maybe Daisi knew something that could be helpful.

"What are you askin', Nicki?"

"Johnny hasn't given out any names. Do you have any?"

"Sure. I've got three. Woody said Clete Gilmore is walkin' around town with a limp and two teeth missin'. And I know Jack Oden has a broken jaw 'cause I saw him in the clinic the other day when I went for my checkup. haven't seen Farrel's broken nose, but I've heard it's worse than the last one Johnny gave him six months ago."

Nicole listened while Daisi spilled every piece of gossip she'd heard on the subject. She didn't say anything, just listened, thinking all the time that Bick had been right— they'd stacked the odds against Johnny from the moment he climbed out of the pickup at the gas station. And the way Daisi talked, it was nothing new.

"I heard Johnny's been flat on his back," Daisi continued. "Is he gettin' better?"

"He's up," Nicole informed her. "Do you know why it happened?"

Daisi leaned forward, lowering her voice. "There doesn't have to be a reason for Farrel to go after Johnny. They've always hated each other."

"Are you sure? I don't think Johnny lies awake nights trying to figure out ways to rearrange Farrel's face."

"Maybe not, but they've always fought."

"Did you know Johnny very well in the old days?"

"We went to school together." Daisi grinned. "I had a bad crush on him when I was in the sixth grade. But then, I think most of the girls in town did. Only, none of them would have wanted to admit it. It wasn't cool to like the poor boy in town, if you know what I mean. And the Bernard family—they were the poorest around." Daisi glanced down the hall. "You can go back and see Sheriff Tucker. He don't have nobody back there with him."

"Thanks." Nicole walked down the hall and stopped at

the first door she came to. After taking a deep breath, she knocked.

"Come in."

"Sheriff Tucker?"

He looked up from his desk as Nicole walked in and closed the door. "Miss Chapman, what a surprise."

"Is it?" She took a seat in front of his desk.

He pointed to his coffee cup. "Can I offer you some?"

"Thank you, no." Nicole gazed around the dingy room, her gaze falling on the news clippings that covered the wall behind his desk. Some of them were yellow with age, making them look twenty years old or more.

Sheriff Tucker sat back in his chair and folded his arms over his thick chest. "So what can I do for you, Miss Chapman?"

"I'm sure you're aware that three days ago Johnny Bernard was badly beaten. I was wondering what you're planning on doing about it."

"The way it works here, little lady, is if there's been a crime committed, I get involved. If there's no proof of one, I don't. And no one has come forward and pressed any charges. My take on the matter is that Johnny and Farrel went a few rounds at Gilmore's. It isn't the first time, and I'm afraid it won't be the last. I don't mind telling you that's why I didn't think too much of this here deal the parole board set up. Johnny back in Common just doesn't make good sense. Actually, I'm giving him the benefit of the doubt in this instance by ignoring what happened."

"Meaning?"

"Fighting is a parole violation, Miss Chapman." The sheriff mopped his brow. "I could have him sent back to Angola if I wanted to."

"But he was a victim," Nicole blurted out.

"Johnny Bernard, a victim? Now that would be a first. I've seen the boy in action."

"He was defending himself," Nicole pointed out.

"You obviously haven't seen Clete and Jack. Farrel won't be winning no prize with his looks for some time, either."

"You're saying Johnny defended himself too well!" Nicole couldn't believe what she was hearing.

"No judge in his right mind would look at Johnny's rap sheet and call that fight one-sided, the deck stacked or not. Johnny got a piece of all three of them boys—a big piece."

"Johnny did not start that fight. He was only acting in self-defense. A man would have to be stupid to pick a fight with three men all at the same time. And from what I've seen, Johnny Bernard is far from stupid."

"You don't have to convince me of that, little lady. No one said Johnny isn't smart. Still, if I pursue this thing, it won't go well for him. Now, you may not like hearing that, but it's the truth. I think leaving it alone would be for the best."

"So there's no recourse?"

"Not at this time."

"And if it happens again?"

"Like I said, Johnny's on parole. He's supposed to be keeping his nose clean. The truth is, Miss Chapman, he's been in trouble most of his life. I think the first time he slept over in my jail was age nine. It's true, some of the things that happened weren't always his fault, but most of the time they were."

He gave her a long look, as if seeing her anew. "The folks in town, frankly, got their bellies full of him years ago. They aren't feeling too charitable where he's concerned, and that's their right. We're all trying to do the best we can around here. Honestly, I'll be happy when the summer's over and Johnny clears out."

"I called Johnny's parole agent and explained the situation,'' Nicole announced matter-of-factly. ''He said he was going to call you.''

The sheriff's blue eyes narrowed dramatically. It was the first time he'd shown any emotion since Nicole had entered the room. ''You seem awfully interested in sticking your pretty nose in Johnny Bernard's business, missy. Does he know?''

''Actually, no, he doesn't. But I imagine with the way the gossip in this town flies, he will soon enough.''

''You can bet on it. In the meantime, I suggest you back off. We're not ignorant around here. We don't need to be told what to think, or how to do our jobs.''

''I have no desire to take over your job, Sheriff Tucker. But Oakhaven has a lot riding on Johnny Bernard's health and his ability to work.'' Nicole stood. ''I apologize if I've offended you. I just wanted you to know that I'm not any more ignorant than you are, and if Johnny Bernard is flat on his back in bed more than he is on his feet, I'm going to be damn mad. My father was a lawyer, and if I need legal advice, I know one of his associates would be happy to give it to me. Have a nice day, Sheriff Tucker.''

''Is that what you wanted, *cherie?*'' Johnny asked that night as he slowly entered the study to find her sitting at the desk going over the figures he'd worked on that afternoon.

Nicole glanced up, surprised that she hadn't heard him enter the room, and even more surprised at how well he was moving. ''You did all this in one afternoon?''

''A few hours.''

''That's amazing.''

He smiled, then stepped through the door and closed it behind him. Holding onto his smile, he moved slowly across the room and rounded the desk. Leaning over her shoulder, he began to point out the additions he'd made on repairs and the cost of each. "The kitchen floor is soft," he said. "It'll need a new underlayment. And you'll need to decide if you want another wood floor laid down or linoleum."

"Wood."

"It'll cost more."

"But it would look better, don't you think?"

"Yes."

"Then if Gran says yes, it's all settled."

"I found several ceiling cracks in the upstairs rooms," he told her. "I added those repairs to the list, and the material to fix them, too."

He was so close, Nicole could feel his warm breath on her neck. One of his big hands rested on the desk, and the size of his arm was twice that of hers. She closed her eyes for a moment and tried not to think about what it felt like being in those powerful arms.

She gazed up at him. "You really are a carpenter, then? It's what you want to do with your life?"

He arched his dark brows as he looked down at her. "Right now Oakhaven needs a carpenter, so I guess that's what I'll be."

"And if we need a plumber?"

"Then I'd go find a wrench," he drawled.

And if I needed a lover? Nicole would never let him know what she was thinking, but since the kiss on the porch she had been thinking about it more and more. It was crazy—insane, in fact—yet she couldn't stop thinking about what it would be like with him.

They stared at each other for a moment. Nicole felt her heart skip a beat. She wet her lips, her gaze drifting over his face, inspecting him slowly. The cut on his forehead was no longer an angry red gash, and his black eye had faded. He certainly had a tolerance for pain, she thought.

Nicole envied that about him. She wished she could

store her pain in a neat little box in the back of her head and open it only when she needed a reality check. Instead she was haunted by it daily, forced into reliving it nightly.

"What are you looking at, *cherie?* What are you thinking?"

Nicole realized she'd been caught staring and musing. "I— You didn't overdo today, did you? Clair told me you went for a walk and that you went alone."

"You worry too much."

He really did look fine in more ways than one, she decided. None of what had happened to him had diminished his sex appeal. He was still affecting her breathing, still making her nervous. Still making her yearn for things she would be better off without.

Nicole shoved the chair to one side and stepped around him. She walked to the French doors and gazed outside. It was another sweltering night, the air heavy, filled with the scent of magnolia blossoms. She'd changed back into a pair of cutoffs and a yellow T-shirt the minute she'd gotten back from town. Her feet were bare. "I've been concerned with the amount of money Gran will need for the restorations. I wish there was some way to recoup the expense."

"Want one?"

His quick reply surprised her, and Nicole turned to look at him. "You have an idea?"

"Why not put cane back in the fields? That way, Mae's savings would stay intact. And Oakhaven stands on its own feet again. It's a profitable business."

The idea had never occurred to Nicole. "A sugar plantation, like when Grandpa Henry was alive?"

"Why not? Griffin Black is making money at it. Why not us?"

Us. He'd said *us.* Nicole's heart started to pound. "But

I don't know anything about running a sugarcane plantation. I don't even know that I want to.''

"It's just a thought. I could look into it, at least, if you'd like. It'll be a pile of work, and this first year all we'd do is get the fields in shape. But by next spring everything would be ready to go. Before I leave I could check out who might be interested in working for you. That way, they'd be lined up for next spring."

When I leave. To hide her disappointment, Nicole quickly turned to gaze outside. Funny how unexpectedly things change, she thought. A week ago all she wanted was Johnny Bernard out of their lives. But now... Now she couldn't imagine him gone. Suddenly she was angry. Angry that he had disrupted her life in the first place. Angry that she had let him.

She faced him. "It wouldn't work. Not without a foreman to keep it all running smoothly. No, forget it. I'll get the money another way."

"At least let me check—"

"I said no!"

He slanted her a puzzled look. "What's wrong, *cherie?* A minute ago you acted like the idea was worth checking out."

"I was being polite."

He started toward her. He looked a little angry, or maybe disappointed. When he finally stopped, he was so close that Nicole could see his pulse throbbing at the base of his throat. So close, she could smell his musky male scent. She took a step back and felt the window against her spine. "Let's just drop it."

She turned her head to avoid his eyes, but he reached out, cupped her chin and turned her face back to his. "Let me help you."

"Me? How can you help me when you can't even help yourself? Half the town hates you, and Sheriff Tucker isn't going to do a damn thing about those men who—'' Nicole knew in that brief second she'd said too much.

''You talked to Tuck today?'' He was frowning.

''Yes.''

''Where?''

''At his office.''

''You went to see Tuck after I told you to keep out of this?'' He released her chin. ''Why?''

''Gran and I have a stake in your well-being. If you can't work—'' She didn't go on. He was glaring at her, so angry he was clenching his teeth.

''Don't worry, I'll make sure I get the work done,'' he told her.

''That's not what I meant. I only—''

She clamped her mouth shut as he turned and headed for the door. After swinging the door open, he turned back to look at her. ''I warned you to keep your opinions to yourself. If you make enemies in this town, *cherie,* you'll have them for the rest of your life. Take it from someone who knows.''

''I'm not afraid of the people in this town,'' Nicole snapped, feeling defensive.

''Well, you should be. These people are a crazy bunch, some more than others. But if they decide not to like you, you won't have a chance in hell of changing their minds later.''

''And what would make them not like me? Speaking out on your behalf? Facing Sheriff Tucker and telling him I think Farrel Craig and his 'boys' were out of line and should be arrested for assault?''

''Dammit, *cherie,* do you have any idea what you've done?''

''Don't tell me, I've just been condemned.'' Nicole

clutched her throat as if someone had ahold of it and was choking the life out of her. "Will they beat me up, too?"

Johnny's answer to her theatrics was dead serious and final. "If anyone lays a hand on you, I'll kill them."

Chapter 9

Two days later Johnny moved back to the boathouse and found a rat snake nailed to the front door. He removed it, tossed it in the bayou for fish bait, then went up to his room. He was getting tired of the harassment. Still, there was more than one reason to keep his cool. There were too many people depending on him right now.

Feeling surly, he scanned the small apartment, found it unchanged, then headed back outside. On the dock, he untied the boat and climbed in, ready to spend Sunday afternoon by himself. He'd had enough of Mae's fussing and Clair's oversize meals. And he'd played so many hands of cards with Bick, the man had nearly lost his entire stash of White Horse.

Mostly, he'd had enough of Nicole and her newfound silence. She hadn't spoken to him since the night they'd fought. Of course, he hadn't tried to speak to her, either. He was still mad as hell at her for deliberately going against his wishes.

The afternoon heat had steadily climbed into the nineties. Johnny stripped off his T-shirt and tossed it in the bottom of the boat, then picked up his pole and thrust it deep into the water. Giving a solid push, the boat surged forward, cutting through a thick patch of spider lilies and pickerel weeds.

He closed his eyes briefly as the familiar bond he shared with Belle wrapped its magical fingers around him, and for a moment he was a kid again, exploring the narrow channels leading everywhere and nowhere. He'd gotten lost a hundred times as a small boy, but eventually he'd learned every secret channel and switchback Belle owned. He'd even braved the black bog long before he'd known it was the nesting ground for monster alligators like old One Eye.

The sky was clear, and there was just enough breeze to keep the heat moving. The bayou branched off in a maze of tiny channels. Johnny maneuvered around the cypress knees, chose the hidden gate most often missed, and in an instant disappeared through a veil of Spanish moss.

Around the next bend stood the old farmhouse. He pulled the boat into the shoreline and tied it to an old post left over from what had once been a dock. Holding his ribs, he hiked the overgrown path, stopping when he'd made it to the top of the hill.

Funny how, standing there, so many memories rushed back to him. The strongest were the Sunday afternoons he'd spent with his mother and father on the hillside. He closed his eyes, remembering how they used to lie side by side and look at the sky. How they would take turns telling each other made-up stories. Once they'd gotten talked out, they would doze off, holding hands.

His family had been beggar-poor, Johnny admitted, but what they had shared so briefly had been worth gold. They had loved one another honestly and completely. God, how they had loved one another.

He took a deep breath, then eased down on the hillside to sprawl in the tall grass. The sun felt good on his face, and he let go of the tension that had been keeping him restless the past few days. After a time he turned his hands palm-side up and pretended *they* were once again beside him holding his hands. He took a deep breath and let it out slowly, allowed the sun's rays to seep into his bones, and damn if he didn't fall asleep just the way he'd done back when he was a kid.

Only, it wasn't his mother's voice jarring him awake an hour later. It was Nicole's.

"Johnny?"

"Mmm…"

"Are you all right?"

Her sweet voice sent pure desire snaking through Johnny's blood. Through half-open eyes, he watched her sink to her knees in the fragrant grass a foot away. After noticing she had on those too-short jean cutoffs again and a skimpy red T-shirt, he reminded himself he was still angry with her, and she with him.

"Johnny, wake up."

"I'm awake. I heard your car a mile away," he lied, rolling slowly to his side and raising up on one elbow to rest his head in his hand. His booted feet, he crossed at the ankles. "So we're talking again, is that it?"

"You walked out on me, remember?"

"With good reason."

She rolled sideways onto one hip and tucked her feet close. "I'm not going to say I'm sorry, because I'm not. You told me if you're not sorry, you shouldn't say it. So it goes for me, too."

Hearing his words thrown back at him made him frown. "Sometimes I should keep my mouth shut," he grumbled.

She smiled, then gazed at the farmhouse. "Are you going to fix it up?"

"The house? Hell, no. There's no point. It needs to be leveled."

She shoved a loose strand of hair behind her ear, and directed her interest to the bayou. "It's beautiful here. Belle is picture perfect."

The bayou was beautiful, Johnny agreed silently. But not as beautiful, nor as perfect as the woman sitting next to him. He couldn't deny how much he enjoyed looking at her. How much he liked being close enough to smell her womanly scent. She was driving him crazy, making him want her more and more with each passing day. It was ironic how one small woman could do so much damage to his insides in such a short amount of time.

Frustrated, feeling suddenly reckless, he reached out and grabbed Nicole's ankle, jerking her off balance and onto her back.

"Johnny! What are you doing?"

She tried to shake off his hand, but he hung on while he got to his knees. Flattening out his hands on either side of her tiny waist, he effectively pinned her to the ground. "So you like me, is that it?"

"What! Are you crazy?"

Grinning, he said, "Why else would you pay a visit to Tuck? Don't be shy, *cherie*. You can admit it to me. It'll be our secret."

A defiant gleam sharpened her blue eyes. "Me, like you? An arrogant ex-marine, ex-con, ex-who knows what else. I don't think so, Johnny Bernard. Now get off me and let me up."

"I've caught you staring," he goaded.

"Neanderthals are rare in California," she reasoned.

Johnny hooted.

She scowled at him. "It's really nothing to be proud of. Or don't you know what a Neanderthal is?"

"So are you interested in kissing this Neanderthal again?"

She went still. A warm flush darkened her cheeks, while at the same time she defiantly answered, "No."

Johnny leaned closer, drinking in the scent of her. "I think you're lying. I think that's why you came looking for me."

"The afternoon sun has cooked your brain," she insisted, squirming beneath him and pushing gently on his chest. "Let me up."

Johnny shook his head, liking her hands on him. "How about we strike a bargain?"

"No." She shoved a little harder.

"Ouch!" Johnny rolled off her onto his side and clutched his ribs, while Nicole scrambled to her feet. "It serves you right. I— Oh, God!" She dropped to her knees beside him. "I didn't mean to— I'm sorry, all right?"

"So she says after she drives my busted ribs into my lungs."

"Busted? They're busted?"

He heard her suck in her breath, and opened his eyes to see her looking worried and afraid. "Hey, I was just kidding."

"No, you weren't. You've known all along, haven't you?"

Johnny sat up slowly. "They're mending fine. You like to fish?"

She wrinkled up her nose. "Not really."

"Boat rides?"

"Sometimes," she said cautiously.

Johnny glanced up at the blue sky overhead. "Great day for a boat ride."

"Are you asking me to take a boat ride with you, Johnny Bernard?"

She cocked her head to one side. Johnny relaxed, enjoying her smile and her shapely curves accented in her well-fitting cutoffs. "Yes, mama, I guess I am," he drawled. "I'll show you a side of Belle that's rarely seen. Cypress trunks eight feet across."

"There isn't such a thing," she challenged.

Johnny stood and headed down the hillside to the bayou. "If I'm lying," he called over his shoulder, "I'll work the next week for no pay."

By the time he reached the boat, Nicole was trailing him. Grinning to himself, Johnny helped her into the boat, warning her to watch her step, then climbed in after her. Knees bent, his balance cemented in the boat, he deftly maneuvered them away from the grassy bank with the long push-pole, then traded the pole for a paddle and sat down.

In the blink of an eye, the shoreline vanished, as Johnny sent them deeper into the swamp where the sun wasn't able to follow. Giant cypress—their massive, twisted trunks submerged in the brackish water—closed in around them, crowding the narrow channel, some stretching eight feet across at the base, just like he'd said.

An hour passed. The scenery turned wilder, more remote. He pointed to an alligator gliding along the muddy bank. "Be a good girl, *cherie,* and keep your hands in the boat."

She did as she was told, inching her tiny backside into the middle of the boat.

They skimmed over a carpet of water lilies so thick it could easily have been mistaken for solid land. "What did you do in L.A.?" Johnny asked, maneuvering them around a cypress knee.

"Does it matter?"

He slanted her a curious glance, detecting a note of challenge in her tone. "Virgil couldn't remember what kind of work you were doing there."

"Virgil?"

"Yeah, I asked him what he knew about you that first day after our phone conversation. I wanted to find out about the woman who was bent on firing me without even laying eyes on me."

"I didn't need to see you to know you were trouble," she told him.

"Still think so?"

"Yes." She paused, then softly said, "No."

"So who's Nik Kelly?"

She'd been enjoying the scenery. Suddenly, she stopped and looked his way. "Are we playing twenty questions?"

"Something like that." Johnny grinned. "So, who's Old Nik? The guy sure has made an impression on somebody around here. There're paintings everywhere by him. One in every room. Mae even insisted I hang one at the boathouse."

"She did, did she? Do you like the painting?"

Johnny liked the painting very much, but if the artist turned out to be a close friend of Nicole's, he wasn't so sure he'd like it for much longer. He said, "It's all right."

"Just all right? Then you're not interested in art?"

"I don't know much about it," Johnny admitted.

"Most people don't. But it's not the knowing that's important. It's whether you like what you see or not. Or maybe it's not even about that. If it makes you give it a second look, makes you stop and think for just a second, then it worked." She ran a hand quickly through her hair, sending it away from her face, only to have her long bangs fall back into her eyes. "Actually, *Old* Nik lives right here in Common. Would you like me to introduce you sometime?"

That the guy lived in Common surprised Johnny. Still,

he shook his head. "No, thanks. I don't think we'd have much to talk about."

"That's too bad. I think *she'd* enjoy showing off her collection of paintings to you."

Johnny's brows knit quizzically. "She?"

Suddenly Nicole extended her hand the small distance that separated them in the boat. "Johnny Bernard, meet Old Nik. The paintings are mine."

She had completely taken him by surprise. "You're the artist?"

Enjoying the trick she'd played on him, an impish smile parted her irresistible lips. Then, like a naughty child, she giggled with delight. It was the prettiest sound Johnny had ever heard. "I really had you going," she boasted proudly. "You should see your face."

Johnny shook his head, finally giving up a grin. "Why Kelly?"

"That was my mother's name. Alice Kelly. Everyone called my father Nik instead of Nicholas. I just put the two together," she explained.

Johnny glanced at the wilderness surrounding them, the gnarled trees, all the shades of color that made up the landscape. "It takes a special talent to make all this come alive with a brush and a bunch of wet, slippery paint."

She considered what he'd said. "I never thought of it quite that way, but I suppose it does."

He looked back at her. "I'm impressed."

"I'm flattered that you are," she admitted. "I've been selling in a gallery in L.A. for about four years. And it looks like I might be doing the same in a gallery in New Orleans if things work out. I've considered turning the attic into a studio. Actually, it was Gran's idea."

She stopped herself from going on. Johnny noted that the animation had drained from her face and that she now looked a little ill at ease. "Fixing the space so it works for you would be no problem. All you have to do is tell me what you want.''

She allowed a small smile. "That's nice of you to offer. Maybe I'll take you up on it a little later. After the more important things at Oakhaven get done. I told Gran I was taking the summer off, so there's no rush." She batted away an irksome fly. "My parents never liked the idea of my being an artist," she confessed. "They said no one would pay me to paint pretty pictures, and I should go to law school so I could become a partner in my father's law firm.''

"Did they eventually understand?"

"Not really. I always wanted their approval, for them to see me as a success. I guess all kids do. Now, hopefully a little wiser, I think what matters most is how you see yourself. If I had children I would…I'd try to teach them that. Try to let them be whoever they need to be, not what I need them to be.''

"Sounds like your kids are going to be lucky having you for a mom.'' His comment made her look off into the bayou, her face as solemn as Johnny had ever seen it. "Sorry, did I say something wrong?"

"No, you didn't. I haven't been around kids much. And I never had a lot of friends.'' She looked back at him. "You were an only child, too, right?"

"Yeah. And you already know my status with friends.''

Aware that her mood had darkened, Johnny was curious why, but he didn't think asking would be wise. This was the most Nicole had talked to him since they'd met, and he wasn't ready to squelch it by getting nosey. She had a right to her past, just like he did. Though he couldn't deny that he was eager to know how *Chad* fit in—and why, when nighttime came, she got as restless as a cat.

"I'm boring you," she said suddenly. "This all must sound ridiculous to you. First I tell you I'm an artist, then

I start getting philosophical. I must sound like a complete idiot.'' She looked away, embarrassed.

"No, don't do that," Johnny drawled, reaching out to turn her face back to look at him. "Don't be embarrassed *cherie*. Not with me. Never with me."

The words hung between them. They stared at each other while a chorus of crickets trilled. Then an alligator's low growl echoed through the channel, sending several birds into flight.

"I don't usually talk so much," she said, still looking embarrassed. "How about if you talk for a while."

Johnny dropped his hand from her cheek. "I've never been much of a talker, either," he admitted.

"Well, since I told you something about me, I think it's only fair you share something with me. One of your secrets."

"Secrets? I don't have any secrets," he told her. "I'm an open book."

She laughed richly. "Liar. A secret," she insisted. Then with more care and in a sultry, quiet voice. "One no one else knows."

The intimate request fell into the silence. It was followed by the two of them sharing another long look.

Finally, Johnny said, "Something no one else knows hmm..." He scratched his chin. "How about I show you instead?"

"I knew it!" Her eyes lit up like those of an anxious child. "You have buried treasure in the swamp?" she speculated. "You buried it long ago and now you've come back to dig it up."

Moments ago they had shared a special heat-filled look; now they were sharing laughter. Johnny couldn't remember when he had really laughed with a woman, when he had felt this damn good.

It would take twenty minutes to travel to the *secret*

Johnny had decided to share with Nicole. Once their laughter died out, he reminded her again to keep her hands in
the boat, then steered them into another hidden channel
and headed north. North into the black bog.

Deeper…deeper still, they slipped through a watery
maze so remote and overgrown, it was like stepping back
in time to a place no human had ever traveled. Only, there
were a few who had braved the bog. Once, Johnny had
tried to outrun the sheriff by way of the bog, only to be
caught and arrested for vandalizing the Saint and Savior
Baptist Church. He hadn't been responsible for the broken
windows, but he had paid for them nonetheless.

The boat cut soundlessly through the water while egrets
and cranes watched from their nests—as did the white
ibises, and the shy night herons. An abundance of bofin,
spotted gar, crayfish and bullfrogs went about their business in the unseen depths beneath.

Nicole's artist's eye absorbed everything as Johnny
pointed, naming various animals one by one—a sleeping
barred owl overhead, a red-eyed slider that had come
alongside the boat, a tree lizard as red as a brilliant sunset.
She seemed genuinely fascinated, and soon began asking
questions—questions Johnny liked knowing the answers
to. He liked the way she seemed openly impressed with
what he knew, and it served to prompt more conversation
between them.

He saw the king snake hanging in a tree long before
Nicole did. It wasn't poisonous, but he pointed it out, anyway. "Harmless," he assured, maneuvering the boat away
from it to ease Nicole's mind.

She nodded, then offered him that impish smile he was
fast growing fond of. "Harmless? Like you?"

"Yeah, just like me." He grinned, steering the boat toward a narrow strip of land. He stood, then leaped onto a
spongy green carpet, watching Nicole's eyes grow wide as

the ground beneath him moved. It sank away slowly bobbed, then stabilized somewhat.

"Johnny! That's not land!" she warned. "Hurry, get back in the boat!"

Her concern was touching. He said, "Easy, *cherie*. It's fen. Moving land." He held out his hand. "Come on."

"Are you crazy? I've heard stories about people thinking they were safe out here, then they disappear and never come back. Get back in the boat!"

"Out here you don't listen to the stories, *cherie*. You listen to me," he told her, holding out his hand. "Always."

She raised her stubborn chin. "Forget it. I'm not leaving this boat."

"Come on, Nik Kelly. Trust me."

"Johnny, please. I can't."

"Yes, you can." He stretched his hand out to her. "Come on, you won't be sorry. Trust me...just this once. Then the next time will be easier."

She chewed on her lip, glanced around. "If I come, will you—"

"I promise."

"You don't know what you just promised."

Johnny shrugged. "It doesn't matter. Whatever you want, I still promise."

She stood slowly, grabbed his hand and hung on tight. "Oh, God! I must be crazy."

Then she did as he'd asked. She trusted him.

The minute her tennis shoes sank into the spongy green fen she let out a startled shriek that flushed a couple of dozen nesting birds from the trees overhead. The sound they made taking off startled her further, and she nearly jumped out of her skin and into Johnny's arms.

She clutched him tightly. So tightly, in fact, that he gritted his teeth against the pain that shot through his vulnerble ribs. But it didn't matter. The warm feeling of her curvy body against him far surpassed his discomfort, and he enjoyed the moment like a greedy beggar.

After she had regained her composure, he tied up the boat and led her into the dense woods, the ground still moving beneath them. "How far?" she asked tentatively, her voice almost a whisper.

"Just a little farther." He squeezed her hand reassuringly, and she squeezed back.

There was no path to follow, and as soon as they reached the woods, they were surrounded by thick, green foliage. After several twists and turns, Johnny drew them to a stop, pointing toward a massive cypress.

For a long time she simply stared. Finally she breathed, "This is...unbelievable."

The amazement in her voice said it all, both her surprise and delight duly noted. Nonetheless, the idea of her seeing such a private piece of his past made Johnny feel as exposed and vulnerable as he knew it would. But maybe it was worth it, seeing her so in awe of something that was his and his alone.

"I said I'd show you my secret," he reminded. "I built the tree house at age eleven."

"At age eleven?" She angled her head to one side, amazement gleaming in her bright eyes. Then she smiled, and Johnny felt as if he'd been born anew. "I take it no one knows this is here?"

"I don't think so."

"So it's a secret only we share?"

He gazed down at her. "That's what you asked for," he drawled softly. He took her hand and tugged her along behind him until they were standing beneath the massive limbs, heavy with tattered moss trailing from its sweeping branches. He hadn't intended to show her this place when he'd bragged about the giant cypress, but here it was for

her to see—a tree that would make a monumental state
ment if he'd ever let anyone know it was here.

He released her hand to let down an old rope ladde
he'd put together years earlier. Finding it still sturd
enough to hold his weight, he climbed on. "I'll go first.'
He looked over his shoulder. "To evict the unwante
guests."

Even with bruised ribs, he scaled the ladder with agility
then disappeared into the moss-covered shack built aroun
and into several high, sturdy limbs. A moment later he
emerged with a snake in each hand. The brown snake
could easily have been mistaken for cottonmouths, excep
for the fact that they were missing the black bands an
yellow underbelly of their deadly cousin.

"Oh, God!"

"Easy, *cherie*. They're friendly. When you meet up wit
a snake remember, don't move fast, but don't freeze u
either." Johnny gave the snakes a mighty heave, and th
reptiles suddenly became airborne. "Okay," he encour
aged, pointing to the ladder. "It's your turn. I'll hold i
steady."

She hesitated only a moment, then grabbed the ladde
and started slowly up. Seeing how delicate she looke
climbing twenty feet into the air suddenly made Johnn
nervous as hell. The minute she was close enough for hin
to lay hands on her, he reached out and snared her aroun
the waist. Then, in one quick motion, he swept her insid
the dark shack.

As she clung to him, her head fell back, her slim bod
molding to his. Breathless, she said, "Your secret is won
derful. Thank you for sharing it with me."

Her eyes were glittering with pleasure, her body warn
and arousing pressed against him. Johnny's blood race
through his veins. "Thank me another way, *cherie*," h
whispered. "Kiss me."

The request smoldered between them, as sultry and poignant as the moody, black bog surrounding them.

A minute lapsed.

Slowly, Nicole went up on her tiptoes and brushed his lips with a seductive feather-light kiss.

Johnny didn't move, didn't breathe. Not until he felt her shudder and move against him. Then he drew her tightly to him and deepened the kiss. In answer, her lips parted, her clever pink tongue turning into a fish lure, dancing and teasing him senseless.

They spent the rest of the afternoon exploring the swamp together. Johnny didn't kiss her again, not after the heated passion they'd shared in the tree house. Not after the way she had sugarcoated the moment by whispering his name and rubbing her soft body against him.

The sun was low on the horizon when they arrived back at the farmhouse. Johnny walked Nicole to her car, where it sat in the driveway, and she left not saying much. He watched her drive away, then returned to the boat, troubled by a vague feeling that someone was watching him.

Nicole closed the book she was reading and glanced once more at the clock on the nightstand. Nine-thirty. Sighing, she swept the sheet aside and climbed out of bed. It was ridiculous to think she could attempt to go to bed at a reasonable hour. The ritual had been set months ago; she needed at least two hours of pacing to unwind. Tonight, maybe three.

She could hear the patter of raindrops on the windows. It was one of those lazy rainy nights, the kind that make a person restless. Anxious. Something she didn't need more of tonight.

She padded to the second-story window and looked out. Her bedroom window overlooked the front yard and offered an unobstructed view of the oak-lined driveway.

Johnny had gone into town. Gran had said he was spending the evening with Virgil.

He'd been gone for hours, and after what had happened a week ago, Nicole didn't see why he didn't just stay away from town altogether. At least until he felt a hundred percent again. What if Farrel tried something a little more creative this time? What if this time he didn't stop at a few broken ribs?

Nicole's stomach knotted as she thought about the possibility of Johnny taking another brutal beating, or worse. She wrapped her arms around herself, not wanting to think about it but unable to think of anything else.

Today had been one of the nicest days she'd had in months. The entire afternoon had been an artist's dream come true. Johnny had taken her places she would never have seen on her own. He had explained so much, made her feel important enough to share his secret, and had completely swept her away on an amazing adventure right in her own backyard. She'd seen cypress that resembled giants, just the way he had promised, and Spanish moss so thick that it had veiled them like a live blanket.

Even before today she had loved Belle, but now she felt oddly connected to it. And she had Johnny to thank for that.

Gran had insisted he was special. Today he had shown Nicole not only Belle, but a side of himself she suspected only a rare few had cared enough to see.

Trust me, cherie, he'd said. And she had; for the first time in months, she had trusted a man. Looking back, she had actually put her life in his hands at least a dozen times today, and he had not once failed her.

She stared out the window, anxious to see lights coming up the driveway, lights that would confirm he was safe. A minute turned into two, then three.

Desperate for a diversion, angry with herself for not

being able to drive Johnny from her thoughts, Nicole stripped off her chemise and grabbed a loose cotton shift from the closet. Abandoning the idea of wearing a bra, and after retrieving a pair of blue satin panties from her drawer, she dressed quickly, then headed downstairs. After finding a flashlight in a drawer in the kitchen, she escaped outside.

Warm raindrops greeted her as she stepped off the porch. At first she thought she would try out the swing in the backyard, but instead she found herself in Gran's flower garden. Another half an hour passed, and soon Nicole left the garden behind and crossed the road. Once she entered the woods she turned on the flashlight and let the shining beam guide her to the swimming hole. If anyone knew what she was planning, they would surely think she had lost her mind.

Over the past few weeks she'd gotten adept at maneuvering the wooded trails. Flashlight in hand, she easily arrived at the swimming hole unscathed. Turning out the light, she laid it down in the grass and waited a moment until her eyes adjusted to the darkness. It only took a few seconds before she could see the shadowy outline of the water lapping the grassy bank. She kicked off her wet canvas shoes, then swept her rain-soaked shift over her head and let it fall at the water's edge. Naked except for her panties, she slipped into the water.

An hour later, feeling less anxious and relaxed enough to maybe fall asleep once she returned to the house, Nicole waded to the bank in search of her discarded shift and shoes. Wringing out her wet hair, she glanced around the dense buttonbush.

"Looking for this?"

Nicole spun around, her wet panties clinging to her curvy bottom, her arms quickly covering her bare breasts. "Johnny? How long have you been standing there?" she gasped, speaking to the ghost who still hadn't materialized but knowing it was him by his unmistakable black-bayou drawl.

"Long enough." The formidable shadow shoved away from the shelter of a tall oak and stepped into the misting rain. "Kinda late for a swim. Weather's not the best, either."

Nicole's heart began to pound wildly. Her body started to tremble when she saw her dress in one of his big hands. "Toss it," she implored.

At the mention of her dress, he glanced down at the sodden garment as if he'd forgotten it was there. Only a few seconds lapsed, but it seemed like forever before he did as she asked and tossed her dress—to the other side of the buttonbush.

Nicole sucked in her breath as he started to advance on her. Stunned, she took a step back and felt the water lap at her feet. "Johnny, what are you doing?"

"What we both want me to do. What your eyes have been begging me to do to you all day." His powerful hands locked solidly around her elbows, and he pulled her up against him. Nicole's eyes went wide. She made a strangled little cry that could easily have been mistaken for that of a creature of the night, but he ignored it and thrust his hand into her wet hair, tipped her head back and quickly covered her trembling mouth.

The kiss was hot. Desperate. Possessive. His tongue probed, searched, forced her mouth open to delve deeply. Not breaking the kiss, his hands slid around her and cupped her behind the knees, lifting her into his arms. Then they were moving, heading in the direction of the boathouse.

Nicole wrapped her arms around his neck and burrowed

her face against his rock-hard shoulder. "Your ribs," she whispered.

"Shh," he silenced.

He smelled earthy and warm. Rain-soaked. Nicole brushed her lips against the pulse throbbing at the base of his throat, whispered more concern for his ribs. He told her again that she worried too much and wrapped his arms more securely around her nakedness, fusing her to him as if she were his most prized possession.

Halfway to the boathouse he stopped. "We're not going to make it, *cherie*. I'm not going to make it," he amended, sliding her from him. He pulled her beneath a live oak with high branches that created a natural umbrella from the misting rain. Backing her against the tree, he sought her lips, giving her no time to think or to question the right or wrong of it. She kissed him back, her fingers sinking into his loose, wet hair. He leaned into her, rotated his pelvis urgently. The feel of his arousal through his damp jeans had Nicole moaning softly, liquid heat bubbling up inside her.

His rapid breathing caused his chest to heave in and out like a bellows, and when his hands closed over her breasts, palming them, kneading her warm flesh, Nicole bit her lip and arched into his big hands. He dragged callous thumbs over both aroused nipples, playing with them, at the same time keeping his eyes on her face, gauging her response, her need.

"You're so beautiful," he drawled, then bent his head and drew one ripe nipple into his hot mouth. Nicole again arched into him as every internal muscle responded all at once.

His kisses trailed lower to her abdomen, licking, stroking. Then he was kneeling in front of her, his hands settling on her waist, his tongue delving into her navel. Nicole gasped and felt her knees go weak. His hands moved lower, brushing the satin wedge between her thighs. "Say yes, *cherie*," he murmured. "Say you want this. That you want me as badly as I want you."

He was giving her a way out, she realized. Letting her escape at the last possible minute, if she needed to. He had stopped touching her, and she looked down to see he was staring up at her, waiting for her answer.

"I want you," he drawled softly, "but if I misread you this afternoon—"

Nicole silenced him by brushing her fingertips over his full mouth. "You didn't misread anything."

He stared at her a moment longer, then his fingers began caressing her satin mound through her panties, keeping his eyes still watchful on her face. Nicole trembled in answer to his silent request, and again felt as if she were being robbed of air.

"Time's up," he drawled. He kissed her flat stomach, his fingers moving past her panties to find her sex swollen and wet with desire. He moaned against the soft flesh of her stomach and gently parted her.

Nicole made a little starved noise in the back of her throat as his fingers entered her, testing, seeking, becoming familiar with her body. He was setting her on fire with one frenzied wave of heat after another. Panting, she twisted her body in a desperate plea. "Oh, Johnny! Ohh—"

The urgency in her voice had him withdrawing his fingers. Standing, he kissed her again, then hooked a finger in either side of her panties and snapped the elastic as if it were a single thread. Pulling the damp satin forward, he let it drop.

"Unzip me," he instructed, tearing his rain-soaked white T-shirt off and tossing it aside.

Nicole ran her hands down his hard belly. With trembling fingers, she worked his zipper down. Another shudder ripped through her as she reached for his rigid shaft, her fingers closing firmly around him.

"No, *cherie*," he groaned, grabbing her wrist. "I won't last two seconds with your hands on me."

He released her wrist and shoved his jeans past his buttocks, then quickly lifted her, urging her to wrap her legs around his waist. Without ceremony, he gripped her naked bottom and guided her down on his erection. Nicole's head fell back and her body shuddered violently. His hips strained upward, eased into her farther. She closed around him, her body willingly accepting him.

He let out a slow torturous moan of approval, and with one powerful thrust he was deeply seated inside her. But he wasn't there long before he lifted her as if he would leave her completely, then swiftly brought her back down over him. The air in his lungs rushed out while his hips strained again, bucking upward. He penetrated her again, then again in several solid mind-numbing thrusts.

He swore she was killing him. But it was Nicole who thought she would be the one to die as passion enveloped her and a flood of liquid heat shot past the burn of being stretched so completely. She gasped in sweet agony and clutched at him as his violent release sent her spiraling over the edge. She caught her lower lip between her teeth, closed her eyes and hung on as he carried them through the tempest, his endurance endless, his hard body controlling the tide, giving and taking at just the right moments. And when it was over, Nicole, shaken to the core, knew she would never forget this moment or the man named Johnny Bernard.

Johnny watched her as he slowly lifted her off him and set her bare feet gently to the ground. Righting his jeans, he kept silent, letting her have time to catch her breath. Feeling shaky himself, he bent and scooped up his T-shirt looking for a cigarette. Realizing he must have lost them in the foray, he swore and tossed the shirt back to the ground.

He couldn't explain why he had ended up at the swimming hole. He supposed the water had simply beckoned, and he had answered the call. The lazy rain was to blame, he decided. It had lured him, tempted him. But the moment he had laid eyes on Nicole gliding on her back in the water, he knew a higher power had brought him here.

He glanced at her now as she reached for his T-shirt and pulled it over her head to conceal her naked body. He'd ruined her panties, but she picked them up anyway and tucked them neatly into her little fist. She didn't look at him as she stepped from beneath the tree and tilted her face up to the night sky. It was still raining, a fine, almost invisible mist. She stood perfectly still like a fragile statue.

Johnny waited for her to say something, anything, so he could gauge her emotional state. But after a minute passed she simply started walking toward the path.

Surprised, he asked, "Where are you going, *cherie?*"

"To find my shoes and dress."

"You okay?"

She turned to face him. "I'm fine."

Was she really fine? He had tried to be gentle, to go slow, but he'd found out the first time he'd kissed her that slow would never come easily where Nicole was concerned. The minute he had her in his arms, all he could think about was having her as quickly and as completely as possible.

"Look, I thought this was a mutual—"

"It was."

"Then what the hell's wrong?" Johnny hadn't meant to

sound so angry, but she was confusing him. One minute she was moaning and saying his name; the next she was acting as if they were strangers.

"Nothing's wrong, Johnny," she assured. "I just don't want to analyze what just happened. It's obvious we both needed a feel-good session. Let's just leave it at that."

Her comment was like a pail of cold water thrown in his face, and Johnny took a step back. He'd heard it called a lot of things before, but never that. Yeah, it had felt good all right, damn good. And he'd be the first one to admit that he'd had a sexual craving the size of the Gulf since he'd gotten out of prison. That, however, had had nothing to do with tonight. This hadn't been planned—but it hadn't just happened, either.

Angry that she had him trying to justify it in his mind, he taunted, "Well, then, the next time you feel needy, you let me know. A 'feel-good' session with you beats the hell out of playing poker with Bick any day of the week. In fact, we could set up a schedule if you like. Twice a week sound good? Or do you get needy on a daily basis?"

"Go to hell," she spat, and spun around to head down the trail.

With lightning speed, Johnny caught up to her, grabbed her elbow and pulled her around to face him. Quickly, he slid his free hand over her bare bottom, and when she tried to wiggle free, he squeezed, restraining her easily. "Don't," he grated. "Once barely took the edge off. Unless you want me inside you again right now, don't fight me."

"It would be by force this time," she snapped.

Johnny felt her tremble. Boldly, he moved his hand over her naked buttock and watched her shudder once more. "I don't think I'll have to force anything, *cherie*. We fit better than my custom-made boots, and like it or not, when something feels that good, that right, you usually get spoiled and don't want to settle for less.''

"You arrogant bast—"

He lowered his head and kissed her hard and fast. Then, releasing her, he left her standing in the sultry mist while he headed down the path to fetch her clothes. Over his shoulder, he said, "I'll be back with your things. Don't move. If I have to run you down, we both know who'll win."

Chapter 10

She'd known him less than three weeks, and yet she'd let him touch her and make love to her with the familiarity of a long-time lover. Nicole could feel her cheeks burn with the memory of what he had done to her and how she'd responded.

She wanted to shift the blame, wanted Johnny's broad shoulders to carry the weight of what had passed between them. She wanted to accuse him of using her, but she knew that wouldn't be fair. Not when she wasn't so sure she hadn't used him a little herself. Exorcising the past from her mind—Chad, specifically—hadn't been painful at all when the man she had given herself to last night had the power to consume her body, mind and soul.

Oh, she would never forget the baby. Nothing and no one would be able to erase the memory or the loss of her innocent baby girl. But since Johnny had entered her life, the pain of Chad's rejection had steadily diminished. And after last night, Nicole was almost feeling as if she owed Chad a debt of gratitude for walking away.

She knew now she had never loved him.

She wasn't proud of the fact that she might have use Johnny, that subconsciously it might have been her inter tion all along. No, it wasn't something to be proud of. B the alternative was much worse: she couldn't possibly b falling in love with him.

Love… No, she wasn't about to let Johnny Berna worm his way into her heart. Though he'd done a goo job so far.

She plopped down on her bed, determined to pull herse together. She rubbed her tired burning eyes, sleep havin eluded her until only a few hours ago. After Johnny ha walked her to the house last night, she had paced in ea nest, until her feet hurt and the lip she kept chewing wa raw.

The thought of seeing him at the breakfast table in few hours was suddenly giving her a stomachache. Wh she really wanted to do was run off to New Orleans agai But what would that solve? When she got back she woul still have to face him.

Their fevered lovemaking flashed in her mind, and N cole squeezed her eyes shut. Normally she didn't like ove powering, take-charge men, but last night Johnny had con trolled her every move, and she couldn't have bee happier. He'd taken her to a place she'd never been befor an erotic haven she had only fantasized about in her mo private dreams. Desire—yes, she desired him in a doze carnal ways.

But she wouldn't love him. She couldn't.

Nicole swore and headed for the closet. She was ha dressed when she heard a loud rumbling noise outside. Sh turned to the window with her T-shirt in hand. When sh drew back the curtain, she wasn't prepared for what sh saw: four huge, green tractors were being unloaded fror long trailers.

"What on earth!" She watched as one by one the tractors were backed off the trailers and outfitted with plows. Moments later they headed into the overgrown fields.

Realization dawned as to what was happening and, just as quickly, as to who was responsible. Furious that Johnny had dared to take charge of another part of her life, Nicole finished dressing in a flurry of motion, jammed her feet into a pair of tennis shoes and raced downstairs.

She crossed the road in a blaze of anger, her arms swinging at her sides, talking to herself as she went—giving Johnny a verbal beating with each step. If and when Oakhaven became a sugar plantation, it would be Gran's decision, not that of some handsome ex-con. And the sooner Johnny Bernard learned his place around here, the better.

Johnny heard footsteps on the stairs just seconds before the door flew wide and banged hard against the wall. There wasn't time enough to pull his pants on. Hell, there wasn't time enough to climb out of bed.

One eye open, he saw Nicole march into the room and head straight for him. He sat up, dropped his feet to the floor. She hadn't been too talkative last night when he'd walked her back to the house. In fact—

He saw her pull her tiny fist back. It registered what she aimed to do with it seconds before she swung at his head. "You've got a lot of nerve...Bernard!"

Johnny ducked just in time, coming fully awake in an instant. "What did I do? I couldn't have done it today because it's—" He squinted at the clock on the wall. "Hell, it's not even six o'clock."

"I know what time it is," she snapped.

He guessed she did. She looked bright-eyed and awake, as if she'd been up awhile. She sure looked pretty in her tight little cutoff jeans and yellow T-shirt with pink lips

tattooed all over the front of it. "So, what's got you s
riled, *cherie?*"

"Four green tractors. That's what!"

Johnny rolled off the bed, dragging the sheet with him
His sore ribs protested the quick movement, and h
groaned as he straightened. "So what's up with the trac
tors? I told them to stay out of the front yard. They didn'
tear something up, did they?"

"That's the problem. You had no business telling then
anything."

"Sure I did," Johnny argued. "I got the okay from Ma
a couple of days ago. That's why I went into town las
night to see Virgil. I knew he would be able to help u
out with a name or two. This time of year most of th
crews are busy with their own crops. I thought he migh
be able to call in a favor for us with his brother, Martin.'

"You cleared it with Gran?"

"Sure. What did you think, that I'd go ahead on m
own?"

"Why didn't you tell me about it last night?"

Clutching the sheet around his waist, Johnny ran hi
gaze down her curvy body. "We weren't exactly talkin
business last night—not doing much talking at all, if yo
know what I mean."

The look she gave him could have boiled water. "
should have expected you to gloat at some point. Well
you had your fun, last night and now this morning rubbin
my nose in it. I hope you've enjoyed yourself because it'
be the last time you will at my expense."

Johnny studied her face. Now that he was awake, h
noticed she didn't look as well rested as he'd first thought
It made sense; he'd lain awake for half the night himself
He turned contrite. "Sorry, *cherie.* I wasn't gloating."

"Save it. It's not worth talking about." She turned an
was out the door more quickly than she'd come.

Johnny swore, dropped the sheet and reached for his
ans. In the heat of pulling them on and shooting the
ipper north, he nearly castrated himself. "Son of a—!"
*arefoot, rubbing his crotch, he took the stairs three at a
me.*

Just as she was about to open the outside door, he caught
with her, shot his hand past her and flattened it against
e door. In her ear, he whispered, "Don't leave mad."

She whirled. "Okay, I won't leave mad. I'll just leave."

"You forgot something."

"I didn't forget anything."

"Well, I did."

"What? Is there something else you've forgotten to
ention about those green monsters in the fields?"

"No." He paused for just a moment, then drawled,
What I forgot was this." He lowered his head and kissed
r. He didn't give her time to protest, and he didn't allow
mself to get carried away. Once he ended the kiss, he
ok a step back and ran the back of his hand along her
eek. "Good morning, *cherie.*" Then he turned and
olled back upstairs, leaving her speechless, the taste of
m on her pretty parted lips.

"I just don't understand why you didn't tell me," Ni-
le demanded of her grandmother. They were on the front
rch, Mae tending to her prize azalea in the corner. The
n was baking the grass in the front yard and baking
icole, too. She would have preferred to be inside in front
the fan, but she was determined to get used to the
essed heat even if it killed her. Which it no doubt would.

"I told you, Nicki, it just slipped my mind."

"Nothing slips your mind, Gran, unless you want it to,"
icole insisted. "I thought something as important as be-
ming a sugar plantation again would be something you'd
ant to share with me."

"Yes, I suppose you're right, Nicki. I should have d
cussed it with you first. I should have explained our fina
cial situation, too. I'm not broke, by any means, but selli
the fields, or making them turn a profit, would certai
help us down the road."

Nicole slipped into the wicker chair next to her gran
mother. "I told you I'd help. You know I've got mon
from Dad's half of the law practice. And when I sold Mo
and Dad's house—"

"Nonsense, Nicki. You'll do no such thing. That mon
is for you and your own family. For your children's
ture."

"I don't plan on having any children," Nicole blurt
out, then wished she hadn't spoke so quickly. Gran w
completely taken aback.

"No children! But children are wonderful little cre
tures, Nicki. They're the future. This doesn't sound an
thing like you. What's happened to change your mi
about a family? About babies?"

"Nothing, Gran. You're right, children are the futu
And someday maybe I'll want to settle down. I just do
think I would be a good mother right now. Not with su
a demanding career."

Gran looked slightly mollified. Nicole felt guilty.
truth, she would never allow herself to go through anoth
pregnancy. She was too afraid.

"You and Johnny didn't say two words to each oth
over breakfast. Has he done something to upset you? Y
two aren't fighting again, are you?"

"He should have told me about the fields," Nico
countered, "as you should have."

"I'm sorry, Nicki. I made the decision by myself, a
that was wrong of me."

"No, that's not what I'm saying. It was your decisi

to make. Only…" Nicole sighed. "I guess I just didn't want to be the last to know."

"You're right, of course. When Johnny brought it up, well, I was just so excited, I told him to see Virgil about it right away. Virgil's brother has a plantation east of here, a very successful plantation. I knew if anyone could help us out and quickly, it would be Martin Diehl." Mae looked satisfied. "I'm so glad Johnny's come home. This is working perfectly. Better than I'd planned."

"Planned?" Nicole stiffened. "What do you mean 'planned'?"

"I know that look. I said I wouldn't do anything sneaky again, and I won't." Mae went back to grooming the azalea. "When I said 'planned,' I was talking about the fields. I think this is going to be the answer to everything. I'm just surprised I didn't think of it myself."

Nicole pulled into Pepper's parking lot and climbed quickly out of her car. Already late to meet Daisi, she hurried inside wearing jeans and a funky scoop-neck ribbed tank in slate blue with two dozen tiny buttons down the front. The bar was darker than she remembered. Except for that one night weeks ago, she'd only been inside Pepper's over the noon hour, when the sun's rays shot through the transom over the double front doors. Gran loved the Wednesday lunch special—sausage gumbo and a slice of Bosco pie made with extra pecans and Pepper's best whiskey. Clair had tried to duplicate the legendary pie, but she still hadn't discovered the secret. Pepper swore he'd disclose it the minute she promised to leave Bick and marry him.

She stood in the doorway until her eyes finally adjusted to the dim lighting. When she spied Daisi at the half-circle bar, talking to her brother, Woody, Nicole started toward them.

The talk in town was that Woody had a terrible crush on her. He looked up, and when their eyes met, Nicole smiled. She seated herself on a red leather barstool next to Daisi. "Hi," she said, when Daisi spun around.

"You made it. Great!" Daisi glanced at her brother. "See, I told you she'd come." She looked at Nicole. "Didn't I tell you he was cute?"

"Oh, hell, Daisi," Woody grumbled, blushing red. "Shut up."

Nicole let her gaze travel the length of Daisi's brother. Yes, he was cute; he had a nice set of dimples, and kind eyes the color of caramel pie. His attractive long blond curls had been bleached from working outdoors in the hot sun, and it accented his tanned cheeks. His body was a working man's body, lean and muscular. The package was fine, more than fine. Still...

She blinked away the vision of Johnny Bernard's face. All day she'd felt depressed, as if she'd lost her best friend. Which was ridiculous—friends didn't purposely keep things from one another. And that's what Johnny had done by not including her in Gran's decision to go back into business.

"Nicki?"

Nicole blinked, then said, "Sorry I'm late."

"That's okay. Woody thought you weren't goin' to show. But I told him you were the type to keep your word."

"I lost track of time," Nicole explained. "I started cleaning out the attic. I've decided to turn it into my painting studio."

"I'll have to come see." Daisi gestured toward her brother. "Woody will bring me sometime, okay?"

"Sure," Nicole said.

Just then Toby Potter, the local loudmouth, walked by and gave Nicole a long, interested look, then a playful wink. "You better watch yourself tonight, gal. Farrel had all the fun last time, but tonight me and the boys won't be sittin' back watchin'." He glanced at his competition. "I see old Woodrow here's got the same thing in mind. There's likely gonna be some scrappin' goin' on to see who wins the first dance."

Woody gave the truck driver with the shaggy red beard a nasty look. "Go cool off, Toby. Miss Nicki's dance card is full up tonight." He glanced back at Nicole to see if he'd overstepped his bounds.

Nicole nodded, then smiled. At the moment she would have agreed to just about anything Woody suggested. Toby Potter looked as if he hadn't bathed in weeks, and the toothpick he was chewing on was as black as the grease under his fingernails.

"Well, Woodrow," Toby was saying, "I'll fight ya for that dance card. Your call—fists or something more meaningful?"

Nicole's eyes widened. Oh, God, she thought, Toby outweighed Woody by at least fifty pounds. And what did he mean by 'something more meaningful'?

"You boys can discuss this without us girls," Daisi said, dismissing Toby as if he weren't even there. "My back's achin', and I need a comfortable chair to sit in." She reached out, grabbed Nicole's arm and hauled her off the stool. "Come on, girlfriend. Let's find a table. Pepper, bring me somethin' pretty. Somethin' sweet—no liquor for me. Nicki, what do you want, wine?"

"No! I mean, not tonight. I'll have the same as you."

"Make that two pink lemonades, Pepper," Daisi hollered.

Pepper had a towel moving on the bar in time to the music playing on the jukebox and a fat black cigar poking from between his fleshy lips. He never looked up from polishing the bar, but he called back, "It's comin' up, darlin'."

"Hey, Pepper, I'm empty," a man yelled from the other end of the bar. "Stop trying to spit shine that old thing and tend to your customers."

"Hold your horses, and say 'whoa,'" Pepper called back. "Ladies come first around here. I'll bother with you soon as I get them settled." He served Nicole and Daisi their drinks moments later. "Here ya go," he said, setting down the drinks. "My specialty. I call it Sunrise on the Bayou."

It looked too pretty to drink, Nicole thought, the glass tall and narrow, a slice of lemon and a slice of orange stacked on a plastic stick topped off with a cherry.

"You need anythin' else, you just give Pepper a holler. I'll be listenin' for them sweet voices."

After Pepper stuffed himself back behind the bar, Daisi said, "Lucas Pelot's band is playin' later. You ever hear them?"

"No," Nicole admitted, pushing the fruit stick aside and taking a sip of her drink.

"They're really somethin'. Lucas can finger that accordion of his better than anyone I know," Daisi boasted.

They were seated at a table just on the outside edge of the dance floor—the floor Nicole recalled being whirled around just two weeks earlier in Farrel's arms. She had been hoping Farrel wasn't here tonight, but she glanced around and, to her disappointment, noticed him standing at the end of the bar with a drink in his hand. When their eyes met, he lifted his glass and smiled. Nicole didn't reciprocate. She had no intention of furthering a friendship with a man who could be party to a gang beating such as the one he and his friends had given Johnny.

He had called her twice, so Clair had said, leaving messages both times for her to call him back. But Nicole had ignored the requests.

"So, how are things?" Daisi asked. "I haven't seen you in days."

Daisi's question forced Nicole to focus her attention back on her new friend. "Like I said, I've been working in the attic, and I've been sketching, too. There's a gallery owner in New Orleans who is interested in my work."

"I bet the sketches are wonderful."

Nicole hadn't told Daisi anything about the past year in L.A. She hadn't told anyone, actually. She'd wanted to, and she really felt that Daisi would be the one to understand. Only, with Daisi being pregnant, Nicole thought it would be too awkward, the part about the baby. And Daisi just might start worrying about her own pregnancy. Nicole didn't want that. The truth was, having babies was as natural as breathing. Just because it hadn't been for her didn't mean Daisi wouldn't enjoy the wonders of motherhood.

"How are you feeling?" she forced herself to ask. "Is the baby moving? She's fine, isn't she?"

"She? I didn't say it was a she." Daisi laughed. "I told the doctor I didn't want to know." She sobered, glanced at her blooming stomach. "Is it the way I'm carryin' it? Have you heard somethin' I should know?"

"No." Nicole felt a little foolish. "I'm sorry, it was just a slip. I think of all babies as girls."

Daisi relaxed. "Don't let Mel hear you say that, 'cause he wants a boy."

Woody suddenly appeared. "Lucas just finished warmin' up." He set his bottle of beer on the table. "You still willin' to dance with me, Nicole?"

The band started things off with a traditional Cajun song called "Jolie Blonde." At Daisi's encouragement, Nicole took Woody's hand and let him lead her onto the dance floor.

A night of dancing was just what she needed, Nicole decided as she settled herself in Woody's capable arms. Only, this time she was going to stay away from the wine—and Farrel Craig.

From his booth on the far side of the bar, Johnny watched Woody Lavel tripping over his grin as he swept Nicole onto the dance floor for the sixth time. He wished to hell he hadn't seen her come in. And he wished to hell that after he had, he'd left Virgil to his own demise and gotten out of here. But he hadn't. And now it was too late; he wasn't going anywhere. Not with the way Woody was feeling more confident with every song. And with Farrel, leaning on the end of the bar and eyeing Nicole the way he was.

"She sure is perdy." Virgil glanced at the dance floor. "Why don'tcha ask her to dance? Yo' want ta. I can see de way ya look at her, boy."

"I don't dance," Johnny drawled. But he did want to hold her close, only not here. Not in a crowded room full of people. He wanted to go somewhere private with her, somewhere he could have her all to himself.

"Well, maybe it's time ta learn," Virgil was saying. "Woodrow's gettin' de cream tonight. Yo' okay with dat?"

Johnny glanced at his friend. "Shut up, old man."

"Doan take my head off 'cause yo' doan know how ta dance. No point. 'Tain't my fault."

Woody's hand captured her small waist and drew her closer. Johnny's chest constricted, as he remembered how it felt being that close to her, touching her, loving her.

"Doan tink she'd mind, do yo'? Thought Mae said yo' two were—"

"Shut up, Virg."

Lucas Pelot's band hit the last chord on a hip-swinging

tune and immediately went into an up-close, touchy-feely ballad. Out of the corner of his eye, Johnny saw Farrel slide off his stool. Virgil saw it, too.

"Now doan go feedin' trouble with stupidity," Virgil warned. "Tuck'll toss yo' in de slammer if'n yo' get crazy."

Johnny watched warily as Farrel shouldered his way through the crowd and tapped Woody on the back. The younger man turned to see who was intruding on his party, and when he realized who it was, his face fell. He wanted to argue with Farrel, but in the end he backed off, and Farrel slipped in to take his place.

Johnny could see Nicole's body tense from across the room. And he would have come to her rescue if he hadn't known her as well as he did. She looked fragile, vulnerable as hell, but she was made tougher than anyone knew. If she didn't want to dance with Farrel, she'd say so.

He got to his feet. "I'm going home, Virg. Thanks again for getting Martin to turn the fields over."

"Does dat mean yo'll be stayin' ta run things for Mae? Folks tink dat's jus what it means. Down at Red's dere takin' bets yo' be movin' back ta de farm soon."

"Don't waste your money on that bet, Virg." Johnny started for the door. He was almost there when he heard *her* above the music and the laughing crowd. "I said I don't want to dance with you. Now let go."

He glanced over his shoulder and saw her struggling against Farrel's hold. He wasn't aware of it at the time, but suddenly he'd changed directions. A number of dancing couples saw him and scrambled back to their seats. The music stopped, a violin chord dying slowly.

Johnny recognized Nicole's fighting stance from that morning. Quickly he grabbed her around the waist and pulled her back against him, just as she was about to drive her fist into Farrel's surprised face. "Easy, *cherie,*" he drawled in her ear. "He's been known to hit back. Even women."

Much to Johnny's disappointment, Nicole didn't appear to be any happier to see him than Farrel. "Let go!" she demanded. "He deserves a black eye, and if he tries to hit me back, I'll blacken the other one."

Johnny hung on to her. "Let's go outside and cool off."

She shook him off. "I'm not going anywhere. He's the one who should go out and cool off. I'm no dumb blonde." She spun around, glaring at all the men enjoying the show. "Did you hear that, guys? Find another game."

"But we like this game, honey," Farrel mocked.

The men at the bar roared with laughter.

Johnny's already crappy mood deteriorated further. He said, "The fun's over. Come on, *cherie*."

"That's where you're wrong, *beggar boy*. It's just beginning," Farrel taunted. He started to reach out and haul Nicole back into his arms, but Johnny grabbed his wrist and squeezed. "The lady's not interested. She's made that clear." He released Farrel's wrist. "Lay a hand on her again, and it'll be the last time you use that hand."

The crowd grew quiet.

"Did you hear that, everybody? He threatened me," Farrel shouted. "Not too smart in front of witnesses, Bernard."

Johnny shrugged, then spun Nicole around to face him. "Come on. Or do you want me to finish what you started?" Grinning for the first time since he'd seen her enter the bar, he added, "One helluva choice, ain't it? Watching a barroom brawl that'll likely end with me in the slammer, or leaving through the front door with the most unpopular man in town. One way or another, come tomorrow, the gossip will be ripe."

She made a face at him, then struck out for the door with her nose in the air.

Farrel called out several vulgar taunts, trying to bait Johnny into a fight, but Johnny wasn't interested. Farrel wasn't worth another jail sentence.

When he caught up with Nicole outside, she was breathing fire. "If you're expecting a 'thank you,' you can forget it. I didn't need your help in there."

Johnny glanced around at the people gawking. "Can we go? Or do you want to make a scene out here, too?"

"I'm not going home with you," she snapped.

"Oh, and why is that? You suddenly afraid of me? Or afraid of what might happen if we're alone?"

"Nothing is going to happen. And, no, I'm not afraid of you."

Johnny started toward the car. "Good. Let's go."

She hurried after him. "I'm driving. Do you hear? It's my car and—"

Johnny called out over his shoulder. "That's a deal. It'll leave my hands free."

She called him a nasty name, made a quick direction change and raced past him to climb in the passenger's side.

Laughing, Johnny got behind the wheel.

Chapter 11

From his perch on top of the roof, Johnny heard a truck shift into low as it headed up the driveway. When it stopped in the front yard, he glanced down and saw it was one of Farrel Craig's delivery trucks loaded down with supplies. It was a surprise, to say the least. He had expected Farrel to cancel the order and refuse their business after what had happened at Pepper's a week earlier.

"I got those shingles Miss Chapman ordered," the man hollered, climbing out of the truck and slamming the door.

The afternoon sun was hot enough to fry spit. Johnny hooked his hammer in the leather pouch strapped to his waist, then backhanded the sweat from his brow. He came off the roof using the extension ladder leaning against the side of the house. Once on the ground, he unhooked a leather tool belt and laid it on the workbench. A jug of water sat nearby, and he lifted it and dumped it over his head. Shaking like a dog, he picked up the T-shirt he'd discarded hours ago, dried his face off, then pulled the shirt back on.

"I could have come in and picked up the shingles," Johnny told the truck driver. "We don't need the added expense of a delivery charge when I got a pickup right here."

"Miss Chapman requested the delivery weeks ago," the driver informed him. "The boss didn't tack on no extra charge. In fact—" he handed Johnny the invoice "—it looks like he gave her a helluva discount."

Johnny took the invoice and scanned it. His nostrils flared when he saw just how generous Farrel's discount was. He jammed the paper in his back pocket, wondering just what the bastard was up to.

The two men worked side by side until the load was off the truck, and when the truck pulled out, Johnny eased into a chair on the front porch. Sweat dripping from his brow, he ran a hand over his face, then through his hair. Eventually his eyes drifted toward the open French doors that led to the study.

He wondered if Nicole was still inside. He'd walked by earlier and spied her seated at the desk. Conversation between them had been reduced to one-liners since he'd driven her home from town a week ago.

He stood, stretched, then sauntered to the open doorway. Leaning against the jamb, he saw she was still there, still punching keys on a small calculator. She made a mistake, swore softly, then repeated the number sequence. Satisfied this time, she wrote the total in the appropriate column in a black ledger.

"Since when do you do bookkeeping?" he asked.

"Since I refused to ask you for a favor." She hit another set of numbers on the calculator.

Her all-business attitude had Johnny's reined-in temper ripping a notch. He sauntered into the room, stopped at the desk and turned off the calculator. "I don't mind doing
"

Her fingers stilled on the keys, and she slowly look
up. "Well, maybe *I* mind."

Damp strands of hair had come loose from the cas
twist she'd secured at the back of her head. The warm d
had flushed her face, adding more color to her alrea
comely complexion. The pale blue sundress she w
made her already stunning blue eyes more radiant. The l
neckline and narrow straps lured his eyes to the expos
swell of her soft breasts and a touch of sun-kissed cle:
age.

Johnny kicked himself for noticing, felt his jeans turni
uncomfortable, but then noted she was giving his v
T-shirt a long, hard look, too.

When she saw that he'd noticed her interest, she sa
"Did you fall in the swamp, or has it started to rain?"

He shrugged off the sarcasm and went looking for
chair to sit down in. He was sweat-stained and dirty,
he chose the wood rocker. "Craig Lumber just dropp
off the shingles."

She arched a brow. "My call must have worked."

"Call?" Johnny dug the bill out of his pocket and toss
it on the desk. "It must have been some call to get t
kind of discount."

She picked up the bill and scanned it. Smiling, she sa
"Yes, it must have made quite an impression."

Johnny stiffened. "Beg forgiveness?"

"Something like that." She sat back in her chair a
folded her hands in her lap. "Driving to New Orleans
supplies would have cost us double. It was much eas
just to make amends."

Johnny tried to keep from getting angry. "I'm curio
What does it cost these days to make amends?"

"I don't know what you mean."

"Sure you do. What did you promise him, *cherie?* D

er and a movie? Or was there something more substantial nvolved?''

"You have a filthy mind," she snapped.

"No. I just know Farrel, and how low he can stoop."

"Think what you want. I really don't care."

Johnny bit down hard on the inside of his cheek. He idn't like feeling jealous, but there it was. That damn reen monster was biting him again. The truth was, if any-ne was going to scratch her itch, he wanted it to be him. he was in his blood now, and there was nothing he could o about it but suffer. "I'm just looking out for you. Mae ould want me to," he reasoned.

"I'm a big girl. Gran knows I can look out for myself."

"That's not what she tells me. Just this morning she sked me if I'd consider driving you to New Orleans next eekend. She's afraid you're going to get mugged, or orse."

Nicole looked stunned. "You told her no, of course."

"No, I said I'd discuss it with you. But I'm game." ohnny allowed himself the pleasure of studying her pretty outh, then he looked back at her eyes. "Maybe a few ays away would do us both some good."

At his words, her face contorted and her lips thinned. "Thank you, but no thank you. My plans are already set. Jow if there isn't something pertaining to your job we eed to discuss, I'd like to get back to work. You should, oo."

"I'm taking my morning break," Johnny informed her, liding more comfortably into the chair.

She shoved back her chair and stood. "Fine. Take it utside."

He knew full well that he should do as she said, but as e got to his feet, instead of heading for the open door, he tarted toward her. When she backed up, he smiled and

helped her along with a little shove that neatly put h
against the wall. "Feel needy today?"

"Stop it."

"It's been a few weeks. You must be—"

"Go away!"

"Can't. I'm yours for the summer, remember?"

His words brought a flush to her cheeks, and sh
squeezed her eyes shut. "Please, don't."

The idea of touching her again had been driving hi
crazy. He'd tried to stay busy, to ignore it, but she was o
his mind twenty-four hours a day. Disregarding how dir
he was, Johnny leaned into her and pinned her more firml
against the wall. "Look at me," he drawled softly in h
ear.

"Johnny, please," she panted, struggling against him
free herself.

He shifted his body more solidly against her, allowin
her to feel his full-blown arousal against her belly. Anglir
his head, his lips brushed her temple. "You feel goo
cherie. Smell good, too."

"You don't," she countered.

"I've been on the roof since six." He ran his hand u
her bare arm and the shiver he felt go through her bod
tormented his condition further. He wanted her, right her
right now.

He moved quickly, kissing her not gently, not exper
mentally, but like a man who had been lying awake nigh
dreaming about what they'd already shared.

The kiss deepened...deepened.

She didn't fight him, and when he realized she wasn
going to, he slid his hands around her waist and pulled h
away from the wall so his hands could glide freely ov
her curves. She sucked in a little gasp when his han
cupped her backside and pressed her more firmly into hir

moment later he felt her small hands drift up to his
ulders.

Rocked by a sudden, swift possessiveness, Johnny
sed her again, then again. He could feel her heart racing.
l her fingers grip his shoulders.

'Johnny…''

He claimed her mouth again, stroking his hands up her
ne, then tangling his fingers in her hair. The fragile clip
ding her hair went to the floor. Minutes ticked by.
nny and Daisy were unaware that they were being ob-
ved from the front porch. Mae Chapman sat silent in
 wheelchair with a satisfied smile parting her lips and
py tears glistening in her aging blue eyes.

Nicole stood at the railing on the front porch and
tched Johnny amble across the lawn toward her with
 loose-jointed gait that made her heart race. She'd been
iding him for days, thinking that if she did, she would
able to forget what was happening. But it hadn't helped;
 knew she was falling in love with him. Hopelessly in
e with a man who intended to leave in less than three
nths' time.

'You get packed?''

'Yes.'' Nicole watched him scale the porch steps. He
s in another white T-shirt, his jeans ragged but clean.
 hair was damp, suggesting that he'd just showered, but
d neglected to scrape off the shadow clinging to his
.

She stepped back from the railing. Her white cotton
ss—a loose shift with an irregular hem—fluttered in the
eze as she turned and slid into one of the wicker chairs.
refoot, she tucked her feet beneath her, then indicated
 was welcome to take the other chair. He declined, opt-
 instead to lean against the railing.

"You still taking off in the morning?" His hand fo
his hip, hooked a thumb in an empty belt loop.

Nicole remembered how taut his muscles were in
area, and the memory made her mouth go dry. "Yes. E
morning. Take care of Gran?"

"Sure."

His response was simple but sincere. He shoved av
from the column and jammed his hands in his back pc
ets. "I called my parole officer. He gave me permiss
to leave town for the weekend." His eyes searched
face.

"No." Nicole shook her head. "I'm going alone."

He nodded as if he'd expected her to hold firm to
decision. "You watch yourself. A lot of crazies living
Sin City."

Nicole closed her eyes briefly. She loved his hus
bayou drawl. Loved the way he showed his concern, e
though it was half hidden behind his tough exterior.
was beginning to read him. Not always, but half the t
at least. And what she'd learned was that there was a s
sensitive side to Johnny Bernard. A side she had war
to deny existed from the very beginning. But Gran
known it was there all along, and that's why she had
he was worth the trouble all those years ago. He wa
good person, honest and noble.

"Things have been going well, don't you think?"

"Seem to be," he agreed.

"I appreciate your working so hard for Gran. Thi
the happiest I've seen her in years."

"It's because you're here that she's happy."

"Maybe it's both of us," Nicole conceded.

"About this party you're going to—"

"It's an art exhibit, not a party." Her teasing tone
meant to lighten the moment, but when his express

idn't change, Nicole wondered what he was thinking. He
looked a little on edge tonight.

"So you're not meeting anyone there?"

Nicole shook her head. "No. I'm going because the gallery owner is interested in handling some of my paintings.
It's called networking."

"Where are you staying?"

"The Place d'Armes in the French Quarter. It's small
and quaint. I stayed there once before with my parents."
He climbed out of the chair. "I want you to do the bookkeeping again. Will you? I know what I said before. But I
was being—"

"Stubborn," he finished for her.

"Yes, I suppose I was."

He stepped forward, and she took a step back.

It just wasn't fair, Nicole thought. God help her, she
didn't want to love this man. He was going to break her
heart, and this time she feared it would never mend.

"I've got to go inside," she offered quietly. "Thank
you for helping Gran out this morning." She gestured to
the treelike azalea in the corner. "I dreaded repotting that
thing. It meant a lot to her that you cared enough to help."

He took another step toward her, invading her space.
They stared at each other for a long, tense moment. Nicole's heart skipped a beat, and she noticed Johnny's
breathing had turned erratic. Finally he said, "Thank me
another way, *cherie*. Kiss me."

The familiar words made her shake her head. "No,"
she whispered. "No, I won't."

He didn't move, didn't ask again, but he didn't back
away, either.

Tomorrow, Nicole reasoned. Tomorrow she would start
weaning herself away from him. Tomorrow she would be
stronger. Tomorrow she would have the distance between
them and she would be able to think more clearly. She

wouldn't have to look into those see-to-the-soul eye
across the breakfast table, or be teased into a frenzy by h
black, hypnotic drawl. Yes, tomorrow would be soo
enough to face the truth.

Slowly she slid her hands up his chest and lifted he
mouth to his. The kiss was warm and sultry. She meant t
keep it simple, uncomplicated. But he had other plans, an
she lingered on the porch much longer than she'd intended
Much longer.

Chapter 12

He fit in as if he were one of them, and no one suspected otherwise. No one, except Nicole.

She stood in the pristine gallery's arched doorway, her knees weak and her heart in her throat. Johnny was at the other end of the spacious room, his back to her, gazing at a portrait of a naked woman draped over a piano as if dead. He wore snug, faded jeans, free of holes, his custom-made boots, and a navy blue shirt that Nicole had never seen before. The shirt looked new, and it clung to him with an expensive sheen that made her breath catch. His hair was loose, riding his shoulders, and the jet-black color in the gallery light made him stand out like a black knight in the crowd.

She glanced around, taking in the room full of artists, and spied Mr. Medoro at the same time he spied her.

"Ah, Nicole, I'm so glad you decided to come," he said as he hurried toward her.

She smiled and forced her legs to move through the doorway. "Yes, I'm here."

"Tomorrow we will talk about your wonderful talent. But tonight—" he gestured to the walls "—we will enjoy the work, no?"

Nicole nodded, accepted the gallery owner's arm, and soon was whisked into a crowd of artists. She was introduced to each one of them, and the circle tightened around her. She answered their questions, smiled and nodded, but all the time she was gazing off in various directions, trying to locate Johnny. At one point she saw him standing with three women. One, a curvy brunette, was clinging, trying to get him to share her glass of wine, which he declined. Another time, he was standing with Mr. Medoro. Together they were studying an abstract wooden sculpture with two heads. Distracted by questions and meaningless conversation, it was almost an hour before she broke free of the crowd to search for Johnny.

"Your paintings are better than all of them."

Nicole closed her eyes as she felt his presence behind her, his warm breath upon her neck. A tingle ran down her spine. She didn't turn around, and instead said, "And you're an expert, right?"

"I know what I like," he drawled, moving closer. His hands came up to stroke lightly down her arms.

Nicole finally gave in and turned. They were toe to toe, so close that his soft shirt brushed her bare arm. "What are you doing here?" she finally asked. "You were supposed to stay at Oakhaven and take care of Gran."

"Actually, she's why I'm here. She was stewing about you all day, sure you were going to be kidnapped or robbed. She insisted I come and be your bodyguard."

Nicole couldn't stop staring at him. He was there, dressed for the occasion, looking remarkably sexy and amazingly relaxed, though she doubted he had ever set foot in an art gallery in his life.

Grinning, he leaned forward and whispered, "Have you networked enough? I'm starved."

"You don't like your catfish?"

"Huh? No," Johnny said, "the food's always good here."

"You've been here before?"

Mulates was one of New Orleans's famous Cajun restaurants. Johnny liked the cozy atmosphere and the dim lighting. That's why he'd suggested it and asked the hostess if they could have a small corner table in the back.

"I lived here for a few years," he confessed. He didn't mention being a dishwasher for this very restaurant at age seventeen.

Her surprise was subtle, a mere lifting of one delicate eyebrow. "After you ran away?"

"It was a good place for a kid to get lost. An easy place to find work."

He tried not to stare too long at her pretty mouth. He wasn't going to make her uncomfortable by ogling her bare shoulders or licking his chops like a hungry dog, either. But the slippery, little black dress outlining her curves continued to raise hell with his heart rate and the comfort of his jeans.

She had twisted her shiny blond hair up in a messy knot that showed off her mole and accented her slender neck. He had always thought she was naturally beautiful. Tonight she was stunning, turning every head at the gallery as well as in the restaurant.

She smiled, sipped her wine. "So what do you think about Mr. Medoro and his gallery? Will I fit in?"

"I think you'd fit in anywhere. In fact, I suggested to him that he give you your own exhibit."

Her eyes widened. "You what?"

"You're too modest about your talent," Johnny scolded

gently. "You've got to speak up. Let them know how goo
you are."

"I speak up," she argued.

"Yeah, when you're chewing me out." He grinned, let
ting her know he was teasing.

She rested her elbow on the table and propped her sma
fist beneath her chin. "If I've ever chewed you out, it wa
because you had it coming."

Johnny sat back and watched her. "You like getting al
dressed up and going to galleries?"

"Sometimes. But I'm not crazy about surprises."

"I suppose now we're talking about me?"

"We're talking about you, yes." Her smile turned imp
ish. Suddenly she giggled. "You looked relaxed, but
think it was all an act."

"Why do you think that? Was my suffering that obvi
ous?"

"Not to that woman cooing in your face."

Her comment about the overbearing woman with hug
red lips made Johnny's grin widen. "She wanted to knov
how long I was staying in town."

"And you said...?"

"I didn't know."

"So have you arranged a late date with her?"

He wasn't sure if she was teasing or if she was jealous
Jealous, he hoped.

She reached across the table and touched the cuff on hi
new shirt. Johnny gazed down at her hand where her sma
fingers played with the fabric. When she realized her erro
she quickly withdrew her hand. "I've never seen you ir
anything but a T-shirt. This is nice."

"I'm not much for clothes. Still, I wouldn't deliberatel
embarrass you, *cherie*." He paused, saw that both thei
plates were empty, and said, "You ready to head back t
the hotel?"

"Yes. I agreed to meet with Mr. Medoro in the morning to discuss some sketches I've done. I'd like to turn in early."

"But you won't. Instead you'll pace the floor, right?"

"Not funny."

A horse-drawn carriage was just passing by as they reached the street. Johnny flagged the driver and lifted Nicole into the white carriage. It felt good to touch her. So good, in fact, that he slipped the driver an extra fifty to take a longer route back to the hotel.

Forty-five minutes later, after enjoying the glowing streetlamps, the music coming from Bourbon Street, and the sweet aromas that were so much a part of New Orleans, they reached St. Ann Street. Johnny lifted Nicole from the carriage, and they entered the Place d'Armes Hotel, a two-story structure in the heart of the French Quarter. It had a historic courtyard brimming with flowers, and was well known for its quaint charm.

Inside the elevator, Nicole unzipped the gold purse she had slung on her shoulder and went fishing for her room key. "Where are you staying?" she asked. "You never said."

"Actually I got a room here," Johnny told her.

She looked up, unable to hide her surprise. "Here? You're kidding."

He took her key from her hand, and, when they stepped off the elevator, he followed her to her room. Once he'd unlocked her door, he stuck his head inside, flicked on the light and glanced around. "Did you remember to lock the balcony door before you left for the gallery?"

"Yes. Well, I think so."

Her hesitation made Johnny scowl. He shoved the door wide and stepped inside. He found the French doors unlocked. Swearing, he made a quick check of the room, then stepped out onto the balcony. It was narrow, surrounded by a wrought-iron railing. A large potted plant in the corner camouflaged the adjoining balcony. Against the aging brick wall sat a small table and two chairs.

He glanced across the lantern-lit courtyard and found all the other balconies empty. Below, two couples relaxed in the secluded octagonal pool, which was half hidden by palmettos and flowering vines.

He stepped back inside, laid her key on the dresser, then headed for the door. "If you need something I'll be—"

"I won't. But thanks, anyway."

She seemed anxious to get rid of him. Disappointed, Johnny stepped into the hall, and, before he could turn around, she closed the door. For a few minutes he just stood there. He didn't know what he had expected, but he knew what he'd been hoping for.

He pulled the key to the room next door out of his pocket and headed inside. It had taken some time to convince the desk clerk to give him the room next to Nicole's, but a few unexpected cancellations had helped out. Fate, again.

The room was dark and cool. He ignored the lights, pulled his shirt from his jeans and unbuttoned it. The balcony beckoned, and he unlocked the narrow doors and shoved them open. Patting his shirt pocket, he took a cigarette and cornered it in his mouth, then slipped into the sturdy wrought-iron chair.

Two cigarettes later, he closed his eyes and breathed in the warm night air. The heavy scent of azalea blossoms, ripe and sweet, drifted to him, and he tried not to think about Nicki for a moment, especially her undressing and getting ready for bed.

He had just lit his third cigarette when *her* balcony doors opened. He sat silently, glad the mammoth azalea plant on her balcony hid him from sight. He watched as she stepped to the railing, the lit lanterns below giving her silhouette golden glow. He noticed she'd let her hair down, but she till had on the skinny black dress.

Mesmerized, he watched her arch her back like a cat nd angle her head to smell the fragrant night air. Her rofile was beautiful, delicate. Curvy. Exotic. When she an her fingers through her hair, he wished it were his ingers having the pleasure.

All evening he had kept his hands off her, but it hadn't een easy. Swearing inwardly, deciding it was too much— vatching and not touching—Johnny stood to go back in- ide.

"I'm not chasing you away, am I?"

He stopped dead in his tracks, glanced down at his cig- rette, then dropped it and crushed it beneath his boot. 'How did you know? The smoke?"

"Yes. It's your brand."

Johnny turned and moved to the railing. "Raunchy abit. I took it up in the joint."

She faced him. Offered him a sultry, needy look. Later ohnny would say it was that *needy* look that had started he next chain of events. But who could say whose need vas stronger?

"You're killing me," he admitted.

"Am I?"

"You know you are. Come here."

She shook her head. "I don't think so. If you're suffer- ng…good. At least that way I don't feel quite so alone."

Her admission was as unexpected as it was arousing. "You don't have to suffer, *cherie*. Neither one of us loes."

She drifted toward the railing, staying just out of reach. "No gloating later?"

"None."

"And I'll stay the entire night?"

"If that's what you want, yes."

"Will we share breakfast in bed?"

"If we wake up before noon."

Johnny sucked in a deep breath as she took two steps closer, making it possible for him to reach out and touch her. But he didn't lay a hand on her. Slowly he leaned into the railing and kissed her. Only after he felt her shudder did he reach for her, and then carefully, so he didn't bruise her body on the wrought-iron that separated them.

After a long kiss, he slid his hands around her waist and lifted her over the railing. She slid against him and wrapped her arms tightly around his neck. They kissed once more, this time hungrily.

His hands tightened, forcing her breasts to flatten against his chest. "I like feeling you against me," he murmured.

Her hands moved from around his neck and slipped inside his open shirt. Gently, her fingertips stroked his flat coppery nipples. "I like the feel of you, too," she whispered.

Johnny closed his eyes and dragged in a ragged breath. "Yes, you're killing me."

Her smile told him she enjoyed his agony. She lowered her head, her lips following her hands in a series of feather-light kisses over his bare chest. "Don't die yet. You promised me breakfast in bed tomorrow, remember?"

He recaptured her velvety lips. Devouring her softness, he plundered her mouth. He felt her arms move back to his neck, her clever little tongue teasing him, inviting him inside.

"Why?" he panted next to her ear. "Why are you letting me have you, *cherie?*"

She ran her fingers through his hair, rubbed her body against him. Nose to nose, lip to lip, she whispered, "Because you take my breath away, Johnny Bernard. You snatched it away from me weeks ago, and you're doing it again right now. No one has ever made me feel the way

ou make me feel. So have me Johnny, if that's what you
want. It's what I want.''

Her admission nearly took him off at the knees. Johnny
pulled her close, kissed her again, then lifted her into his
arms and carried her back inside. He laid her on the bed
and stretched out beside her. She turned into his arms,
arched against him and said his name. His fingers caught
the hem of her dress. Drawing it upward, he stroked her
silky thigh.

At the feel of her, eager and needy, Johnny rolled to his
back and pulled her on top of him. ''Straddle me,'' he
murmured.

She shoved her dress clean to her waist, then did as he
asked. When she lowered herself over him, the feel of her
slender thighs brushing his hips made him groan, and he
gritted his teeth against the sweet agony of it all.

She spread his shirt wide and trailed light, teasing kisses
across his hard chest. Johnny moaned again. ''More,'' he
demanded. ''More.''

In answer to his plea, her hands continued to caress the
hardness of his chest; at the same time her knees squeezed
his waist, and she moved against him. ''Yes, more,'' she
whispered. ''More than once. Promise you'll love me all
night long, Johnny.''

''All night,'' he promised. ''Take your dress off.''

''Help me,'' she sighed breathlessly.

At her entreaty, he pulled her dress farther up her slender body. Then, giving the slippery thing a fast jerk, he let
it fly. ''Drop the lace,'' he said, staring at her full breasts.

She reached around, unhooked the black bra and let it
fall to his chest. Brushing it aside, she leaned close and
teased his chest with her aroused, hot nipples. Another
ragged moan ripped from his chest as Johnny felt her se-
duction take him past the brink of sanity. She tortured him

further by sliding her hand along the inside of his thigh
Her fingers flattened out to cup him through his jeans.

He heard her breath catch with the realization of how
badly he desired her. *Needed* her.

Before he lost his head and took her too fast, Johnny
quickly pulled her off him and heaved himself from the
bed. Gazing down at her, he said, "We're going slower
this time. There's no reason to hurry. We've got all night.'

She smiled a slow, sexy smile. "I had no complaints
about the first time."

"Is that right?" He grinned. "You liked me acting like
a wild animal?"

"Actually, I did."

He pulled off his boots, then unzipped his jeans and sent
them to the floor along with his underwear. Standing in
front of her in all his naked glory, he watched as she
slipped off the bed, slowly hooked her fingers into her
panties and shoved them past her thighs. Before they
reached her knees, he had her on her back once more and
was peeling the satin past her ankles.

"You've changed your mind, then?" she asked when
he covered her quickly.

"What?"

"I thought we were going slow," she teased.

"Next time," Johnny promised. "Or the next."

Nicole blinked awake. She lay still for a minute, aware
sunlight poured through the open balcony doors. Slowly
she rolled to her side. Johnny lay on his stomach, one arm
draped over his head, the other dangling off the side of the
bed. His lips were parted, his eyes closed. His broad, naked
back beckoned her to reach out and touch him, but she
held back, intrigued with the idea of watching him sleep
without his knowing.

He stirred, and the movement drew Nicole's attention

his long, powerful legs. Even relaxed in sleep, he looked
ough as nails.

She inched closer, his heat drawing her body like a mag-
et. The way he had made love to her last night had been
ncredible. She closed her eyes for a brief moment, unable
o fight her feelings any longer. It was true, she loved him.
Loved the way he made love to her. The feel of him. The
way he smelled, talked, tasted.

She simply loved every inch of Johnny Bernard.

His eyelids fluttered, and he rolled over. "You like
watching naked men sleep, *cherie?*"

Nicole smiled. "It has a certain appeal, yes. How long
ave you been awake?"

"Long enough." He stretched, rolled sideways. Eyes
miling, he stole a kiss. "Good morning."

Nicole arched into him and felt his arousal against her
elly. "Johnny..."

"Shh. Don't say anything. Not yet."

"Breakfast in bed. You were serious?"

The door between the two hotel rooms stood open. Ni-
ole, freshly showered, struck a pose wearing a short
avender satin robe. "Of course, I was serious."

"How long?"

"How long?"

"How long before they come knocking with the food?"

"Thirty minutes."

"Come here."

"No."

"Why not?"

"I have an appointment with Mr. Medoro in two hours.
have to get dressed soon."

She wasn't going to make the appointment. Johnny had
plans of his own. He loved loving her, loved making her
igh and say his name. He loved her eyes, her sweet lips.

Touching her soft skin drove him crazy. No, she wasn'
going to make her appointment with that long-haire
Frenchman.

"Come here."

"Johnny…"

"Okay, I'll come to you."

In an instant he was out of bed, stalking her. Nicol
whirled around to dash back into her room. The minut
Johnny realized she was heading for the bathroom, he cu
her off, forcing her back toward the bed. She stumbled jus
as he reached for her, and together they landed on th
unused double bed.

They were laughing as their eyes locked. Slowly, si
multaneously, they sobered.

"I want you again. In *your* bed this time."

"Johnny…"

An hour later Johnny watched Nicole rescue their break
fast tray, which had been left outside his door a long hal
hour ago. When she returned, she placed the tray in the
middle of the bed and sat cross-legged, tucking her robe
around her.

"The food's cold," she grumbled, lifting the cover of
the seafood omelette.

"Still looks good," Johnny said, popping a slice of ba
nana from the fruit cup into his mouth and chewing with
a satisfied grin. He had pulled on a pair of white underwea
and now stretched out on his side across the bed.

Nicole cut a small piece of the omelette and sampled it
She speared another forkful and offered it to him. "Wan
some?"

For an answer, Johnny opened his mouth, took hold o
her wrist and steered the fork between his teeth.

She fed him two more bites, then set the fork down, he

attention averted by the puckered scar on his thigh. Slowly, she traced it with her finger. "Where did you get this?"

"In prison."

"A knife fight?"

"No." Johnny picked up the fork and gripped the handle. Raising it, he acted out the scene. "A lot of guys in the joint use whatever they can steal and make them into weapons—forks, spoons, a scrap of metal."

"That's awful. It must have hurt terribly. Did you provoke someone?"

Johnny grinned. "No, I didn't."

"But you did fight back, right?" She gestured to the fork. "With one of those?"

Johnny laid the silver fork down. "No weapon. I'm an ex-marine, remember? If you know how to use your hands, they can be just as deadly as any knife."

"And are your hands deadly?"

Johnny gave her body a long heated look. "I don't know, are they?"

She blushed red. "You are really bad."

"You didn't think so a little while ago," he teased.

She motioned to his scar again. "Stop trying to distract me. What happened after the guy stabbed you?"

"We went a few rounds, then afterwards he spent a couple of days nursing a half-dozen busted ribs and a bruised windpipe, and I got a week in solitary for defending myself a little too good."

"Solitary? That wasn't fair."

Johnny laughed. "Fair? Not much is fair, *cherie*. When I was a kid there was always somebody wanting to see me facedown in the dirt. It wasn't fair, but it didn't change things."

"Farrel?"

"He was a regular. That's how I first met Mae," Johnny admitted. "I used to sneak through the cane fields to keep from being beat up by Farrel and the boys. It usually worked, hiding out in the fields. When it didn't, I hid in Henry's pickup. She found me there once. I guess I'c fallen asleep. After that, she used to leave apples and oranges in the pickup for me. Sometimes comic books. I'c lay on the floor, have an apple, and read until Farrel go tired of looking for me and went home. Then I'd stuff the comic books under the seat and head home.''

When Nicole lowered her eyes, Johnny reached out and gripped her chin. "I didn't tell you that for pity, *cherie.*"

"I don't pity you, but I do feel bad. Didn't your father or mother ever try to stop them from persecuting you?"

"My father was being harassed most of the time, too. He would come home from work some nights with his face so black and blue, I wondered how he could see to walk home." Johnny glanced around, feeling the need for a cigarette. "Don't go anywhere, I need to find my smokes."

She put a hand on his arm. "Last night you said it was a bad habit. So today, do something about it."

"I suppose a deal's a deal."

"Meaning?"

"You didn't pace last night 'til midnight did you?"

She smiled. "No, I didn't, did I?"

"Slept straight through, as I recall," Johnny confirmed. Sobering, he said, "I'd still like to know the story behind it."

"The story?"

He knew she knew what he was talking about. He drew her close, kissed her. "Who's Chad?"

She gave him a look of surprise. "How did you know his name?"

"The night you got drunk you mentioned him. Not enough to explain anything, but enough for me to know he hurt you somehow. Who is he, *cherie?*"

She glanced away, then faced him again. "Chad was one of my college professors. When my parents died, he was there for me. At the time, I needed someone older and wiser. He fit the bill perfectly."

She tried to leave the bed, but Johnny hung on to her. "What happened?"

"He changed his mind. Maybe he got bored. I don't know. The reason isn't important."

"Hard to believe that it was boredom. There had to be more to it."

She narrowed her eyes, bit at her lip. Finally she lowered her eyes and stared at her hands folded in her lap. "He wasn't honest with me. He talked about the future, even mentioned marriage. I got careless."

"Careless?"

"All right. Pregnant."

Johnny tensed. "And?"

"You should see your face. Why is that such a scary word for men to hear?" She laughed bitterly.

"I'm not scared. Surprised, is all. You don't look the careless type."

"Well, don't worry, having sex with me won't make you a daddy. You can breathe easy."

Johnny frowned. "I don't deserve your anger. I'm not Chad. Now finish the story."

"It's the old story, really. Student falls for her art teacher, gets pregnant, and he walks. That's it." She turned away.

Johnny sat up, gripped her arms and forced her to look at him. "That's not the end of the story. What happened to the baby?"

She tried to pull away, but he wouldn't let her. "Easy, *cherie.* Take it easy."

"I—I lost her, okay! I lost her in the fifth month." She swatted at his arm to make him let go, but instead Johnny pulled her close and cradled her in his arms as she started to cry. He didn't know what to say. *I'm sorry* seemed inadequate, so he opted to say nothing. He just held her.

They fell asleep in each other's arms. Some time later, Nicole woke up and realized she'd missed her appointment with Mr. Medoro. "My appointment," she sighed. "I forgot my appointment."

Johnny continued to hold her close. "Shh. He'll understand. We'll call him later."

She sat up. "You knew I had an appointment. Why didn't you wake me?"

He tugged her back into the circle of his arms. "I was hoping to convince you to spend the day in bed with me."

"All day?"

"All day." He swept her robe off her shoulders to expose a perfect breast.

"Johnny…"

"The first time I saw you," he said huskily, "I wanted to throw you to the floor in the boathouse and rip your clothes off. Did you know that?"

"You did?"

"Those long legs of yours, your pretty knees. I had just gotten out of prison, *cherie.* What the hell were you thinking of, showing up dressed like that?"

"You weren't supposed to be there, remember? You said three-thirty or four. I had given myself plenty of time to drop Gran's note off, open the windows, and leave well before you ever saw me."

"Then I guess it was fate."

"No, just bad timing."

"*Bad* timing?" Determined to put the sparkle back in her blue eyes, Johnny pretended to be offended. Then, just as quickly, his grin turned mischievous, and he lunged at her. Nicole screamed as he began tickling her and wrestling with her on the bed. It wasn't long before he had pinned her beneath him. Seconds later the laughter ceased. Slowly, he kneed her legs apart and eased himself between them. "Spend the day in bed with me, *cherie?* All day?"

"All day?"

"Starting now."

"Now?"

Johnny glanced down at her naked breasts, and before his eyes her nipples pebbled. Smugly, his gaze locked with hers once more. "I'll take that as a 'yes.'"

Chapter 13

After taking a dozen pictures of Belle and the old farm house on the hillside, Nicole found herself inside Johnny' childhood home. She'd decided days ago on the way back from New Orleans that she wanted to paint it. Johnny had been talking about tearing it down, and she wanted to capture it on canvas before it was gone, or at least have photos to work from later.

It was just the sort of picture that would sell at the gallery in New Orleans, she thought, though she wasn't so sure she would be able to part with it once it was finished.

And she would finish it. She was back working again, spending at least five hours a day secluded high in the attic. Since she and Johnny had returned from New Orleans, it was as if a great burden had been lifted from her shoulders. She was working daily, and sleeping through the nights, and it was absolutely wonderful.

How and why it had happened, she wasn't sure. But she knew Johnny was partly responsible. Or maybe he was entirely responsible. He'd filled up the empty hole in her life, and in her heart, as well.

The interior of the house was dark because the windows had been boarded up. Nicole carefully walked through each room; the crude, less-than-efficient kitchen, the adjoining living room with just a few dilapidated furnishings. Two small bedrooms, one with a ragged mattress rotting in the corner.

She realized something that she hadn't been aware of until now—Johnny's childhood had been more than simply hard; it had bordered on child neglect. He'd lived without running water or electricity, and most likely without a real bed, if the tiny room with the old mattress in the corner was, in fact, his.

In that moment, her heart went out to that small boy who must have ached for a normal life. Was that why Gran had worked so hard to befriend him and then to protect him? Was that why Johnny had finally given in and accepted her in his life all those years ago?

Since they had returned from New Orleans, he seemed different. Up by six, working shirtless until supper time. He hardly stopped to rest. And after supper, instead of relaxing on the front porch or playing cards with Bick, he spent hours in the study tending to the bills and renovating costs.

He hadn't brought up leaving Oakhaven in a very long time. Still, Nicole was sure he intended to go back to Lafayette as soon as his parole was over. Just thinking about it made her want to cry, but the truth was, Johnny had never made any promises to her. She had known all along that he would be leaving at the end of the summer. She wouldn't pressure him into staying. Yes, if he told her he had changed his mind, she would be thrilled. She might even be brave enough to confess her feelings. But it was just wishful thinking, his staying. Wishful, dangerous

thinking, when the odds were that he would leave as sud
denly as he'd come.

When the door groaned open, Nicole was just returnin
to the living room. Face to face with Johnny, she stoppe
dead in her tracks.

"What are you doing here, *cherie?*"

"I—I was photographing the outside of the house
and…" Nicole flushed. "I was curious."

"Curious?"

"Maybe that's the wrong word." She noticed he wa
sweat-stained and dirty. His bare chest gleamed with
sheen of perspiration. She didn't care. In a second, wit
the slightest encouragement, she would slip into his arm
and forget everything but the feel of his powerful arm
around her.

"No, I think *curious* is the right word," he said, closin
the door. He glanced around, his eyes taking in the star
surroundings. "It looks bad, but it really never looke
good." He gave her a half smile.

"I'm sorry."

"I told you before, I don't want your pity."

"I don't pity you, but I do wish things had been differ
ent for you." She broke eye contact with him and move
to stand near a small stone fireplace. She wasn't there lon
before she felt him come up behind her. "I saw you fron
the rooftop," he said softly. "I wondered where you wer
off to, so I followed." He nosed in close. "I'd like to touc
you, but I'm ripe."

Nicole turned around. "It never stopped you before.
like you any way you are, even 'ripe.' We haven't hac
much time together since we came back from New Or
leans. You've been working day and night."

"So, the pretty lady is feeling needy today, is that it?'

"Don't tease me, Johnny."

He bent forward and kissed her without laying a hanc

on her. "We could go to the swimming hole. I could wash up, and you could strip for me." He wiggled his dark eyebrows. "I'd like that."

"I'd like that, too."

He moved in to steal another kiss, then hesitated. "Do you smell smoke?"

"Smoke?" She watched him turn away and stride quickly back to the door. He tried to open it. No success. "Johnny?"

"Dammit!"

"Johnny?"

He slammed his shoulder into the door. Then again.

"Johnny! Is the house on fire?" Nicole could smell the smoke now. She hurried to one of the boarded-up windows and tried to peek out through the slats, but had no luck. "When did you board up the windows?" she asked.

He spun around, his gaze taking in the windows one by one. "Hell, when was that done?"

"You didn't do it?"

"No."

"Oh, my God, Johnny. We're trapped!"

Johnny rammed the door once more before he gave up and hurried to one of the newly boarded-up windows. He couldn't believe he hadn't noticed them before now, but he'd followed Nicole, and all he'd been thinking about was catching up with her and getting some time alone with her. Checking the windows, he found they had been nailed shut from the outside, making them impossible to open.

A rumbling noise alerted him that the fire had taken root and was growing fast; the smell of gasoline confirmed things were going to heat up in a matter of seconds. The moment he thought it, he saw live flames eating through the wall. As they licked across the tinder-dry ceiling, black smoke began to fill the room. He dragged Nicole to the floor. "Stay down," he instructed.

He remembered the old root cellar, just as an explosion rocked the building and a spray of live flames sailed through the air. Quickly, he pulled Nicole beneath him to shield her. He grunted as something solid struck him low on his back, but he didn't take time to acknowledge the searing pain. A thick fog of gray smoke was filling the room, blinding them. He knew they were running out of time.

Dragging Nicole with him, he belly-crawled toward his childhood bedroom, hoping against hope that he hadn't gotten turned around in the smoke-filled room. Overhead, the trusses were creaking, only seconds away from crashing down on them.

"Come on," he shouted, demanding that Nicole follow him as he felt his way toward his small bedroom. His throat was on fire; his eyes felt like two hot coals. He knew Nicole must be feeling the same way, and he was afraid for her. Moving faster, he dragged himself deeper into the pea-soup smoke, knowing that if they were going to survive—and by damn, they were—he had to get them into the root cellar.

When his shoulder banged into something solid, he swung his right arm to the side and confirmed, with great relief, that it was the doorjamb.

"Johnny…"

Nicole's voice sounded weak. He hardly heard it for the roar of the wild flames eating up the wood. With urgent purpose, he pulled her close, just as another explosion sent more debris crashing down around them. Quickly, he flattened himself out on top of Nicole, until he was sure no more flying debris would harm her. Then he swiftly hauled himself upright again.

Swinging his arm out like a blind man who'd lost his

cane, Johnny made contact with his old mattress. The minute he had his bearings, he located the trapdoor beneath it and thrust the heavy door open. "Come on, *cherie,* we've got to hurry. Down here."

When she didn't respond immediately, Johnny scooped her up, drew her close to his body, then dropped into the hole, cradling Nicole against him.

The force of the ten-foot drop ended with a bone-jarring jolt. It knocked the wind out of Johnny, and he groaned in agony as he lay there trying to get past the pain. Just as he was sitting up, another explosion ripped through the house, verifying that the ceiling had caved in.

"Johnny, where are we?" Nicole began to cough.

He pulled her close and hugged her tightly. "We're in the cellar. Catch your breath. We can't stay here long."

When he could move, he got to his feet and ushered Nicole to a safe corner of the cellar, then he climbed up the skeleton ladder, half eaten away by age, and pulled the trapdoor closed. Feeling the heat in the floorboards, he dropped back into the hole, knowing they didn't have long before the floor overhead caved in on them.

Anxiously, he began to search for the tunnel he'd dug as a kid. It had been useful when Farrel and the boys were hot on his trail, had saved his hide a number of times when he was too far from the house to escape them. He sighed with relief as he found the narrow tunnel, then checked to see if he could still fit through it. To his surprise it seemed wider than he remembered, but he didn't consider why that was, only that it was the only escape route they had, and that he was thankful for it.

He heard her coughing again and hurried back to her. "This way, *cherie.* There's a tunnel."

She squinted up at him. "A tunnel? Down here?"

"I dug it when I was a kid. I hope you're not claustrophobic," he teased halfheartedly, trying to pull a smile from her frightened face.

"Would it matter?"

"No. Where I go, you go." When she said nothing, Johnny reached down and hauled her up. She was trembling, completely exhausted, but she was *alive,* doing better than he had expected. He gave her a quick kiss, then urged her toward the tunnel. "I'll go first, just in case there's an animal living in there."

Johnny saw what looked like artificial light soon after they entered the tunnel and made the first turn. The distant glow became brighter as they crawled toward it. Five minutes later, on hands and knees, Johnny and Nicole entered a tiny underground room lit by a single lantern burning in one corner.

In the other corner, clutching a bottle of whiskey, sat Jasper Craig.

Chapter 14

ohnny took in the small hand-dug room with keen inter-
st. When his gaze moved back to Jasper Craig, the town
runk was sitting straighter, his back against the dirt wall.
"What the hell are you doing in here, old man?"

"I'm doing nothing," Jasper mumbled, glancing at Ni-
ole, then back to Johnny. "I—I heard loud noises. Some-
ing happened, didn't it?"

"Yeah, something sure as hell did," Johnny agreed.
"Somebody just set fire to my house with a gas can. That
s, after locking us inside. You know who would want to
o that, or am I looking at the man responsible?"

"Me?" Wide-eyed, Jasper shook his head emphatically.
"Not me. I'd never burn down Madie's house. Never."
He licked his pale lips. "I wouldn't hurt her son, neither."

The mention of his mother made Johnny frown. "Why
would you care one way or the other?"

Jasper suddenly surprised Johnny by offering him a
mile. He relinquished his hold on his bottle, setting it
eside him, and reached for a covered wooden box.

"Easy, old man," Johnny warned.

Again he said, "I'd never hurt Madie's son." He flippe open the top of the box and began fumbling through a array of possessions. Finally he found what he was search ing for and pulled a gold locket from his stash.

Johnny recognized the locket immediately. It had bee his mother's, but it should have been in his drawer bac at the boathouse along with his father's cheap watch. H reached out, snatched the older man's wrist and took th locket. "This is mine. What the hell are you doing wit it? You steal it, old man?"

"I didn't steal it," Jasper argued. "I took it back, is al It ain't yours. I bought it, paid top dollar years ago. Ha it engraved. Madie would want me to have it back."

Johnny examined the locket, but saw no signs of en graving.

Jasper said, "Look behind the picture."

Johnny opened the locket and carefully peeled out th small picture of himself. Sure enough, as Jasper had prom ised, Johnny found a small engraved inscription: *To m Madie, Love J.P.*

Jasper wiped his nose on his sleeve. Then, in a con spiratorial whisper, he said, "We were in love." Pointin to the locket, he said, "That proves it." He dug once mor into his box and handed Johnny a picture. "This is m favorite, but I got lots more if you want to see."

Rocked off balance by Jasper's claim, Johnny stared a the two people in the framed photograph. It was easy t recognize his mother. Jasper was a little harder to iden tify—the years hadn't been kind. *We were in love.* Th possibility of that seemed remote, but then, his mother wa awfully young in the picture.

Nicole leaned over and eyed the picture. "Is it you mother?"

"Yeah, it's her," Johnny confirmed. He tossed the
cket back to Jasper, but hung on to the picture.

Jasper caught the locket, stared at Johnny for a minute,
en tucked it back in his box.

They were three feet away from where Jasper sat. He
nelled bad—a mix of stale liquor and urine. His pale blue
irt was soiled with dirt, his gray pants torn at the knees.
he first time Johnny had seen Jasper in Tuck's office he'd
oticed the dirt on his pants, and now he knew why—the
d man had been spending his days in the tunnel with his
hiskey and that box of memories.

His gaze shifted deeper inside the tunnel. A draft of air
oated into the small space, causing the light to flicker and
e foul smell to rise and drift. An old cooking pot sat on
dead fire, a gunnysack not far from it. Johnny asked,
What's in the sack?"

"Supper," Jasper answered. "Frogs, mostly."

Johnny heard Nicole suck in her breath, and he squeezed
er hand to reassure her that it was all right. "Farrel know
out the tunnel, old man?"

"No. He comes looking for me sometimes, though. I
ear him calling to me, but I don't answer. He don't like
e being here."

"Anyone else come around?"

The old man hesitated, looked away. "No. No one
se."

"You sure?" Johnny watched the old man's eyes blink
everal times. "Don't lie to me," he warned.

"No one else knows I come here. Just Farrel."

The sack moved, and Nicole gasped.

Jasper turned and whacked it hard. "No reason to be
fraid," he said. "They're just frogs."

"So tell me your story, old man," Johnny encouraged,
nally handing the portrait back. "Tell me about my
other and you."

Jasper nodded, the topic obviously one he enjoyed. "W grew up together. I lived on the hill just out of town. St do. I don't know if you knew your mama was adopte Old Glady Keen took her in, mostly to have someone do her work for her, I always thought."

"I knew about Mrs. Keen."

Jasper scratched his chest. "I wanted to marry her, b my folks didn't think she was right for me. I had to snea out of the house to see her." Jasper sniffed, then wipe his nose again on his dirty shirtsleeve. "It was all n fault," he muttered. "We were gonna run away and g married. But first I had to take a trip to Baton Rouge wi my folks. I met Farrel's mother there." He shrugged de jectedly. "I ended up getting Nora pregnant. I could sa she tricked me, but I was a young buck back then. thought I could have whatever I wanted. An affair out town didn't seem all that terrible. A lot of men kicked u their heels before they tied the knot. Only, I got caugh In those days you did the right thing and owned up to yor mistakes."

Johnny vaguely remembered Farrel's mother. A fanc dresser. Skinny. A blonde with a plastic smile and col green eyes. She'd left Jasper before Farrel turned ten.

"Madie was my only love," Jasper admitted, "but ruined it. She refused to talk to me after I came home an word got out that I was engaged to Nora. A few month later there was talk she was seeing Delmar Bernard. didn't make any sense. Sure he was a good-looker, but h was Carl Bernard's son. She had no business getting mixe up with a Bernard, and I told her so. Only, she told me didn't have any right to tell her nothing. She said Delma was a good man, honest, and that all the rumors were ju that—rumors." Jasper flushed. "You won't like to hea this, boy, but those stories weren't rumors. They were a true. I know 'cause I seen it with my own eyes."

Johnny held up his hand. "What rumors?"

"Your grandpa Carl was a womanizer. A no-good wife stealer! That's what." Jasper's nostrils flared. "He busted up half a dozen families in this town, sweet-talking the women into forgetting who they had promised themselves to. Nobody in town talks about it anymore, but that don't mean it didn't happen. We that knew the truth just let it die along with your grandpa."

"Only, you didn't let it die, did you?" Johnny accused. "My father and I paid daily for that old sin."

Jasper lowered his eyes. "That's true. In some ways you're right. But the pain ran deep, boy." He faced Johnny once more. "Your daddy could have passed for Carl any day of the week. That black hair and those eyes kept the memory alive for many of us."

"My father was a decent man," Johnny argued. "He loved my mother and was faithful to her."

"I believe he was. Only, to me, that just made things worse. I was angry that he had won my Madie, and every chance I got, I beat the hell out of him for it. The truth is, I hired him at the lumberyard just so I could take him apart whenever I wanted to. And I did, plenty of times. I'm not proud of it, but he had my Madie. Don'tcha see, boy? He owned my life."

"So you beat him up because *you* made a mistake." Johnny shook his head, so angry that he could hardly sit there a minute longer. If Jasper weren't so pathetic, Johnny would have reached out and strangled the bastard.

Jasper's face twisted in pain. "I don't deserve to live. I know it. You'd have every right to hate me. I hate myself." He squeezed his eyes shut, the pain of living continuing to tear him in two. "She was mine, she'll always be mine," he mumbled.

Johnny never once glanced Nicole's way, but he knew she was silently absorbing everything Jasper Craig said.

Unconsciously, she had slid close to him, her small har
tightly clasped in his, her shoulder pressed against his arr
"So who set fire to my house, old man? Farrel?"

"No. My son hates you, but if he was going to kill yo
I think he would have done it long ago."

That made sense—Johnny felt much the same way. .
fact, that's what he'd told the judge at his trial. "The
who?"

Jasper's eyes widened. "I don't know. I—I can't say.

"Can't...or won't?"

"Carl had a lot of enemies. Some of those men cou
never forgive their wives. I don't know, boy. I don't kno
who it is," he said again. "I'd never hurt Madie, and hur
ing you would hurt her. I come here to talk to her and t
with her. Farrel won't let me keep this stuff in our hous
I have to leave it here. I hide in the tunnel so Farrel can
find me when he comes looking for me, but I don't hu
nobody."

"Farrel knew about my mother, didn't he?"

Jasper nodded. "He overheard me and Nora arguir
about her when he was real young. I was sorry about that.

After Jasper stubbornly refused to leave the tunnel wit
them, Johnny and Nicole belly-crawled a quarter mile, ar
emerged from the underground hole just west of the hous
a few yards from the shoreline of Belle. Gazing towar
the hillside, Johnny saw there was nothing left of th
house, just a pile of rubble.

The past was starting to make sense now. Johnny ha
always wondered why the town had hated the sight of
Bernard, and now he knew. He turned back and stared .
Nicole. "How are you?" He gently touched a nasty bruis
on her shoulder. "That's going to hurt like hell in th
morning."

She looked him over in much the same manner, concer
in her eyes. "You look worse than I do. You've reopene

e old cut on your arm.'' She spun him around and ex-
mined his back. ''And there's a bloody gash on your back
at needs tending.''

He turned and took her hands in his. Slowly, he brought
em to his lips and kissed each palm. ''I'm not worried
bout me,'' he drawled. ''You sure you're not hurt any-
here else?''

''No, I don't think so.''

''Maybe I should have a look-see to make sure,'' he
ased, trying to lighten the moment. ''Come on. Mae must
ave seen the smoke. She'll be worried.''

They started toward the driveway. Nicole said, ''Will
ou report this to Sheriff Tucker?''

''I suppose so, but it won't do much good. We don't
ave a suspect.''

''Should you call your parole officer?''

''It wouldn't hurt.'' He glanced at her once more. ''You
re you're okay?''

''Yes.''

She had dirt smeared on her face, her clothes were torn,
nd she had a number of tiny cuts and bruises on her arms
nd legs. ''Starting now, I want you to stay close to Oak-
aven. Until I get some answers, we're going to have to
e extra careful.''

''All right—as long as you promise to be careful, too.''

''I promise.''

''If Sheriff Tucker turns a blind eye like last time, who
ill help us?''

That was a good question. Johnny didn't know how to
nswer, but he didn't intend to worry Nicole about that
ght now. Again he was struck with how close he'd come
losing her. He had never minded putting himself on the
ne before, facing bad odds or worse. But gambling with
icole's safety was one thing he wouldn't do. He was in
ve with her, had been for weeks, maybe even from the

moment he'd laid eyes on her. But today, those feelin
had been magnified, and the fear of losing her had shak
him like nothing else ever had. It had also opened his ey
to a new truth—one that would change his life forever
he was brave enough to face it head-on.

"This is Detective Archard from New Orleans, Gran
Nicole said by way of introduction. "He's a friend
Johnny's parole officer. He's here to investigate the fire

The tall sandy-haired man shook Mae's hand. "Sure
a beautiful place you got here, Mrs. Chapman." Fro
where he stood on the front porch, Ryland Archard gaz
out over the freshly plowed fields. "Looks like good s
out there."

"If you don't mind me saying so, how would a Ne
Orleans detective know anything about it?"

The detective smiled and turned to give Mae his fu
attention. "I'm from Texas, Mrs. Chapman. We did
plant much for crops, but we sure grew a lot of beef."

"So can you help us, Detective?" Nicole asked. John
had joined them on the porch, and she found herself drav
to him for moral support.

"Like I told Johnny, Miss Chapman, I'll try my best
Detective Archard said.

Fifteen minutes later Johnny and the detective were
their way to see Sheriff Tucker, leaving Mae and Nico
alone on the front porch.

"I just can't believe someone set fire to the farmhouse
Mae sighed. "Thank God, Johnny followed you, and tha
God, he dug that tunnel years ago."

"Did you know about Carl Bernard?" she asked. "W
Jasper Craig telling the truth? Were there women in tov
who were intimate with Johnny's grandfather?"

She was standing at the porch railing, and when Gr

made no comment, she turned around. "Did you hear what I— Gran, what's wrong? You look as pale as a sheet."

Mae turned her head away and gazed across the front yard. The sun was setting and the sky was streaked pink. "Carl was a handsome man, Nicki. Just like Johnny. He could charm a woman out of her dress before she realized what she'd done. His only crime was liking women and enjoying their company too much. All women—short, tall, thin, heavy. He didn't discriminate, and I truly believe he loved them all in his own way. He had such a smooth way about him—a gentleman in rags, I used to call him."

Mae's voice had turned wistful, as if she felt the need to speak reverently about a man the entire town thought was the devil himself. Nicole's heart started to pound. "Gran…?"

"Yes, Nicki. I was one of those women. I cheated on my Henry with Carl Bernard."

The shocking admission momentarily stole Nicole's voice. Finally, she said, "Gran, you don't have to say any more. It was a long time ago, and he probably tricked you. He—"

"No, Nicki, he didn't trick me. He may have seduced me a little with his smooth manner, but I knew what I was doing. He was the kind of man a woman just had a hard time saying 'no' to." She turned to look at Nicole. "I'm sorry if I've shocked you. You must think I'm a terrible old woman."

Nicole didn't think that at all. Gran had just admitted to being human. Everyone made mistakes. Nicole herself had made several in the past year. "I don't think you're terrible." She spoke quietly. "I love you and think you're wonderful—that will never change. You could have ignored the truth, but you didn't. You didn't put all the blame on Carl."

"It was time I told you."

"And I need to tell *you* something," Nicole said sud
denly.

"What is it, Nicki?"

"Remember when I told you about Chad? Well, I lef
out the most important part." She stopped suddenly, too
a deep breath, then charged on. "I got pregnant, Gran
That's the real reason he walked out on me. He didn't wan
to be a father, and I—I wasn't so sure I wanted to be
mother, either. But there I was, pregnant, and in a blin
of an eye, alone."

"Oh, Nicki, you should have told me. You must neve
think you're alone. This is your home, I'm family."

"I know, but I was ashamed." Nicole wiped the tear
from her eyes. "After weeks of crying my eyes out, I go
angry. Angry at Chad and then at myself. Even angry a
the baby. But then the most wonderful thing happened. A
few months later I felt her move inside me. My baby
moved. From that day on, my life meant something
Then—" Nicole turned away, stared out into the fron
yard. "Then one night I woke up with violent stomac
pains. By the time I got to the hospital, I was already i
labor."

She forced herself to face her grandmother once more
"I lost my little girl, Gran."

"Oh, Nicki, I'm so sorry. Come here, dear."

Nicole wiped the tears from her cheeks, then knelt by
Gran's chair. "I should have told you sooner. I just didn'
know how. But when you told me about Carl, I—"

"You didn't feel like you were the only imperfect on
in this family."

"Oh, no, Gran. I would never judge you."

"Hush, dear. It's all right. Life is hard to live, but w
do the best we can. And whether we want it to or not, life
goes on."

"Did Grandpa Henry forgive you?" Nicole asked.

"Yes, he did. Many of the men in town didn't, though. Griffin Black disowned his wife. Pearl Lavel's oldest sister left town in shame, not telling a soul where she was going. Frank Gilmore's wife left four small children behind. And here were many others who sold their homes and moved away. Some with their husbands, some without. It was a horrible time for this town, but Henry and I got through it together."

"You didn't end up hating Carl Bernard, though? Blaming him just a little?"

"No. Like I said, he never forced me into anything I didn't want to do. I could have said no."

"And he was married, too?"

"Yes. His wife left him finally, when Delmar was in high school. Like some of the others, she ran off in the middle of the night and never let Carl know where she'd gone. Delmar turned out as handsome as his father, and I think that was salt in everyone's wounds. Delmar in Carl's image only kept the scandal alive. Carl died of a stroke at fifty-five. Delmar stayed on the farm, and not long after high school he married Madie. The rest you know."

Nicole moved to the wicker chair next to Mae and sat. "So do you think maybe Griffin Black or one of the others is responsible for the fire?"

"It's very possible. But Griffin remarried soon after, and now all he thinks about is buying up more land and making money so that fancy young wife of his can spend it. I don't believe he's living in the past any longer."

"So who else, then? Think, Gran. Who have you forgotten about?"

Mae sat quietly for a moment, thinking. Disgusted, she said, "I just don't know. Most of those people moved away or are as old as I am."

"Then maybe the person we're looking for isn't old,"

Nicole decided. "Maybe Jasper Craig is lying to protec Farrel."

Suddenly, Nicole wanted to speak to Johnny, to touc him and make sure he was all right. He had told her t stay close to Oakhaven, but she felt he should be takin his own advice. Glancing toward the road, she prayed h would come home soon.

Nicole paced the floor in the study. It had been hour since Johnny and the detective had gone to town. Wha was taking so long? Three full hours had passed.

She stopped in front of the window and looked out. Th sky was dark, and it had started to rain. She was growin anxious. *Terrified* was a better word. Had something hor rible happened to Johnny? No, she wouldn't accept that He was with Detective Archard. What could happen?

Again she searched the long, dark driveway, hoping t see lights. "Where are you, Johnny? What's going on?"

Twenty minutes later, Nicole snatched up her keys an headed out the front door. It took her less than ten minute to get to town. Once there, she checked the police station only to find it dark; the green Blazer the detective owne was nowhere in sight. She decided to drive the streets i search of them, noting it wouldn't take very long since th town was so small.

She ran the streets north and south first, then started o the east-west route. She was ready to give up when sh noticed the Blazer parked in the back lot of the Pass-B Motel. Relieved, she pulled in alongside the Blazer, the got out of her car. The lot was dark, and the hotel was li by a single light coming from Virgil's office.

Nicole was headed for the office when she heard a noise Spooked by what had happened at the farmhouse two day earlier, she flattened herself against the building and clung here a minute. Frustrated, she hissed softly, "Damn you, ohnny. The things I do for you."

"Are you keeping a record so you can get paid later, *cherie?*"

Johnny's silky drawl was right next to her ear. Nicole gasped and nearly jumped out of her cutoff jeans and tennis shoes. She whirled around to find him standing with his hands on his hips and his dark eyes narrowed.

"I thought I told you to stay put." His voice was tight and not at all friendly.

"I've been waiting at home for hours. I thought you were probably lying in some ditch somewhere. Honestly, couldn't you have called?"

"And tell you what?"

His inconsiderate answer struck a nerve, and Nicole turned defensive. "Sorry for cramping your style." She glanced behind him to see if they were alone or if Detective Archard was close by. As far as she could tell, they were alone.

He saw her glance over his shoulder and turned slightly. "You expecting someone?"

"No. Are you?"

"What kind of question is that? I've been with Ryland Archard since I left Oakhaven. He's one helluva cop. Best of all, he's in my corner."

"But would he be if he knew the whole story?"

"Meaning…?"

Nicole knew she shouldn't have brought up his grandpa. Still, it made her angry that the man had dared to disrupt so many lives and hurt so many people, her own family included.

"I asked you a question, *cherie.*"

"I just meant your grandfather was a…"

"A womanizing bastard," he finished for her. He stood

tall and straight, towering over her, his hands on his lea▮
hips. "Are you suddenly thinking I'm the same?"

"That's not fair." Nicole felt the challenge and didn'
back down. She jammed her hands on her own waist and
glared back at him. "I didn't say that. I'm not comparing
you with him."

He moved closer, so close Nicole was forced bacl
against the wall. "Am I scum in your eyes now, *cherie*
Have I soiled you?"

"Stop it. I'm just upset and worried. And—"

"And that's why I want you back at Oakhaven. Ry
land's been picking Virgil's brain about the old days, try
ing to get a lead on who this crazy might be. So until we
know who it is, I want you home where you'll be safe
Now, be a good girl and do what you're told."

Nicole resented his condescending words, as well as be
ing sent home like a naughty little girl. "Okay, fine." She
moved past him.

He grabbed her arm. "Don't do that. Don't walk away
mad."

"Let go, Johnny. I'm not some helpless child who need▮
to be told when to go home. I sure as hell don't need you
telling me to be good and do what I'm told, either. Now
get your hands off me!"

When he released her, she started back to the car. She'd
only taken three steps before he caught up with her. He
didn't touch her, but he kept pace.

They reached her car in short order, and to Nicole's
surprise, as she attempted to open the door, Johnny cap
tured her around the waist and whirled her into his arms
Holding her next to his hard body, he nuzzled her neck,
then kissed her ear before whispering, "I don't want any
thing to happen to you, dammit. Right now that's the mos▮
important thing to me. If I'm acting a little crazy, *cherie*,
it's only because I care. But that doesn't give me the righ▮

talk to you like I did. I'm sorry." He pulled back to gaze down at her, then he lowered his head and kissed her.

Nicole didn't want to be a clinging vine, but she gave in to her emotions and slipped her arms around Johnny's waist. Soon the kiss turned long and deep, and when they finally parted, Johnny said, "We might be out half the night. If I find out anything, I'll call you. I promise."

"Just don't be a hero, Johnny," Nicole pleaded. "Don't take any chances. I don't want to add more pressure to the situation, but you have to know I love you." When he would have said something, she quickly pressed her fingers to his warm lips. "No, don't say anything. I didn't come here to spill my guts, and I don't expect you to say anything back. Just be careful."

Nicole met Daisi Buillard in front of her house on Mill Street at ten-thirty. Unlike the other times they'd met, tonight Daisi wore sloppy jeans and a T-shirt, her feet shoved into a pair of black tennis shoes. Her pretty hair, she'd stuffed under a baseball cap.

"I can't believe I'm doin' this," she said, climbing into the car and handing Nicole the key. "If you get caught, both our backsides are gonna be lunch meat," she said bluntly.

Nicole took the key. "I appreciate your lending me the key. I couldn't have broken into the police station without it."

"Are you sure you should be doin' this? Why not just wait until tomorrow?"

"Sheriff Tucker hates me. He wouldn't help me any more than he'd help Johnny. I have to do this tonight." Nicole glanced at Daisi, suddenly not so sure she should have involved her friend in something illegal. Especially breaking into the very place where she worked.

"Woody doesn't have a chance, does he? You reall
got it bad for Johnny Bernard, don't you?"

Nicole's smile was a little sad. "I love him, Daisi. Bu
I'm not so naive as to think that love will get me what
want. I've resigned myself to the fact that Johnny's leavin
soon. It hurts—only, it would have hurt so much more i
I hadn't gotten to know him. He's a good man, Daisi. H
truly is a wonderful man."

"Woody's goin' to be heartsick. Oh, well, I'll still b
your friend," Daisi teased, "even though I was hopin
we'd be sisters someday."

"You're the best, Daisi." Nicole leaned across the sea
and hugged her friend. "I'll get the key back to you.
promise."

She left Daisi at the curb and turned the corner on Coo
per. Avoiding Main Street altogether, she turned off th
headlights and headed into the alley. After parking unde
a massive weeping willow, she slipped from the car an
crept along the side of the building, keeping a watchfu
eye out for any passerby. If she saw someone, she intende
to walk past the station house and round the block as i
she were just out for a stroll.

Luckily, the streets were empty as she neared the door
and she slipped inside with relative ease. She locked th
door from the inside, then stuffed the key in her pocket.

She had been ready to head home just as Johnny ha
instructed when she decided there might be something i
the files in Sheriff Tucker's office that would shed som
light on who might be out for revenge.

The small flashlight she'd taken from the glove com
partment would come in handy, and she snapped it on an
directed the narrow beam down the hall. With hurrie
steps, she passed Daisi's desk and headed for Sherif
Tucker's office. Outside his door, she stopped to catch he
breath, then turned the doorknob. She sighed with relie

when the door opened, and she eased into the office. As he scanned the room with the flashlight to get reacquainted, the beam of light passed over the file cabinets along one wall, then the sheriff's desk, strewn with papers. She was moving toward the row of files when she heard a noise—

Oh, God! She froze, then turned off her flashlight.

Holding her breath, she listened as footsteps started down the hall. She knew whoever it was had to have a key, and it didn't take too much imagination to figure out who that was. Nicole scrambled toward the file cabinets to hide. She nearly fell on her face in the dark as she tried to reach the narrow space along the wall. Sucking into the tight gap, she crouched low and held her breath.

The door creaked open moments later. A flashlight—the beam the size of a searchlight—illuminated the room. Panic seized Nicole when the flashlight zeroed in on her hiding place. "You really are starting to annoy me, Miss Chapman," Sheriff Tucker said. "Crawl out of there."

Nicole felt herself shudder as Clifton Tucker strolled forward, roughly gripped her arm and hauled her out of her hiding place. "I'm sorry," she said, trying to think of a way to explain. "I know this looks bad, but—"

"Nothing happens in this town without me knowing about it, Miss Chapman. Nothing."

Nicole snapped her mouth shut, surprised by the deadly tone in his voice. His eyes had taken on a glassy quality, she noted, and had narrowed in the bright light. At that moment she realized the truth. "It's you, isn't it? You're the one—"

The words barely out of her mouth, Nicole swung her flashlight at Clifton Tucker's head as hard as she could. The weapon made a sickening *thud,* and the sheriff groaned in pain and staggered back. Free, Nicole scrambled for the door. Just as she thought she would escape, he lunged at her and grabbed her around the waist. Her flashlight clattered to the floor as his strong arms lifted her and threw her into one of the metal file cabinets along the wall. The impact made Nicole see stars.

Then nausea rose up in her throat—and everything went black.

Chapter 15

Farrel had an airtight alibi for the afternoon of the fire, as did Clete Gilmore and Jack Oden. The last name on Johnny's list had been an old-timer who lived in Assumption Parish, some thirty miles away. But Tweed Bowdeen hadn't even remembered who Carl Bernard was—Tweed had had a stroke and had been housebound for several years. Johnny and Ryland were forced to admit they had hit a dead end.

"It's late," Johnny said, once they were back on the road heading home to Common. "Let's call it quits for tonight."

"Sounds good," Ryland agreed. "We'll sleep on it, and get an early start in the morning."

Ryland Archard was one of the NOPD's toughest, and he was used to getting stonewalled. But he was also used to working a number of angles, and looking at trouble from both sides of the law. He said, "I've got two days before I have to be back. There's still time, and a few rocks we haven't overturned. Keep the faith, Johnny."

Johnny had never had much faith in cops, but then, he'd never met a cop like Ryland Archard. The man was honest and straightforward. A regular guy with a normal-size ego.

Johnny checked his watch and found it was past eleven. The weather had turned sour, with thunder rumbling like a bowling alley on a Saturday night, and sheet lightning dancing across the black sky.

Ryland reached over and snatched a cigarette from Johnny's T-shirt pocket. "I need to quit, but it's not going good."

Johnny nodded. "I've quit."

"The hell. What are you doing with smokes in your pocket, then?"

"As long as I know they're there, I don't need them. Sounds crazy, I know. But it's been working so far." Johnny grinned. "It was Nicole's idea."

The detective grinned back, flashing his straight teeth. "You meet a woman, and she helps you quit smoking. I meet a woman, and start up. Lucky bastard." Ryland's smile widened, then he took a long drag off his cigarette.

Johnny's thoughts turned to the dilemma he'd been wrestling with all day. Finally, he asked, "If we can't solve this thing, what are the odds of getting my parole moved somewhere else, real quick-like?"

"It can be done," Ryland assured. "I'll work on it, if and when you decide that's what you want."

"I think I do. Nicole and Mae have been put in an awful position since I came to town. I don't want to see either one of them hurt any more." Johnny cracked the window to let the smoke from Ry's cigarette filter out, then sank into the seat and closed his eyes. "Wake me when we get back to town, will you?"

They were on highway 20, Johnny dozing, when Ryland hauled on the brakes and pulled to the side of the road. "Hey, partner, your lady's car just sailed by."

Johnny suddenly came awake. "Can't be—I sent Nicole home hours ago."

"No mistake. She just sped past us like a lightning bolt."

"Then run it down," Johnny demanded. "Move!"

Ryland did an on-the-spot U-turn while dropping the clutch from first into third. Within seconds the Blazer was in fourth gear, the accelerator on the floor. When the Skylark slowed down to turn off the highway onto the county road, Johnny said, "It's her car, all right."

When the car hit a straight stretch, Ryland saw his chance to floor the Blazer and speed past it. Once out in front, he cut right and skidded to a stop, forcing the Skylark to the side of the road. The Blazer was still bouncing when Johnny leaped out into the rain and angrily stalked toward the car.

Before he reached the door, however, it was thrust open, and he came face to face with a wide-eyed Jasper Craig. "It's good to see you, boy. Thought I'd have to take him on by myself."

"What's going on, old man?" Johnny hollered over the thunder.

"He's got her. Cliff took your lady."

"What?"

"I was scared. I should have told you he was the one. He's the one who burned down Madie's house. He's done other bad things, too. Real bad things."

Johnny froze, feeling his world tilt. A moment later, he rallied. "When? How?"

"I saw you two in the parking lot at the Pass-By. I heard what you told her about going home, but she went to Daisi Buillard's house instead, then to the police station. She had a key, and I watched her go inside. Then Cliff showed up. When he left a little while later, he had your lady with him. I'm scared he might already have hurt her, boy. She

wasn't moving when he put her in the trunk of his car.'
Winded, Jasper gasped for more air; his breath was lace
with whiskey. "I didn't know what to do. I waited a bit
then got in her car and decided to follow Cliff. It's just
good thing she left the key in the ignition."

Fear gripped Johnny, and he squeezed his eyes shut fo
a minute to absorb Jasper's words. If anything happene
to Nicole he'd never forgive himself. If anything happene
to her, he didn't want to live.

Johnny and Ryland rushed back to the Blazer an
Johnny directed him to the farm. Jasper followed at high
speed in the car. They found Sheriff Tucker's car parke
there.

"See," Jasper pointed, "I was right."

With a flashlight Ryland had produced, Johnny tracke
Clifton to Belle Bayou. Needing a boat to follow him, the
backtracked quickly to the boathouse, and untied tw
boats.

"Follow me," Johnny instructed as he sent the pol
deep into the water and pushed one of the boats away from
shore into the black bayou. He knew full well how dan
gerous the swamp could be, especially at night. But h
wouldn't let it end like this, he promised. He had been
fool tonight not to tell Nicki he loved her, but he *woul*
tell her. He'd tell her everything he'd been holding bac
since he'd made love to her at the swimming hole week
ago.

It wouldn't be too late, he promised. He wouldn't let i
be too late.

Nicole woke with a pounding headache and rain show
ering her face. Her head spun, and she moaned softly. Fo
a minute she couldn't think, then she remembered wha
had happened, and with the memory came the realizatio

that she was no longer in Clifton Tucker's office, but in a boat. Slowly, she sat up.

"It's about time you woke up. Just so you know, I didn't want any of this to happen. The score was already settled years ago. I just wanted Johnny to go away and never come back."

"Why is it so important that Johnny leave town?" Nicole winced as pain shot through her temple. The slightest noise, even her own voice, made her head want to split in two. "He's a good man."

The sheriff swore. "Them Bernards—they were always good at getting the women to fall for them."

"You don't want to hurt me, Sheriff Tucker. Take me back."

"I can't. They're on to me by now. That damn fool Jasper has probably told them how Delmar really died."

"What do you mean how Delmar really died? Johnny's father died in a hit-and-run accident on Bayou Road, that's what Gran told me. Are you saying it didn't happen that way?"

"No, it was a hit-and-run." The sheriff grinned. "Just not an accident."

A lump formed in Nicole's throat. Was he saying he'd killed Delmar Bernard—that he'd run Johnny's father down on the road? Or had he covered for the man responsible?

Another bolt of lightning ripped across the black sky as Clifton Tucker, caped in a black slicker, poled the boat deeper into the bayou. Nicole shivered as the rain soaked her to the bone, making her clothes feel like a cold, wet blanket.

She didn't want to surrender to this madness, but if she jumped from the boat she would surely die. The swamp was full of alligators and poisonous snakes. The least bit of splashing would bring them to investigate. She shuddered at the thought, remembering Johnny's words. *Be a good girl and keep your hands in the boat,* cherie. *No sudden moves.*

The image of an alligator clamping its jaws around her or a snake touching her with its kiss of death had Nicole feeling dizzy with fear. She squinted into the darkness, trying to grasp where they were, but it all looked the same—a bleak promise of black water and certain death. She felt tears sting her eyes. She didn't want to cry. Didn't want to die.

There had to be a way to escape. There had to be something...

Shaking violently, Nicole squinted into the darkness, noting that the boat was gliding very close to a stand of cypress. Was there a shoreline close by? The swamp was so deceiving, she couldn't be sure.

She studied the water, then felt the boat bump into something. It wasn't exactly solid, but— Fen? Could it be fen? With no time to debate her decision, Nicole said a silent prayer, then exploded off the wooden seat and grabbed a passing tangle of vines. The boat tilted as she caught a fistful of the thick, ropelike vines and hung on.

"No! Come back. No!"

Clifton's angry voice only spurred Nicole on, making her more determined than ever to get away from him. Head still spinning, she didn't look back as she swung her body into the air, then let go of the vine. Keeping her shaky knees bent, she set her feet. The ground beneath her bobbed once, twice. The third time she went down and came back up, the ground stabilized.

A flood of emotion engulfed her as she realized she was, indeed, standing on fen. Sweet, wonderful, *fen.* She could have cried out with joy, but there wasn't time. She turned and ran, fighting her way through the thick vines, determined to get as far away as possible before Sheriff Tucker came after her.

She found the tree house by accident, practically stumbling into the giant cypress facefirst. When she gazed up and saw massive limbs supporting Johnny's tree house, she started to cry. Leaning against the giant tree, she worked at catching her breath.

"Miss Chapman. Do you hear me? I would have done it quick, killed you fast and painlessly. Now the swamp will make you suffer."

His voice urged Nicole into action, and she jerked the rope ladder down and began to climb. Refusing to consider what she might find inside the tree house, she stepped into the shelter just as a flash of lightning lit up the sky. For no more than a brief second, she saw the snake coiled up in a dry corner, and it stopped her in her tracks.

This one's a harmless milk snake, cherie.

Well, it was too dark to see underbellies, Nicole noted. *Think,* she told herself. What else had Johnny said?

Don't move fast, cherie. *But don't freeze up, either.*

Nicole forced herself inside, taking slow, even steps. "You can stay right there," she told the snake, "and I'll stay over here."

Unable to see whether the snake had moved, she had to blindly trust the reptile—and fate. "Fate and Johnny," she whispered softly. "He'll come for me. I know he'll come."

She forced herself to breathe evenly, and began to pray that Johnny would find her sooner rather than later. She refused to think negative thoughts. Instead, she wedged herself into the corner and clung to the wall. At least she didn't have to worry about freezing up; she couldn't have stopped shaking if she tried.

Clifton's voice above the thunder was the lucky break Johnny needed. He turned the boat toward the black bog and sent the pole into the murky water with swift, strong, purposeful strokes. Five minutes later, he heard Clifton's voice again. This time he was calling to Nicole, taunting her about dying in the swamp.

The reality of the situation made Johnny's blood run cold. With renewed energy and his keen sense of direction, he pushed on. He told himself the swamp was his home; he'd traveled every inch of it in daylight and darkness. He would find Tuck, but most importantly he would find Nicole. He had to.

He spotted Clifton's boat pulled into shore some ten minutes later. They ran their boats onto land, and Johnny led Detective Archard and Jasper through the thick woods. It was Johnny who first saw the sheriff stumbling around as if he himself were lost.

"Tuck!"

The sheriff spun around, drawing his gun at the same time, his flashlight zeroing in on Johnny's face. "That you, Johnny boy?"

Johnny squinted through the misting rain. "Why, Tuck? What's going on? Where's Nicole?"

"It ain't my fault she's gonna die, it's yours," Clifton said. "None of this is my fault. If you had stayed away, this wouldn't be happening. It was all over. The debt paid."

"Tell him all of it." Jasper suddenly appeared alongside Johnny. "Tell the truth, Cliff. Tell him how his daddy died."

Clifton angled his head and stared at Jasper. "You wanted Madie for yourself as much as I wanted justice for my daddy. It wasn't my fault she got sick and died before you could marry her. If she had lived you would have called me a hero instead of a murderer. Don'tcha see, J.P., we had to do it."

Jasper shook his head. "I didn't do nothin'. I didn't know what you'd done until after. I would have never agreed to murder. Never!"

"But you kept my secret for twenty-two years."

"What secret?" This time it was Ryland's voice.

"Carl Bernard seduced my mama, and my daddy shot himself when he found them together. I had no choice after that. The Bible says 'an eye for an eye.' That's why I ran Delmar down on the road that night."

Johnny was sure he hadn't heard right. It was too crazy. Sheriff Tucker was responsible for the hit-and-run accident. "You killed my father?"

"Delmar always walked home from town. No one questioned it." Sheriff Tucker raised his gun and pointed it at Johnny.

Detective Archard said, "You've just confessed to murder, Sheriff Tucker. It's all over. Put the gun down."

It was then that Johnny came out of the gray fog that had enveloped him. Crying out, he charged Clifton, knocking the bigger man off his feet. He threw a hard punch to the man's jaw and reached for the gun.

"No, boy. No!" Jasper hurried forward. "Don't hurt him, Cliff. He's Madie's son. Don't hurt the boy."

The gun went off, a deafening *crack*. It all happened so fast that in a matter of seconds it was all over. Johnny threw a hard right to Clifton's jaw and then muscled the gun out of his hand. When he looked up, he saw Jasper crumpled on the ground, a bullet hole in his chest.

"Old man!" Johnny crawled over to where Jasper Craig lay unmoving on his back, vaguely aware of Ryland rushing to apprehend Sheriff Tucker.

"Boy?" Jasper fought for air. "Listen now. There ain't much time. You tell Farrel I'm real sorry. Tell him you two are even now, that it's time to make peace. Go to the tunnel and get my things. I want them with me." He

reached for Johnny's hand and gripped it urgently. "Prom
ise me, boy. I need my things."

Johnny nodded. "You have my word, old man. You'l
have them."

Jasper smiled, then nodded. "Good boy. Your mama
was a fine woman. You remember that. Your daddy, too
We just wanted the same thing, and I was a sore loser."

"You should have stayed back, old man. Kept clear."

"It was time I did something right. Selfish, really. I've
been needing to see Madie real bad for a long while now
This time, when we meet, she'll be happy to see me. She'll
know I did something good for a change. She'll smile
maybe even forgive me. You remember my box, boy. I
need my box with me."

Those were the last words Jasper Craig ever spoke.

Johnny looked over at Clifton Tucker. Ryland was putting handcuffs on him. "You bastard! Why?" Johnny
scrambled to his feet, his fists raised.

"Johnny, no!" Ryland grabbed him by the shoulder.
"Listen to me. He's crazy. What you do to him now won't
make any difference. Let the law handle it. Remember
what we came here for. Nicole's out there somewhere, and
she needs you to find her. Go!"

Ryland's words shocked Johnny back to reality. He
turned and scanned the darkness once more, then yelled,
"Cherie!" He wiped tears out of his eyes as he struggled
into the woods. He couldn't remember the last time he'd
cried. His mama's funeral, he supposed.

"Johnny!"

"Cherie!"

"Here, Johnny. I'm in the tree house!"

Moments later he was standing beneath the giant cypress. When he saw her appear in the doorway of his tree
house, he nearly collapsed with relief. A moment later he
was lifting her off the rope ladder and hauling her into his

arms. Cradling her against him, he buried his face in her hair.

"Johnny? I heard shots. Are you all right?"

"I'm fine," he drawled, still holding her close. "Give me a minute, *cherie*," he said, unable to let go of her just yet. When he finally loosened his hold minutes later, he told her what had happened.

"I'm so sorry, Johnny. It's all so terrible."

"He's crazy." Johnny hung his head. "Jasper's gone. The old fool was trying to help me and Tuck shot him."

Raw emotion took him over the edge. Johnny pulled Nicole close and buried his head in her hair once more. After a few minutes passed, he set her away from him and smiled down at her. "The good news is you're safe. You aren't hurt, are you?"

"A bump on the head is all. I'll be fine now that you're here. I knew you'd come. Thank you."

"Thank me another way, *cherie*. Kiss me."

The townsfolk were in a state of shock. And yet the gossip lines were humming; the phone at Oakhaven hadn't stopped ringing all morning.

What had amazed Nicole most about the people of Common was their sincere effort to make amends to Johnny.

The truth was, for years Sheriff Tucker had manipulated the people of Common, and they had come to realize that fact quickly, with alarming clarity—something that more than convinced Nicole they were genuinely good people. Yes, the truth had shaken the town of Common to the core, but it had also given the people back their dignity. And for that, Nicole believed they truly thanked Johnny.

Last night, when they had gotten back to the house, they'd spent an hour explaining to Gran what had happened and why. Next, Farrel had to be called, and Johnny and Ryland had spent several hours closed in the study with him. Nicole hadn't asked Johnny what had happened between them, but she knew whatever had been said, their feud had ended.

Ryland had been wonderful handling all the details last night, and again this morning. The incarceration of Sheriff Tucker had gone smoothly, and before he'd left to go back to New Orleans he'd promised to look into Johnny's parole deal. It was amazing how quickly things could be expedited when you knew the right people, Nicole thought. And Ryland Archard certainly knew the right people. Good, honest people—people like himself.

All in all, last night had ended the hostility toward the Bernards. It had also explained Jasper Craig's self-destructive obsession with liquor, and Farrel's constant need to wreak vengeance on Johnny. Sheriff Tucker had been a victim in many ways himself. Though Nicole was glad he would be locked up, she found it hard to hate him.

She parked the car at the end of the driveway and walked up the road leading to the hill where the farmhouse had stood. As she neared the hillside, she saw Johnny sitting in the grass overlooking Belle. The morning sun was hot, but there was a gentle breeze, and his loose, gorgeous hair moved freely around his shoulders.

He had been so protective of her last night, and she of him. She supposed they had looked ridiculous clinging to each other the way they had, but no one had said a word. Later, in the early hours of the morning, he had come to her bedroom and made love to her. Such fierce, passionate love that she had cried the entire time.

She reached the hillside and silently sat down beside him. Just being near him made her happy, made her thankful to be alive. God, how she loved this man.

He turned to look at her. "So, *cherie,* what's so important that it couldn't wait until noon? I told Mae I'd be back by lunchtime."

"Yes, I know. Ryland called from New Orleans. He said he parole board will be reviewing your case. He says ou'll be a free man in a matter of weeks, if he has anyhing to say about it. I thought you'd want to know."

He dismissed the news with a slight nod. "You feel like alking?"

"If you want."

He turned and looked straight into her eyes. "I wanted o talk last night, but you couldn't stop crying." He grinned. "That was new. At first I thought I was hurting you."

"You stole my breath again," Nicole confessed. "My eaction was just a little different this time. So, what is it you want to talk about?"

"Last night, before all hell broke loose, you told me you loved me. Remember?"

"Yes." Nicole wanted to reach out and touch him, but he held back. He looked suddenly very serious, and it made her nervous. Was this it, then? Was this where he old her he appreciated the time they'd spent together, but hat he was leaving nonetheless?

"Do you still?"

Of course, she still loved him. "More than ever," she admitted. "But I told you—"

"Shh." He reached out and touched her lips with two fingers. "It's my turn. I've been sitting here trying to figure it out. How best to say what I need to say."

Nicole couldn't keep quiet. "I know you plan on leaving. I've always known. I've been preparing myself." She offered him a soft smile in the hope that he hadn't heard the lie in her voice. "It's okay, really. I—"

"Is it? You want me to go?"

"No!" Nicole said in a rush. "But I don't want you to feel—"

"To feel what?"

He brushed her hair out of her eyes, and Nicole welcomed his warm touch. Savored his gentle side. "I—I want you to do what you want," she said. "That's all."

"Whatever I want?"

"Yes."

"It's all up to me?"

"Yes."

"So I can love you?"

Nicole couldn't breathe. Did she dare hope?

"I love you, *cherie*. 'You've got to know that I do' is what you said to me last night. Well, you've got to know that I love you, too."

He *loved* her. Nicole could hardly sit still a moment longer without touching him, without knocking him over and kissing him senseless. "And?"

"And if I stay, I'm not living in the boathouse. And I'm not sleeping alone, either."

He was moving in. That was doable. More than doable. Nicole tried to contain her smile, but it was spreading fast. "So?"

"So, *cherie*, what do you think? Are you going to marry me so Mae can stop matchmaking?"

Nicole couldn't believe what she was hearing. "This isn't some guilt thing, is it?" she asked suddenly. "I mean—"

With one quick movement, he had her on her back, and he was towering over her, his dark eyes narrowing slightly. "No guilt." His eyes softened. "And about kids…we'll go slow. If and when it happens, it'll be because you're ready. No pressure."

"No pressure," Nicole agreed, so in love with Johnny that she could hardly contain her tears. "You can't take it back," she whispered, feeling the first tear wet the corner of her eye. "Now that you've asked, it's a done deal. Right?"

"Are you going to cry?"

"Probably."

He grinned. "Because I'm stealing your breath again?"

"Yes." Nicole squirmed beneath him, running her hands down the length of his strong back, needing so badly to feel his strength. "Should we seal the deal with a kiss?"

"Just a kiss?" Johnny's eyes turned heavy-lidded, and as needy as Nicole's. She wrapped her arms around his neck as he eased his weight onto her prone body. It was going to be gentle and tender this time. He whispered the promise in her ear. Unhurried, he swore. But as usual the kiss turned hot and demanding the minute their lips touched, and what followed sizzled, then burned.

They ended up late for lunch to tell Mae the good news.

*   *   *   *   *

Look Who's Celebrating Our 20th Anniversary:

Celebrate
20
YEARS

"Working with Silhouette has always been a privilege—I've known the nicest people, and I've been delighted by the way the books have grown and changed with time. I've had the opportunity to take chances...and I'm grateful for the books I've done with the company. Bravo! And onward, Silhouette, to the new millennium."

—*New York Times* bestselling author
Heather Graham Pozzessere

"Twenty years of laughter and love... It's not hard to imagine Silhouette Books celebrating twenty years of quality publishing, but it is hard to imagine a publishing world without it. Congratulations..."

—International bestselling author
Emilie Richards

INTIMATE MOMENTS®
Silhouette®

SILHOUETTE'S 20TH ANNIVERSARY CONTEST
OFFICIAL RULES
NO PURCHASE NECESSARY TO ENTER

. To enter, follow directions published in the offer to which you are responding. Contest begins 1/1/00 and ends on 8/24/00 (the "Promotion Period"). Method of entry may vary. Mailed entries must be postmarked by 8/24/00, and received by 8/31/00.

. During the Promotion Period, the Contest may be presented via the Internet. Entry via the Internet may be restricted to residents of certain geographic areas that are disclosed on the Web site. To enter via the Internet, if you are a resident of a geographic area in which Internet entry is permissible, follow the directions displayed on-line, including typing your essay of 100 words or fewer telling us "Where In The World Your Love Will Come Alive." On-line entries must be received by 11:59 p.m. Eastern Standard time on 8/24/00. Limit one e-mail entry per person, household and e-mail address per day, per presentation. If you are a resident of a geographic area in which entry via the Internet is permissible, you may, in lieu of submitting an entry on-line, enter by mail, by hand-printing your name, address, telephone number and contest number/name on an 8"x 11" plain piece of paper and telling us in 100 words or fewer "Where In The World Your Love Will Come Alive," and mailing via first-class mail to: Silhouette 20th Anniversary Contest, (in the U.S.) P.O. Box 9069, Buffalo, NY 14269-9069; (In Canada) P.O. Box 637, Fort Erie, Ontario, Canada L2A 5X3. Limit one 8"x 11" mailed entry per person, household and e-mail address per day. On-line and/or 8"x 11" mailed entries received from persons residing in geographic areas in which Internet entry is not permissible will be disqualified. No liability is assumed for lost, late, incomplete, inaccurate, nondelivered or misdirected mail, or misdirected e-mail, for technical, hardware or software failures of any kind, lost or unavailable network connection, or failed, incomplete, garbled or delayed computer transmission or any human error which may occur in the receipt or processing of the entries in the contest.

. Essays will be judged by a panel of members of the Silhouette editorial and marketing staff based on the following criteria:

Sincerity (believability, credibility)—50%
Originality (freshness, creativity)—30%
Aptness (appropriateness to contest ideas)—20%

Purchase or acceptance of a product offer does not improve your chances of winning. In the event of a tie, duplicate prizes will be awarded.

. All entries become the property of Harlequin Enterprises Ltd., and will not be returned. Winner will be determined no later than 10/31/00 and will be notified by mail. Grand Prize winner will be required to sign and return Affidavit of Eligibility within 15 days of receipt of notification. Noncompliance within the time period may result in disqualification and an alternative winner may be selected. All municipal, provincial, federal, state and local laws and regulations apply. Contest open only to residents of the U.S. and Canada who are 18 years of age or older, and is void wherever prohibited by law. Internet entry is restricted solely to residents of those geographical areas in which Internet entry is permissible. Employees of Torstar Corp., their affiliates, agents and members of their immediate families are not eligible. Taxes on the prizes are the sole responsibility of winners. Entry and acceptance of any prize offered constitutes permission to use winner's name, photograph or other likeness for the purposes of advertising, trade and promotion on behalf of Torstar Corp. without further compensation to the winner, unless prohibited by law. Torstar Corp and D.L. Blair, Inc., their parents, affiliates and subsidiaries, are not responsible for errors in printing or electronic presentation of contest or entries. In the event of printing or other errors which may result in unintended prize values or duplication of prizes, all affected contest materials or entries shall be null and void. If for any reason the Internet portion of the contest is not capable of running as planned, including infection by computer virus, bugs, tampering, unauthorized intervention, fraud, technical failures, or any other causes beyond the control of Torstar Corp. which corrupt or affect the administration, secrecy, fairness, integrity or proper conduct of the contest, Torstar Corp. reserves the right, at its sole discretion, to disqualify any individual who tampers with the entry process and to cancel, terminate, modify or suspend the contest or the Internet portion thereof. In the event of a dispute regarding an on-line entry, the entry will be deemed submitted by the authorized holder of the e-mail account submitted at the time of entry. Authorized account holder is defined as the natural person who is assigned to an e-mail address by an Internet access provider, on-line service provider or other organization that is responsible for arranging e-mail address for the domain associated with the submitted e-mail address.

. Prizes: Grand Prize—a $10,000 vacation to anywhere in the world. Travelers (at least one must be 18 years of age or older) or parent or guardian if one traveler is a minor, must sign and return a Release of Liability prior to departure. Travel must be completed by December 31, 2001, and is subject to space and accommodations availability. Two hundred (200) Second Prizes—a two-book limited edition autographed collector set from one of the Silhouette Anniversary authors: Nora Roberts, Diana Palmer, Linda Howard or Annette Broadrick (value $10.00 each set). All prizes are valued in U.S. dollars.

. For a list of winners (available after 10/31/00), send a self-addressed, stamped envelope to: Harlequin Silhouette 20th Anniversary Winners, P.O. Box 4200, Blair, NE 68009-4200.

Contest sponsored by Torstar Corp., P.O. Box 9042, Buffalo, NY 14269-9042.